Blood Feud

A Scottish Dark Ages Romance

The Warrior Brothers of Skye
Book One

Jayne Castel

WINTER MIST PRESS

Historical Romances by Jayne Castel

DARK AGES BRITAIN

The Kingdom of the East Angles series
Dark Under the Cover of Night (Book One)
Nightfall till Daybreak (Book Two)
The Deepening Night (Book Three)
The Kingdom of the East Angles: The Complete Series

The Kingdom of Mercia series
The Breaking Dawn (Book One)
Darkest before Dawn (Book Two)
Dawn of Wolves (Book Three)
The Kingdom of Mercia: The Complete Series

The Kingdom of Northumbria series
The Whispering Wind (Book One)
Wind Song (Book Two)
Lord of the North Wind (Book Three)
The Kingdom of Northumbria: The Complete Series

DARK AGES SCOTLAND

The Warrior Brothers of Skye series
Blood Feud (Book One)
Barbarian Slave (Book Two)
Battle Eagle (Book Three)
The Warrior Brothers of Skye: The Complete Series

The Pict Wars series
Warrior's Heart (Book One)
Warrior's Secret (Book Two)

Warrior's Wrath (Book Three)
The Pict Wars: The Complete Series

Novellas
Winter's Promise

MEDIEVAL SCOTLAND

The Brides of Skye series
The Beast's Bride (Book One)
The Outlaw's Bride (Book Two)
The Rogue's Bride (Book Three)
The Brides of Skye: The Complete Series

The Sisters of Kilbride series
Unforgotten (Book One)
Awoken (Book Two)
Fallen (Book Three)
Claimed (Epilogue novella)

The Immortal Highland Centurions series
Maximus (Book One)
Cassian (Book Two)
Draco (Book Three)
The Laird's Return (Epilogue festive novella)

Epic Fantasy Romances by Jayne Castel

Light and Darkness series
Ruled by Shadows (Book One)
The Lost Swallow (Book Two)
Path of the Dark (Book Three)
Light and Darkness: The Complete Series

***

For Tim—my lover, my editor, and my best friend.

***

Maps of The Winged Isle

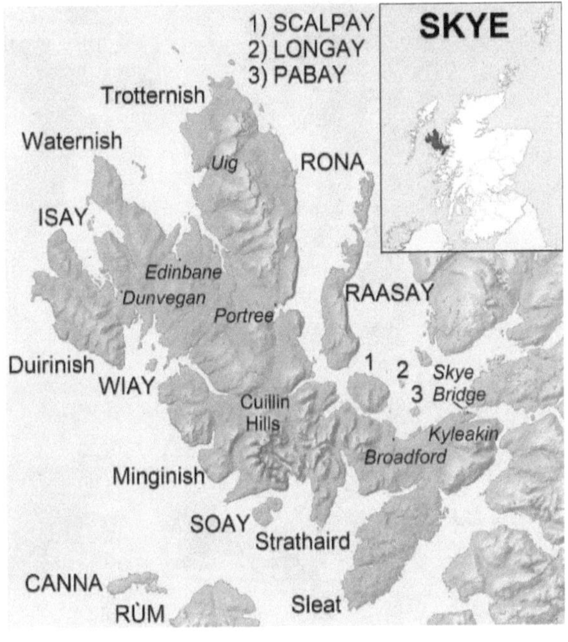

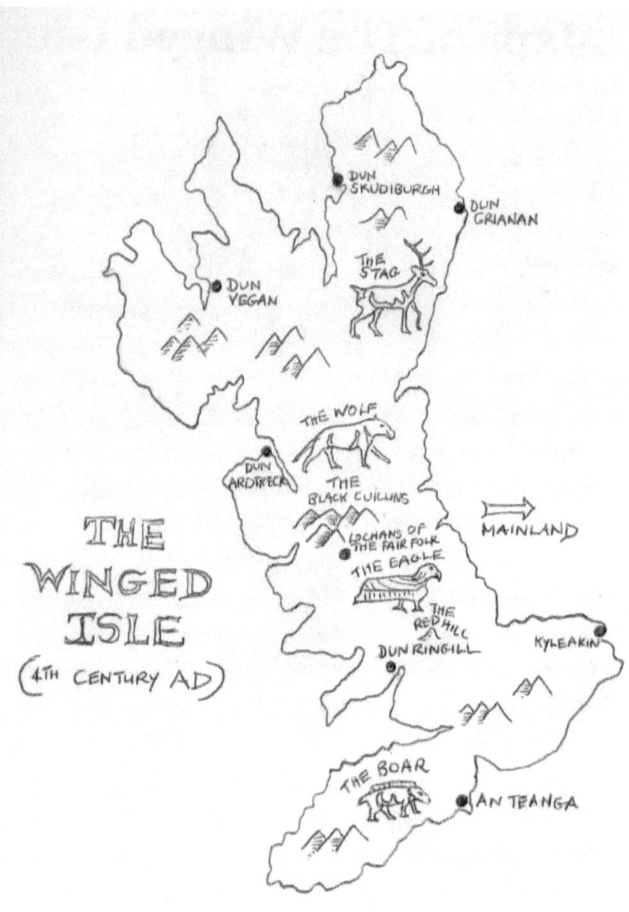

DUN SKUDIBURGH
DUN GRIANAN
THE STAG
DUN VEGAN
THE WOLF
DUN ARDTRECK
THE BLACK CUILLINS
LOCHANS OF THE FAIR FOLK
MAINLAND
THE EAGLE
THE RED HILL
DUN RINGILL
KYLEAKIN
THE WINGED ISLE
(4TH CENTURY AD)
THE BOAR
AN TEANGA

Background notes for BLOOD FEUD

Glossary

All-Heal: old name for Valerian root
Aos Sí or Fair Folk: fairies
bandruí: a female druid or seer
Broch: a tall, round, stone-built, hollow-walled Iron Age tower-house
Caesars: the Ancient Romans
Cruthini: the name the mainland Picts gave to themselves
drualus: mistletoe
The Land of the Cruthini: Pictland

Place names

An t-Eilean Sgitheanach: Gaelic name for the Isle of Skye
Beinn na Caillich: the Red Hill of Skye
Black Cuillins: mountains in the west of the Isle of Skye
Dun Ardtreck: a broch located on the Minginish Peninsula of Skye (home of the Wolf tribe)
Dun Ringill: an Iron Age hill fort on the Strathaird Peninsula of Skye (home of the Eagle tribe)
Dun Skudiburgh: a fort on the north-east edge of Skye (a Stag tribe stronghold)
Kyleakin: a village on the south-east edge of Skye
River Brittle: the river beneath the Fairy Pools
The Lochans of the Fair Folk: the Fairy Pools

The four tribes of The Winged Isle*

The People of The Eagle (south-west)
The People of The Wolf (north-west)
The People of The Boar (south-east)

The People of The Stag (north-east)

Gods and Goddesses of The Winged Isle*

The Mother: Goddess of enlightenment and feminine
energy—the bringer of change
The Warrior: God of battle, life and growth; of summer
The Maiden: Young goddess of nature and fertility
The Hag: Goddess of the dark—sleep, dreams, death,
winter, and the earth
The Reaper: God of death.

Festivities on the Isle of Skye*

Earth Fire: Salute to new life and the first signs of spring
(February 1)
Bealtunn: Spring Equinox
Mid-Summer Fire: Summer Equinox
Harvest Fire: Festival to salute the harvest (Aug 1)
Gateway: Passage from summer to winter (October
31/November 1)
Mid-Winter Fire: Winter Equinox

* Author's note: I have taken 'artistic license' when it
comes to the names of the tribes, festivities, and gods
and goddesses upon the Isle of Skye. The historical
evidence is very scant, making it a challenge for me to
get an accurate picture of what the names of the tribes
living upon Skye during the 4th century would have
been. Likewise, I could not find any references to their
gods and festivities. The Picts were an enigmatic people,
and we only have their ruins and symbols to cast light on
how they lived and whom they worshipped. To make my
setting as authentic as possible, I have studied the rituals
and religions of the Celtic peoples of Scotland, Ireland,
and Wales of a similar period and have created a culture
I feel could have existed.

Cast of characters (in alphabetical order)

Alia: midwife at Dun Ringill
Cal, Namet, Lutrin, and Ru: Galan's four most trusted warriors
Deri: young woman married to Cal, one of Galan's warriors
Domech mac Bred: Wolf Chieftain, Tea's father (deceased)
Donnel mac Muin: youngest son of the Eagle chieftain
Eithni: Tea and Loc's younger sister
Fina: Tea's mother (deceased)
Forcus mac Vist: Wolf warrior, Tea's ex-lover
Galaith: Galan's mother (deceased)
Galan mac Muin: eldest son of the Eagle chieftain
Loc mac Domach: Tea's brother and new Wolf chieftain
Luana: Donnel's wife
Mael: Luana's sister (married to Maphan)
Muin mac Uerd: Eagle chieftain, Galan's father (deceased)
Ruith: the seer at Dun Ringill
Talor: Luana and Donnel's infant son
Tarl mac Muin: middle son of the Eagle chieftain
Tea: (pronounced Teeya) the daughter of the Wolf chieftain
Wid: Tea and Loc's cousin

Prologue

Broken

Late summer, 366 AD—the Isle of Skye

The fort of Dun Ardtreck

TEA STOOD HIGH on the walls of Dun Ardtreck and watched the men bring her father's body home from battle.

Her brother wept as he led the shaggy pony pulling a litter up the incline. The other warriors trailed behind Loc and his pony, many of them limping or cradling injured limbs. From her vantage point atop the stacked-stone wall, Tea could not see the face of the corpse upon the litter, but she knew it could only be her father. She had not seen her brother weep since they were children. Ice-cold dread slithered down her spine.

"Father," she whispered, her voice catching in her throat.

She did not want to believe it.

Domech mac Bred was a true warrior of An t-Eilean Sgitheanach—The Winged Isle that lay just beyond the edge of the mainland. He had been destined to die protecting the island from invaders, not in some bloody skirmish with the Eagles of Dun Ringill.

Shock chilled Tea to the core, and for a moment she forgot to breathe.

Then she swept her heavy fur cloak close and descended the stairs from the high wall. Her leather foot coverings scraped on rough stone as she flew down the steps and sprinted toward the gates of Dun Ardtreck.

Behind her rose a great stone broch—a round tower-house made of stone—and beyond that a sheer rock face rose higher still. Shaped like an enormous beehive, Dun Ardtreck perched upon a rocky knoll, on the edge of a cliff, smoke snaking from the two slits in its great roof.

To the west the waters of Loch Bracadale glittered in the late afternoon sun. A chill breeze blew in from the same direction, a sharp reminder that summer was ending and Harvest Fire was on its way. To the north lay the mouth of Loch Harport and the naked brown crags of the headland beyond. Loch Harport itself stretched east, cutting inland in a long finger and forming the Minginish Peninsula where Tea's people ruled.

Breathing hard, Tea reached a dry stone wall and passed through a wide archway. There she waited at the entrance to the cleft between two rocks—the only entrance to the fort—for her father's party to arrive.

Loc had wiped the tears from his face by the time he emerged before the gates. Tall and dark, like Tea, her brother walked as if he carried a great weight upon his shoulders. He was limping and leaned against his pony for support. Blood encrusted his right leg, and he bore a nasty gash to his left shoulder.

Their cousin, Wid, a burly young man with long, black hair, walked a few paces behind Loc. Barely out of boyhood, Wid looked badly shaken. His youthful face, with just a fuzz of dark beard starting to grow on his chin, was ashen beneath a layer of grime and blood.

The procession inched closer, and then Loc was standing before her.

"Tea." Her brother's gaze met hers. They had the same colored eyes—those of their dead mother—deep midnight blue. His red-rimmed eyes and swollen face told the story Tea had been dreading to hear. "Father fell."

She stared at him, horror rendering her speechless. Stiffly, as if she was sleep-walking, she stepped around him and stopped before the litter.

Domech son of Bred, chieftain of her people, lay there—as dead, grey, and cold as stone. Blood was splattered over his pale face from the slash wound across his throat.

"Who did this?" she finally croaked.

"Their chief, Muin," Loc replied, his own voice rough with grief, "but not before father delivered a fatal blow to his belly."

Forcus, a warrior with curly brown hair and pale blue eyes, stepped up beside Loc. The man's gaze met Tea's, direct and bold as usual. A year earlier she and Forcus had briefly been lovers. Although their union had ended, the pair had remained close ever since.

"Muin died screaming," Forcus informed her. "Domech made him suffer before the end."

Tea stared at him, barely able to take the words in. Then she looked down at her father's face. Even in death he looked formidable: a warrior to strike fear into the hearts of his enemies.

Her gaze shifted away from her father to the last stragglers, as they limped their way into the fort. The other warriors walked by them. Bloodied and beaten, they were a sorry sight. "So few have returned," she whispered.

"It was an ambush," Forcus told her, his voice flint-hard. "They were waiting for us."

Tea stepped back from the chieftain's corpse, her attention shifting to her brother. Such was her shock at seeing her father dead that she had barely noticed Loc's injuries.

"You're hurt." Her gaze travelled down from the blood-soaked leg of his plaid breeches to the deep laceration on his shoulder. "Eithni needs to tend your wounds."

Loc shook his head, brushing off her concern. He did not want a fuss made of him, not when their father lay dead just a few feet away.

Speaking of their sister made Tea's belly twist. Eithni would be broken by the news—and it would fall upon Tea to tell her.

Tea brushed out her father's long, dark hair and marveled at how little grey he had in it. At forty three winters, he still looked to be in the prime of life.

She and Eithni stood in an alcove within the broch, where they were preparing Domech mac Bred for his burial. Beside Tea, Eithni wept as she painted curling blue designs over her father's chest. He bore a number of tattoos, including a wolf's head on his right arm, but many of them had faded with age—the paint brought them back to life.

Tea blinked back tears of her own and slid silver and gold rings studded with amber onto her father's fingers. They had dressed him in his finest clothes, before adding a long robe that reached his ankles. The robe was trimmed with a fur collar and hemmed in gold.

Tea inhaled deeply and scrubbed at the tears that trickled down her cheeks. *Stay strong.* Grief sat like a boulder in her chest, but she would not succumb to it.

Eithni drew back from her father and put aside her brush and clay pot of woad paint. Her face was wet, her eyes swollen—yet Eithni's grief had not prevented her from carrying out her duties.

Silently, the sisters now made the final touches to their father's appearance. Tea placed Domech's iron sword, which he had carried through so many battles, upon his chest, and folded his hands across its bronze pommel. His wooden shield, covered with leather and stained with the mark of The Wolf, she lay across his legs.

Their father would go to meet The Mother looking his finest.

Dusk was settling over Dun Ardtreck as the procession of mourners carried the chieftain's body out to the barrows. Domech mac Bred would now join his forefathers in a stone cairn to the south east of the broch. The men held him aloft upon a bier.

Tea and Eithni walked behind the warriors bearing the chieftain, at the head of the group of mourners. Her sister was weeping again, yet Tea was dry-eyed.

Tears would not help now. Only vengeance would soothe her aching heart.

They reached the row of stone mounds and brought the chieftain's body to the closest of the cairns. Its entrance was a gaping, dark mouth, yawning to receive him.

As the eldest daughter, Tea stepped up to sing the lament. Had her mother still been alive, this would have been *her* role. Inhaling deeply, Tea steeled herself for the outpouring of emotion that was to follow.

She began the song. At first her voice was low and tremulous, but then it rose to great heights, soaring above the mourners and becoming part of the grey dusk.

Great Domech mac Bred
Go to your long sleep.
Taken cruelly
Slain without honor
Too soon

Too soon.

The last strains of Tea's voice died away, and behind her she heard quiet sobs. Her own heart was racing, slamming against her ribs like a battle drum. The warriors slid the chieftain's body into his final resting place, sealing the entrance with a heavy slab of stone. Beside Tea, Eithni gave a choked cry of grief and buried her face in her hands. Tea stepped close to her and wrapped an arm around her sister's shaking shoulders.

Bile rose in Tea's throat, and her chest ached from the force of the rage and sorrow that warred for dominance within her.

The People of The Eagle had no honor. Tea would have her reckoning. She would see the earth stained crimson for this treachery.

One month later ...

Chapter One

Sacrifice for Peace

HARVEST FIRE ARRIVED upon the isle with shorter days and a chill to the air. The folk of Dun Ardtreck celebrated the changing of the seasons with a great slaughter of animals—sheep, goats, and pigs—for the coming winter. After the blood-letting ceremony at dusk, Tea and her sister helped the other women carry pails of blood and entrails back up to the fort, while the men carried the carcasses. Days of work lay ahead when the women would make blood pudding and sausages. Once the meat had hung, they would need to salt much of it to ensure they had food for the bitter months.

As dusk fell, the folk of Dun Ardtreck lit great fires on the slopes beneath the fort. Harvest Fire was just one of the many days the folk of The Winged Isle celebrated. At Harvest Fire, night and day were of equal length—and this balance meant the night was a powerful, magical time. Druids and healers would be out tonight, making divinations about the months to come or asking favors of the gods.

The revelers drank newly pressed cider before the fire and danced around the flames, the boom of drums thudding through the gloaming. Afterward they wandered indoors to enjoy a great feast.

Inside the great circular feasting hall lined with alcoves, folk sat at long wooden tables, perched upon low benches. They feasted upon roast goat, braised beans, salted pork, and fresh bread. Mead and ale flowed, while a harpist played near the crackling fire pit in the center of the hall.

Loc had taken his father's place at the head of the chieftain's table. His young cousin, Wid, and most trusted warrior, Forcus, now sat at his right hand. It still felt odd to sit here without Domech's booming voice. Loc's was a quieter, more brooding presence.

The roar of voices was deafening inside the stone space, but Tea felt apart from it all. She sat near the head of the chieftain's table. Next to her, Eithni took listless bites of meat, her heart-shaped face pale and strained. A month had passed since their father's death, yet Eithni was not bearing up well. Three years younger than Tea, Eithni was small and delicate with fine, light-brown hair the color of walnut—the same looks and coloring as their mother. Like her mother, Eithni was a sweet, gentle soul. Tea shared her sister's melancholy this eve, for she too still felt her father's loss keenly. She could not bring herself to smile and share in the revelry of Harvest Fire.

Tea sipped at a cup of mead, ignoring the chatter of conversation around her, and glanced up at the carved wooden beams that ran overhead. They depicted the gods and the special times of year folk honored them. As always, the carved figures drew her in.

There was The Mother, presiding over Mid-winter; and The Warrior taking part in the Mid-Summer Fire. Nearby, a carving showed The Maiden dancing at Earth Fire and Bealtunn. Directly overhead, Tea spied The Hag watching over tonight's celebration—Harvest Fire. The only god not honored above was The Reaper, the god that ruled Gateway—the festival that marked the beginning of the dark, bitter months. It boded ill for any who tried to depict his likeness.

Tea's gaze lingered on the stooped figure of The Hag, an aged crone bent over a cauldron—a symbol of both life and death that reminded Tea of her father. She hoped he was being treated well in the afterlife.

"Tea."

She dropped her gaze from the ceiling and glanced at her brother, realizing that he had been trying to catch her attention. She met his eye and gave an apologetic smile. "Aye, Loc."

"Did you hear what I was saying?"

Tea blinked. "No, I was far away—sorry."

Her brother's face was tense, his blue gaze clouded. "No matter—it bears repeating anyway."

Next to him, Forcus was scowling. "Spare us," he muttered. "I've already heard enough."

Ignoring the warrior, Loc focused on his sister. They were only eighteen months apart and had always been close. Yet ever since his father's death there had been something different about him. It was something she could not put her finger on: a tension, a resolve.

"I was saying that this feuding must come to an end," Loc said quietly, spearing a piece of meat with his knife.

"Aye," Tea replied with a sharp nod. "With the destruction of our enemies."

Forcus gave a grunt of approval. "At least one of you sees sense."

Tea frowned, her gaze flicking between him and Loc. "Excuse me?"

Around them, the feasting hall had quietened. Although Loc's voice was not as loud as his father's had been, the tone of it commanded respect. However, some of the warriors were exchanging wary glances in a way that immediately put Tea on guard.

Her brother sighed. "I'm not talking about war, Tea. This blood feud is a beast devouring its own tail. If we continue to feed the beast, it will never die." He gave her a long, hard look. "I'm talking about peace."

Tea stared at him a moment before giving a disdainful laugh. "Over my dead body."

Loc shook his head, making it clear it was he who led here, not his spirited sister. "No, for what must be done this tribe needs you to live."

Tea stiffened, while beside her Eithni had stopped pretending to eat and now watched her brother and sister keenly. Opposite Tea, Forcus had gone still. The cold, hard look on his face made it clear that Loc had not shared these thoughts with him. Not heeding the deathly silence at the table, her brother continued.

"I will not make the same mistakes as my father," he said, his voice low and flat. "I will not leave wives without husbands and families without fathers." Loc's gaze fused with Tea's. "You will wed the chieftain of The Eagle and bring peace to The Winged Isle."

For a few moments, Tea did nothing. She merely sat there, reeling at her brother's proclamation.

"What?" she finally rasped, her fingers curling around the bone-handled knife she had been using to eat her meal.

"I sent word to Dun Ringill and have just heard back," Loc continued, seemingly unaware of the hostility that crackled in the air around him. "Their new chief, Galan mac Muin, is of the same mind as me—he wants peace and is willing to wed you if that means no more blood will be shed between our tribes."

Tea's lip curled. "The son of a butcher? I'll not wed him."

"Yes, you will."

Tea struggled to her feet, shaking from the force of her rage. "Betrayer!" she shouted. Around them the entire feasting hall had gone silent. The revelers stopped eating and drinking and turned to watch brother and sister lock horns. "Father would kill you for your weakness … your cowardice!"

Loc rose to his feet, his face thunderous. "Bravery isn't always measured by how many men you slay," he growled. "Sometimes it takes courage to choose peace."

Tea resisted the urge to spit at him, to rake his face with her nails and kick him in the cods. "I'll not wed that murderer's spawn. Father would never have allowed this."

Loc's gaze went hard. "Father is dead." His voice was cold and flat. "I'm chief now—and my word here is law."

Tea left the feasting hall then—it was either that or attack her brother. She was not so incensed that she forgot her place. Like her, Loc was proud and stubborn. He would never back down, especially in front of his warriors. She would shame him at her peril.

She stormed out of the warm, smoky interior, crushing rushes underfoot as she went. Outside a cold wind whistled around the broch's solid base, causing the peat braziers to gutter and spit. On the hill below, the Harvest Fire bonfires were burning down to glowing embers.

Tea had come outside without her mantle, but despite that she wore only a sleeveless woolen tunic cinched at the waist with a heavy bronze belt, she barely noticed the chill. The wind whipped her hair into her eyes, and she pushed it aside, blinking back tears of rage as she did so.

How dare he?

It was unthinkable that she would marry The Eagle chieftain—utterly unthinkable. In the days since burying her father, all she had thought about was revenge. She had lain awake in her alcove and imagined the day her brother would lead his men against the People of The Eagle and slaughter them all. Instead, he had been plotting peace, using her as his pawn. He expected her to live among them, to bear her enemy's children.

Tears now scalded her cheeks. He could not send her away. Dun Ardtreck was her world. She would not leave her sister alone, could not abandon the people here who depended on her. As her mother had done with her father, Tea co-ruled the fort with her brother. However, like Domech, Loc had the final say.

Her belly twisted painfully. She felt like a fat lamb about to be sacrificed at Earth Fire. And it was her own brother who whetted the blade.

"Tea ... are you well?"

She turned to see a man's broad silhouette emerge from the broch behind her. Forcus stepped up beside her. The guttering braziers illuminated the masculine lines of his face but threw his eyes into darkness. Like her, Forcus had come outside without his cloak. Wearing only leather breeches, he did not even flinch at the cold. Dark swirls inked his broad torso, and around his neck he wore a leather thong with an amber pendant carved into the shape of a wolf's head.

Tea shook her head and looked away. She did not wish for company. She never let others see her upset—tears were for private. Even Forcus, who had been her lover for a time, had never seen her weep.

"Your brother is a fool," Forcus said finally.

In other circumstances, Tea would have railed at him for insulting her kin, but not this evening. Tonight he spoke the truth.

"Does he really believe what he's saying?" she asked, her voice husky with the effort she was making to control her panic. "Does he really trust them?"

Forcus barked a laugh. "Of course not. He's desperate for peace and will do anything to achieve it."

"But Muin's son—why has he agreed to this?"

"It seems that he too has lost his stomach for war."

Tea turned to face him. She refused to believe that her brother could get away with this. "But surely, Loc stands alone? His warriors won't follow him."

"Many agree with him, including Wid."

Tea stared, aghast. "But why?"

"Seems they are tired of war. They believe Loc can give them a better life."

Dread crawled over her skin at this news. Loc's warriors had been her last hope; her only chance that her brother's mind could be changed. Without their support, she was lost.

Hopelessness swamped her—for the first time in her life she despaired. She had been through much in her twenty winters. Her mother, Fina, had died young. Tea had been barely ten winters old when the enemy attacked Fina and her escort on her way home from visiting relatives on the north-east of the isle. Muin, The Eagle chieftain, had raped and murdered Fina. Domech had never been the same since.

Was it any wonder he had sought to destroy the man responsible for his wife's death?

Tea knew she was strong, yet the desire to throw herself off the cliff outside the fort walls overwhelmed her.

I'll not wed Muin's whelp.

Sensing her desperation, Forcus stepped quietly forward and placed his hands on her shoulders. "Forget about all this. Let's leave it behind," he said, his voice low and urgent. "Come with me. We'll go tonight ... cross to the mainland and begin a new life there."

Tea stared up at him, blinking. She was in turmoil over Loc's decision, and Forcus was proposing she run away with him? He spoke as if they were still together. She and Forcus had ended their affair over a year earlier, for his domineering ways had made her feel suffocated. Once more he reminded her why she had left him.

Tea twisted away from him, anger rising. "Are you mad? I'm not leaving this isle."

He watched her, his broad, heavily-muscled body going still. "You'd rather wed that Dun Ringill dog then?" Each word cut like a knife blade, but Tea did not flinch.

"I'll not wed anyone." She choked the words out, rage strangling her. "I won't be any man's slave."

He gave a cold laugh and turned away from her. "That's exactly what you'll be."

Chapter Two

Rage

"I"LL NOT WED him."

Loc mac Domech sighed and looked up from the game of knuckle bones he was having with Wid. His gaze settled upon where his sister stood, hands on hips, before him.

"I'll take my life if you force me."

Loc watched his sister silently for a few moments, taking in her blazing eyes, pinched lips, and rigid stance. He did not believe for a moment that Tea would do such a thing, yet the paleness of her face and the hollows under her eyes worried him somewhat. He did not like to see her suffer.

Guilt needled him. He did not want to do this to his proud sister, but he would not cast away this opportunity to forge peace.

"Do I need to confine you to your alcove until we leave?" he asked, deliberately keeping his voice low, his tone neutral. If he responded with anger, Tea would merely use it as an excuse to rage at him again. Their arguments since his announcement five days earlier had been blistering. Now, every time the siblings entered the feasting hall together, the inhabitants of the broch cast wary glances their way—holding their breaths till the next tempest.

"Did you just hear me?" she ground the words out, a nerve ticking in her jaw as she sought to restrain her temper. "I said I'd—"

"I heard you," Loc cut her off, aware that Wid was now shifting nervously on the bench opposite him. His cousin knew there was another storm brewing. Loc rose to his feet and met his sister's eye. "But I tire of having the same argument, day after day. It will not change my mind."

Tea stepped close to him. She was tall and met his eye easily. "Muin mac Uerd raped and murdered our mother. Have you forgotten that?"

Loc inhaled deeply. This was the argument she used most frequently against him, the one she knew wounded the deepest. Yesterday she had slapped him when they had discussed this. His jaw still ached from her blow. He did not want to raise his hand to his sister—but if she lost control again, he would have no choice.

"I could never forget it," he replied softly, "but Galan is not Muin. Why should he pay for his father's crimes?"

"He fought at the battle where father fell, did he not?"

"He did."

"He has killed our people too. He's our enemy," Tea concluded.

Loc remembered Galan there in that steep vale strewn with boulders—a tall, broad-shouldered warrior with long, dark hair who fought with cold, precise brutality. Yet the two of them had not crossed swords that day. After the ambush, once both chiefs had fallen, Galan had the chance to slay Loc and his men—instead, he had let them live, had given them time to escape. Loc had known then that Galan mac Muin was different to his father.

Loc sighed. He was wearying fast of this discussion. "Battle is different, Tea," he replied. "You know that."

"How is it different?"

"It just is. When two war parties clash, they know there will be death on both sides—it's expected."

Tea glared at him, incensed now. "I'm not some goose-brained woman you can patronize. I've been trained to fight—and I would have been with you that day if father hadn't forbidden it."

Loc's mouth thinned. "He was right to forbid it. You and Eithni are all that is left of our family's female line. You must be protected."

He watched her hands clench and unclench at her sides. He could see the fury that pulsed through her. Even before their father's death, Tea had been so full of anger, so embittered for one so young. She had been young when they brought Fina's mutilated body back to Dun Ardtreck—but that day Loc had seen his sister change. Overnight, she went from an energetic and mischievous lass, to a self-contained, angry girl who wanted to fight with the world.

She had trained as a warrior alongside Loc, and was as good as any of the men, but Domech had insisted she stay behind whenever he led a war party out. Tea had raged at her father's decision, but Domech would not be moved.

Looking into his sister's blazing gaze, Loc realized there would be no reasoning with her—instead, her continued defiance forced him to be harsh.

"You will wed Galan mac Muin," he growled. "Even if I have to drag you into his bed myself."

Tea reeled back as if he had struck her, nearly colliding with Eithni who was sitting upon a stool behind her, winding wool onto a wooden spindle. Tea's sister cried out, toppling off her stool onto the rushes. However, Tea was so incensed that she did not even notice.

"You're a disgrace to his line," she snarled. "I'm ashamed to call you my brother."

Then she spat on the rushes between them and stormed off to her alcove, the goat-skin hanging swishing shut behind her.

Tea was sitting upon a pile of furs inside her alcove, staring blankly at the pitted stone wall, when Eithni poked her head inside.

"Can I come in?"

Her sister's face was pale and pinched, her hazel-green eyes wide with fright. Tea felt a rare pang of remorse. Tea and Loc's fights of late had reduced Eithni to tears more than once, and although Tea had no intention of relenting, she was sorry to see her sister so upset.

"Aye," Tea replied, her voice husky from shouting. Now that her anger had burned itself out, she felt exhausted, drained.

Eithni stepped into the alcove and let the hanging fall shut behind her. Then she padded across to Tea and sat down on the furs next to her. Wordlessly, she reached out and took Tea's hand.

Tears prickled Tea's eyelids. Her sister's gentleness was disarming. She squeezed Eithni's hand in silent thanks.

After a few moments her sister spoke. "Please don't fight Loc any longer," she murmured. "It will not change things—it will only make you hate each other."

"I don't hate him," Tea replied, "but I can't let him do this to me—to us."

She glanced over at Eithni and saw that she was watching her steadily. They were so different—Tea was like a tempest, Eithni a summer breeze—and yet they had always been close. Tea kept herself apart emotionally from most people. She only let her brother and sister into her private world, and now that Loc had betrayed her, Tea was starting to feel as if no one but Eithni cared what happened to her.

Eithni held her gaze, her own calm and resolute. "I can make it easier for you," she said softly.

Tea frowned, not understanding her sister's meaning. When she did not respond, Eithni continued. "I can make you a special potion—one that will soothe your nerves and make the handfasting easier to bear."

Tea stared at Eithni, swallowing the hysteria that bubbled within her. She had not even thought that far ahead, for in her mind she still refused the match outright. Yet her sister's words reminded her of what lay ahead. She would wed this enemy, would have to lie with him as his wife and bear his whelps. Eithni had not meant to alarm her, but she had.

Her sister was a healer. Since girlhood, she had helped Old Maud, the cunning woman who tended the ill at Dun Ardtreck. Maud had died last winter, and now Eithni had taken over as healer. Tea knew Eithni took her role seriously; however, her skills could not mend what ailed her sister.

Tea removed her hand from Eithni's and stood up. She then began to pace the narrow space, her bare feet sinking into the thick furs that covered the floor of the alcove. Panic made it hard to breathe.

"Give me something to stop my heart," she choked out the words. "Prevent this handfasting from ever taking place. That's the only thing that can help me."

"I won't do that." Eithni jumped to her feet and grasped Tea by the arm, forcing her to turn and face her. Despite her small frame, she had a surprisingly firm grip. "I'd take my own life before I'd ever harm you." Eithni's eyes glittered with tears. "Please stop fighting this, Tea. Whether you wish it or not, Loc will insist you wed The Eagle chieftain. Don't make this any harder than it needs to be—don't ruin the few days we all have left together."

Tea stared at her. If Loc had spoken those words, she might have lashed out at him. Yet she would never do so with Eithni—and her sister knew it. Eithni was only trying to help her, only trying to mend things between Tea and Loc. But she did not understand that some rifts could not be bridged. Some wounds cut too deep.

Tea's throat constricted, and she felt tears sting her eyelids. "For your sake, I'll stop raging," she agreed finally, "but it changes nothing. I'll not pretend to welcome this union, and I'll not forgive Loc for giving me to the enemy."

Chapter Three

The Gathering at the Pools

GALAN MAC MUIN reined in his pony and glanced up at the darkening sky. He did not like the look of those roiling purple clouds to the east, or the ominous rumble of thunder in the distance. However, the bleak crags of the mountains, the Black Cuillins, loomed overhead, telling him that their destination was near.

Glancing over his shoulder, his gaze slid over the procession behind him. Only a few of them—him, his brothers, and his proven warriors—rode on horseback. The rest of his band travelled on foot. It took half a day to reach the gathering place, the half-way point between Dun Ardtreck and Dun Ringill. They had been climbing for a while now, crossing rivers, peat moor, and rocky hills covered in heather, to reach the sacred pools.

Behind Galan his brother Tarl met his eye. "I can hear the first waterfall," he said, raising an eyebrow. "Your bride is near."

Galan cocked his head. He too could hear the low roar of water tumbling down from a great height. His chest tightened slightly in response—suddenly this was becoming real. When a warrior had arrived from Dun

Ardtreck a month earlier with word that The Wolf chieftain wished to make peace, Galan had been initially suspicious. However, Loc mac Domech's emissary was an articulate woman who put forward a strong, convincing argument—and Galan was of a mind to believe her.

Now that they were just a short distance from their destination, Galan's suspicions rose once more.

I hope I have not brought my people into a trap.

The youngest of the three brothers, Donnel, drew up alongside Tarl then. His wife, Luana, pregnant with their first child, rode double with Donnel, her slender arms wrapped around his waist.

The sight of Luana gave Galan a pang of misgiving. Donnel's wife had insisted on accompanying them—but what if they were riding into an ambush?

"Why have we stopped," Donnel asked, his face troubled. "Is something wrong?"

Tarl grinned at his younger brother. "Looks like Galan's having second-thoughts."

Donnel smirked. "Bit late for that now."

Ignoring them both, Galan swung down from Faileas—'Shadow'—the shaggy, heavy-set stallion that had carried him here. "We go on foot from here," he announced.

Ignoring his brothers' grins, Galan turned and led the way up the rocky incline. The path was steep and rough, but his pony managed to pick its way up the hillside. Finally, the first waterfall hove into view: a frothing column of water thundering down from craggy grey rocks.

Mist from the fall drifted across the path and caressed Galan's face. He inhaled deeply. The air smelled perfumed here. He had not been to the pools in a long while, but this place touched him, as it had on his last visit.

He turned then to Tarl, who stepped up beside him. His brother's teasing expression had been replaced by one of wonder. His gaze travelled over the waterfall for a few moments before it flicked to Galan.

"Are you sure this place is as sacred to them as it is to us. What if they've laid a trap?"

Galan gave a tight smile. "The Lochans of the Fair Folk are revered by us all," he reminded his brother quietly with more confidence than he actually felt. "They will not shed blood here."

Tarl snorted. "You have more trust in them than me."

Galan favored his brother with a long look. "To forge peace, I must." He paused here, his gaze shifting to the column behind him. Trust was one thing, stupidity another. "Tell everyone to have their weapons within easy reach though … just in case Loc mac Domech turns out not to be a man of his word."

They continued on their way farther up the hill, alongside the River Brittle, to the remaining lochans—pools—beyond. Their destination was a large, clear blue pool framed by a natural stone arch. Known as The Wishing Pool, it was a favorite spot for handfastings among the four tribes that lived upon The Winged Isle. It also was a place favored by the Fair Folk—the Aos Sí—the fickle, magical creatures that cohabited the same earth as men. As such, it was wise to treat this spot with respect.

As they approached The Wishing Pool, Galan spied a cluster of hide tents pitched on the hill above it. A row of figures stood there, their dark, cloaked figures outlined against the stormy sky, watching the party approach.

Galan's body tensed at the sight of them. He had faced these people in battle countless times, but this meeting would be different. The daughter of his people's enemy awaited.

He could not imagine she was looking forward to this union.

Not that Galan was either. He did not like the idea of wedding a woman he had never met. She might look like the rear end of a goat or have a shrewish temper and a voice that could shred a man's nerves to dust. However, this was a sacrifice he was ready to make.

The memory of his father, screaming as he tried to push his entrails back inside his body, still haunted his dreams. Despite his father's death, The Eagle had won that day—but for Galan it had been a hollow victory. That was why he had let the rest of the enemy war party flee with their lives. The price had been too high. Too much blood had been spilled; too much hate had festered between the tribes for decades now.

Galan was ready for peace.

He led Faileas up the hill toward The Wolf camp. Ahead, a group of men came out to greet the newcomers. Galan was aware that his brothers now flanked him. He stole a glance behind to see that his four most trusted warriors—Ru, Namet, Lutrin, and Cal—had ridden up to the head of the column. Their faces were stern, their gazes watchful.

Despite that he had agreed to this meeting, Galan shared some of their tension. This was the first peaceful meeting between The Wolf and The Eagle for at least two decades. It felt strange—almost unnatural—to approach without his sword unsheathed and ready for battle.

A man stepped forward from the crowd at the crest of the hill and strode down to meet him.

Galan recognized Loc mac Domech immediately. He had seen him during their last skirmish; the pair of them had fought at different ends of the rocky ravine where their war parties had met, yet even then Galan had known him to be the chieftain's son.

Tall and lean, with a shock of black hair and piercing dark-blue eyes, The Wolf chieftain's face was stern as he approached. Galan sensed his wariness but hardly blamed him; this meeting was new territory for them both.

Since The Wolf chieftain was walking toward him alone and unarmed, Galan decided to pay him the same courtesy. He passed Faileas's reins to Tarl and walked forward to meet Loc.

The two men halted about four feet apart.

"Good day," Galan greeted him.

Loc favored him with a tight smile. "You came—I'm glad."

Galan smiled back, a little of his own tension easing as he realized that Loc mac Domech was indeed sincere. "Aye—I gave my word."

Loc's mouth quirked slightly, before his gaze flicked to Galan's escort waiting a few yards behind him. "I won't lie to you, Galan. Many of my people are against this union. I hope yours took the news better than mine did."

Galan's gave a humorless laugh. "No—they didn't."

"And your brothers?"

"Tarl and Donnel are more skeptical than me, but they will accept the new way of things in time. We are all tired of war."

Loc nodded. "As are we. This feud has gone on for so long, none of us know why we hate each other, only that we do."

Galan inclined his head slightly, studying Loc. Here was a man who would make a great leader. A man who understood the price of war on his people. Galan was glad Loc had sent word to him, and glad that he had agreed to forge peace between their tribes.

"And what of your sister?" Galan did not want to ask the question but knew he must. "Does she hate my people?"

Loc's mouth thinned, giving Galan his answer. "I wish I could say she is of the same mind as me," he admitted, "but she is too much like her father to let the past go so easily."

"Yet she has agreed to wed me?"

Loc gave a bitter smile. "Aye—under duress."

This news did not please Galan, although he had not expected any different. He did not want to share the furs with a hissing and spitting she-cat. Even so, it could not be helped—at least she understood her duty to her people.

Galan's gaze slid over the crowd amassed behind Loc. "Where is my bride?"

"Getting ready for her handfasting," Loc replied, "as must you. Come—we have ale, wine, and mead to share with you and your people."

Galan nodded before turning back to where his brothers and warriors stood. He beckoned them forward and then followed Loc up the slope to the tents. It looked as if the People of The Wolf had arrived here at least a day earlier; the grass underfoot was crushed and slightly muddy in places, and a village of hide tents now covered the hillside.

The aroma of roasting venison, no doubt for the handfasting feast, wafted through the camp. It was a delicious aroma, but Galan found he was not hungry; he was too tense to think about food.

"Here." Loc poured Galan a cup of frothy ale and passed it to him before holding up a cup of his own for a toast. "To lasting peace."

Galan was aware of the hostility around them—from the men and women of his own band, and from Loc's. There were two hulking warriors standing a few feet behind Loc, who did not look friendly. Galan did not like the cold, assessing way the men's gazes moved over him and his escort. Loc mac Domech may have been ready to make peace, but some of his warriors clearly were not.

Casting a look behind him, at where Tarl and Donnel were accepting cups of ale, Galan noted their hard faces and narrowed gazes. Things were not so different in his own camp—it had taken a while to convince his brothers to come here. Behind Tarl and Donnel, some of Galan's warriors looked uncomfortable. He had bid them to leave their weapons with the ponies, but they clearly were not pleased to be facing the People of The Wolf without a sword, axe, or spear grasped in their hands.

Galan stepped close to his brothers, his own brow furrowing.

"Would the pair of you try smiling?" he growled. "I don't want a fight breaking out before I wed."

Tarl snorted, glancing over at where the big warriors still stood eyeballing them. "If those bastards stop staring at me, I might."

"Ignore them."

Donnel rolled his eyes and raised the cup of ale to his lips. "I hope you know what you're doing."

Chapter Four

The Potion

TEA SAT IN stony silence as her sister washed her feet.

It was a ritual before handfasting for the bride to have her feet washed, so she could step out onto the path before her with confidence and make a clean start to her new life.

Tea's heart pounded throughout the rite, her body rigid like a doe ready to flee.

She had fought Loc, but in the end he had gotten his way. Brother and sister were both rulers at Dun Ardtreck and equally respected by their people. Yet when it came to marriage alliances, Loc commanded. After many ugly scenes, and tears from Eithni, she had finally submitted to her brother's will. Tea knew that many at Dun Ardtreck sided with her: to see the chieftain's sister wed an Eagle would be hard to stomach. However, Loc had refused to change his mind.

She hated Loc for it—she would never forgive him.

Sensing her sister's tension, Eithni glanced up, her face creasing with concern. They were alone inside the tent. The Eagles had arrived, and Loc was welcoming them, while Tea prepared for her handfasting.

Eithni gestured to the low wooden table beside them, where a cup sat next to a clay vial. "Tea ... I've prepared a drink for you."

"I'm not thirsty," Tea replied stiffly.

"It's All-Heal," Eithni explained with a tense smile. "Remember I said I'd fix you a potion? The calming herb should make the ceremony easier. I've added a few extra herbs of my own; it should soothe you."

Tea swallowed her rising nausea and forced a smile. She appreciated the gesture—Eithni was only trying to help.

Eithni finished washing Tea's feet before drying them with a strip of linen. "Will you wear mother's necklace?" she asked.

Tea nodded. "It's over there." She gestured to where the leather pack that she had carried from Dun Ardtreck sat.

Eithni rose to her feet and crossed to it. She began rummaging through the pack. While her sister's back was turned, Tea looked down at the cup Eithni had handed her. She was not sure she would be able to get through the coming ceremony without her sister's help. Her instincts told her to leap to her feet and run. Yet Eithni's potion was the only chance she had, if she was not going to shame her kin.

Bile filled Tea's mouth. *I shouldn't worry over shaming them. Loc's shamed us all with this truce.*

Still, it had to be done. Tea lifted the cup to her lips and drank deeply.

Eithni returned to her, carrying the heavy gilded necklace. It was an elegant coil, resembling a curled serpent. Tea's eyes filled with tears at the sight of it. She remembered her mother wearing the necklace at feast days, the gilded surface gleaming in the firelight as she laughed and sang at Domech's side.

"Here." Eithni knelt before her and slid the coil around her neck. Her eyes glistened as she gazed at it. "It suits you," she said softly.

Tea reached up, her fingers tracing the necklace's cool surface. It was one of the few items she had of her mother's—the rest had been buried with her.

"She would not want this," Tea said, bitterness turning her voice brittle. "To see me wed the son of the man who defiled and murdered her."

Eithni stared back, her expression pained. Tea could see she did not want to pursue this conversation, especially now. A moment later Eithni tried to steer her sister away onto another topic. "Did you see them arrive earlier?"

Tea shook her head. She had retreated inside her tent the moment someone told her of the enemy's approach. She had no wish to set eyes on any of them until she was forced to.

"I did," Eithni pressed on. "I saw him, Tea, the man you're going to marry."

Tea swallowed painfully. "And?"

Eithni met her gaze, her cheeks reddening slightly. She gave a small smile. "He's handsome at least."

Tea's lip curled. He could be a fire-breathing demon for all she cared. "He's an Eagle maggot," she replied. "I care not if he's got a pretty face. I'd sooner wed a turd."

Eithni gave her a pained look but said nothing.

Tea sighed; she could feel the All-Heal taking effect. Her body was slowly relaxing, although she was still too lucid. She needed to blunt the sharp edges of the world further if she was to go through with this.

She leaned forward and grasped her sister's hands. "I'm sorry, Eithni. I didn't mean to snap at you. I'm just nervous. There's a skin of wine in my pack, can you pass it to me?"

Eithni frowned. "I don't think wine mixes well with the potion I just gave you. It could make you light-headed."

"Please." Tea hated the desperation in her own voice. She had never felt like this, out of control—weak. She did not trust herself.

Would she be able to face her husband-to-be without knifing him?

Her sister's mouth thinned before she relented. "Very well, just a couple of sips." Eithni rose to her feet and reluctantly went to fetch the wine. She returned to Tea's side and handed her the skin, her brow furrowing. "Just don't drink anymore wine at the feast this evening—it's best to be careful."

Tea was just about to tell her to stop fussing, when the flap covering the tent's entrance opened, and Loc ducked inside.

Tea stiffened at the sight of him. Ever since his decision at Harvest Fire there had barely been a civil word between them. Loc's face was serious, his lean body tense, as he straightened up before his sister.

Tea's lip curled at the sight of him. "What do you want?"

Loc sighed, his gaze meeting hers. "I didn't come here to fight, Tea. We only have a short time left before you wed—let's not sour it."

Anger choked her for a few moments, and it took three deep breaths to master it. "Don't expect me to pretend I'm happy about this—I won't."

He looked steadily at her, sadness on his face, before answering. "I've spoken to Galan mac Muin—he seems a decent man ... a good choice for you."

"I should be able to make that choice for myself," she hissed back.

Loc's jaw clenched. "Let's not go into this again. You know why you must do this."

Tea lurched to her feet. "Don't stand there and tell me this man seems decent. You know who sired him—a murderer and rapist. The same blood runs through his veins, and you're giving me to him."

Loc ran a frustrated hand through his long dark hair. "For the love of the gods, Tea, you test my patience. I've told you—Galan isn't his father."

Tea straightened up, her anger warring with the numbing effects of the potion, which now settled over her like a soft fur mantle. "And you are nothing like ours," she snarled.

Color flared in Loc's cheeks, and he grabbed her by the shoulders, shaking her hard. "Enough!" he ground out between clenched teeth. "I've listened to your venom for too long now. You will do your duty, and there will be no more defiance!"

His fingers bit into her shoulders, hurting her. Still she stared back at him, refusing to back down. Their gazes held for long moments. Then with a look of disgust, Loc released her, turned on his heel and stalked from the tent.

Tea glared at his retreating back, angry words still burning within her. She glanced over at Eithni. Her sister gave her a reproachful look, which only served to fuel Tea's rage further. Gritting her teeth, Tea unstoppered the skin of wine and drank deeply.

Chapter Five

Handfasted

GALAN STOOD AT the edge of The Wishing Pool, watching the water glisten in the dusk, and waited for his bride to join him. The storm was getting close now. The sky overhead had deepened to slate grey, and there were specks of rain in the cool wind that had sprung up.

His people had made camp on the south-east slope of the hill, next to the tents of The Wolf. Tarl and Donnel had wanted to erect their tents farther away and place sentries on the edge, but Galan had refused. They needed to make a show of trusting their neighbors or the coming ceremony would mean nothing.

"Here she comes," Tarl murmured from beside him.

Something in his brother's voice, a note of surprise, made Galan glance up from the water. His gaze travelled over the waiting crowd to where a woman walked toward him.

Galan's breathing caught in his chest.

Tall and statuesque, her long jet hair flowing over her bare shoulders, his bride was a wild beauty. A band of supple leather bound her full breasts, leaving her midriff bare. A long woolen skirt hemmed in gold swished around her ankles as she walked barefoot over the grass. Her garb was simple, the addition of a heavy coil about her throat and heather threaded through her hair the only concessions to the special occasion. Unlike some of the women present, she did not bear many tribal tattoos—the symbol of The Wolf on her right bicep her only marking.

Galan stared at her, his gaze resting upon her face. She had high cheekbones and blue eyes the color of a summer's day sky just before dusk. Her mouth was full and soft, although the firmness of her jaw and chin hinted at a strong character. Holding his gaze, she lifted her head slightly in wordless challenge.

Galan slowly let out the breath he had been holding. He felt like he was coming out of a trance; this woman had held him spellbound for a few moments, as if she were one of the fair folk come to enslave him.

Another young woman followed his bride, a smaller female with brown hair and a pretty heart-shaped face. Galan assumed she must be kin, although she bore no resemblance to the majestic beauty before him.

His bride stopped before him at the edge of The Wishing Pool.

They would wed here, surrounded by nature and under the sky. Like his bride, Galan was barefoot. Clad in plaid breeches, his chest decorated with blue swirls and coils, he had removed his fur mantle before the ceremony.

Loc stepped up with a ribbon of plaid, to perform the handfasting. Usually, an older member from one of the tribes would lead the ceremony, but it had been a harsh past few years. Both Galan's parents were dead, as were Loc's.

"Join hands," Loc commanded softly.

Galan reached out, fastening his hand around his bride's wrist. Her eyes widened as she wrapped her own fingers around *his* wrist. Galan felt her pulse flutter against his fingertips. He looked into her eyes, searching for the hostility he expected, but was surprised to see that her gaze was slightly unfocused. She seemed to look straight through him. Had she been drinking ale before the ceremony?

"Galan mac Muin, Chieftain of The Eagle, I join you with my sister Tea, daughter of Domech mac Bred of The Wolf," Loc began. He started to wind the length of plaid around their hands, joining the two of them together. "May The Mother light your way. May The Warrior protect you. May The Maiden grant you healthy children. May The Hag bless you with long, healthy lives—and keep The Reaper from your door."

Galan inhaled deeply as Loc finished. It was now his turn to speak. "I, Galan mac Muin, pledge to protect you, Tea, daughter of Domech mac Bred, with my body and my life."

Silence fell then, long uncomfortable moments, before Loc fixed his sister in a hard stare. "Tea, it's time for you to say your words."

She blinked as if trying to concentrate and wet her lips before speaking. "I, Tea, daughter of Domech mac Bred, pledge to honor you, Galan mac Muin, with my body and my life."

Her voice was low and musical. So much for his fears that his new wife would be ugly with a voice that could curdle milk. Instead, Tea's voice was like a caress. Just the sound of it filled him with desire for her.

Relief flooded through Galan. The last few years had been hard, with bitter winters, poor harvests, and endless warfare. There had been little time for Galan to indulge himself, to take a lover, to enjoy the passing of the seasons and forget about survival. Looking at the wild dark beauty in front of him, he dared believe that was all about to change.

Around them the gathered crowd waited expectantly. Galan knew his brothers and sister-by-marriage stood directly behind him, while his warriors looked on silently father back. The tension that had settled over the groups after their first meeting had followed them to The Wishing Pool. Even a handfasting ceremony could not ease the simmering hostility on both sides.

Galan was relieved the initial greetings were over. Later, Loc would host a great feast where the two tribes would finally break bread together. Galan just hoped that the rich food and mead would help build a bridge between them. Even so, he was not foolish enough to believe that a wedding would end years of hatred; it was just the first step on a long road.

"You are now wed." Loc mac Domech's voice intruded, bringing Galan back to the present. The Wolf chief fixed him with a cool stare. "You can kiss your bride now."

Galan nodded and stepped forward, close to Tea. Gently, he reached down and cupped her chin with his fingertips, raising her face to his. She was a tall woman, so she did not have to angle her chin far in order to meet his gaze.

Like before, he noted her midnight blue eyes held a glazed, slightly unfocused look. Wordlessly, he leaned down and kissed her. However, it was like kissing a warm corpse. Her lips were soft, and she smelled of rosemary and lavender, but she did not move—did not respond.

Trying not to frown, Galan straightened up.

What's wrong with her? His earlier suspicion, that she had been drinking, increased. Had the thought of wedding him been so odious that she had downed a horn of mead?

At that moment thunder boomed loudly overhead, and the spitting rain grew heavy, stippling the still surface of The Wishing Pool.

Galan stepped back from his bride, blinking water out of his eyes as Loc quickly unwrapped the braided cord of plaid that joined them.

The handfasting was done; they were now man and wife.

Tea sat next to her husband and tried to focus.

They had retreated out of the driving wind and rain to a large conical-roofed tent. Loc had overseen its construction as soon as they arrived at the lochans. A large fire pit sat in its center and long tables formed a square around the hearth. Conversation rose and fell around them, mingling with the boom of thunder as the storm raged outside. At one end of the tent, two harpists had taken their places and were playing a pretty tune. Two lads had just carried in a haunch of venison which had been spit-roasting outside for the best part of the day—fortunately it had finished cooking just as the storm unleashed its fury.

Tea took a bite of venison and chewed slowly, struggling not to sway against Galan. She was not sure what other herbs Eithni had added to that draft, but she was starting to feel very strange. Her body felt boneless, weightless, her mind lost in a dreamy fog. All the anger she usually carried with her, the tension she wore like a mantle about her shoulders, had dissolved.

She felt free, wild ... and aroused.

Galan mac Muin was not what she had expected. Not at all.

She had not believed Eithni, had not cared, when her sister told her that he was handsome. Yet when she saw the tall broad-shouldered man waiting for her by The Wishing Pool, she had gone weak at the knees.

It was that potion, she was sure of it. Men did not affect her like this—and certainly not at first sight.

Nonetheless, Galan cut an imposing figure. Heavily muscled, with a brooding presence and eyes the color of slate, he had stared at her as if a goddess walked toward him.

He was handsome, but not in a chiseled way. Instead, he had strong, slightly hawkish features, which only added to the intensity of his gaze. His long dark hair was unbound this evening, falling down his back in glistening waves. He bore a large tattoo of an eagle on his right bicep, and tribal paintings traced the lines of his smooth bare chest.

Since their handfasting, Galan had said little. He sat beside her now, unspeaking, waiting while a woman—one of his relatives—poured a cup of mead and placed it between them. The woman was small and dark with a large pregnant belly. After she had served them, she took a seat to Galan's left, farther down the table.

"Drink!" someone shouted from across the tent. "Drink to your health and happiness."

Galan picked up the cup—bronze and decorated with garnets—and passed it to Tea.

Eithni had told Tea to avoid strong drink tonight, but Tea could not refuse to sip from her husband's cup.

Her fingers brushed his as she took it from him, and her heart started to race. The merest touch from this stranger excited her beyond reason. The pit of her belly had turned molten and need suddenly pulsed between her thighs. She squeezed them hard together, denying her body's violent reaction.

Damn Eithni and her potions.

She cast her sister a look of censure. Eithni was sitting between Loc and Forcus. Was she imagining things, or did her sister look worried? A crease had formed between her finely drawn eyebrows, and she watched Tea with a slightly narrowed gaze.

Feeling the weight of her husband's stare upon her, Tea turned her attention back to Galan and raised the cup to her lips. She held it with both hands and took a sip of mead. Then, as tradition dictated, she passed it to

Galan. His dark-grey gaze snared hers, and Tea felt her breathing still for a moment. Then he took the cup from her and completed the ritual.

A roar went up inside the tent. A cup of mead and good food had eased the tension between the two tribes a little, although Tea found it difficult to concentrate on anything except the brooding, virile man seated on the bench next to her. They sat so close that their thighs accidently brushed every time he leaned forward to help himself to more meat.

Tea took another bit of venison and inhaled deeply. *Breathe.*

She trusted her sister with her life—otherwise she would have thought Eithni had played some cruel trick upon her and given her a love potion rather than a draft to calm her nerves.

Her skin felt heated and sensitized. Her nipples chafed under the supple leather wrapping, and sweat beaded upon her skin when she thought about Galan freeing them and suckling her.

Gods, no—stop it.

Blinking, Tea reached for a tureen of braised onions and immediately regretted the action when her leg shifted against Galan. She felt his hard, muscular thigh against her thigh and lost all train of thought. Fortunately, he had not noticed. Galan was speaking with one of his warriors, who sat directly to his left.

In an effort to distract herself from her body's traitorous response to her new husband, Tea took a moment to observe his escort. Galan had introduced his brothers to her before they took their seats at the table. The three of them had the same slate-grey eyes and muscular build, but the similarities ended there.

Tarl, the brother who sat nearest to Galan and Tea, had a cocky, swaggering manner, shaggy dark brown hair, and the kind of brash self-confidence that Tea had never liked in men; it reminded her too much of

Forcus—who was sulking this evening at the end of their table, stabbing at his venison as if he wished to kill it twice.

Next to Tarl sat the youngest of the three, Donnel. With long eyelashes, a sensual mouth, and a cleft chin, he was the most handsome of the brothers. Donnel had dark hair, like Galan, but he wore his short. He had a calm, self-assured manner, and Tea noted how much attention he paid his pretty, dark-haired pregnant wife. The woman smiled back at him, letting him feed her choice pieces of meat. Clearly, they were very much in love.

Tea looked away, dropping her gaze to her half-eaten meal. The Warrior preserve her, how she wished she did not feel so odd. She could have burst into tears, she felt so emotional. Where was her fire, her anger? She felt naked without it.

Chapter Six

A Stormy Night

THE FEASTING AND drinking continued late into the evening. Outside, a violent storm battered the large tent, causing its hide covering to billow and snap. Yet inside, no one seemed to notice. The men passed a large drinking horn around the table—and many of the warriors grew raucous and red-faced as the night stretched out.

Galan was expected to drink twice as much as any of the men here, yet he refused the drinking horn more often than he accepted it. This was his wedding night; he wanted to be lucid when he took his bride to the furs. No woman wanted to be plowed by a swaying, drunken oaf. Galan wanted to remember this night.

Mid-way though the feasting, a fight broke out.

Tarl, who often got mouthy when he was in his cups, had been trading insults with a Wolf warrior across the table. The situation escalated when Tarl got over-exuberant and told the man his mother must have rutted with a hog to produce such an ugly son. In response, the warrior bellowed a curse, leaped to his feet, and launched himself across the fire at Tarl.

Food and drink went flying, and Donnel, who was seated next to his brother, barely avoided getting punched in the face as he yanked Luana to one side. A roar went up in the tent—but Tarl and The Wolf warrior were oblivious to it. Teeth bared, fists pummeling, they were still snarling insults and threats when other warriors pulled them apart.

"Enough!" Loc shouted. The Wolf chieftain had risen to his feet, his high cheekbones flushed with rage. "There will be no fighting here—not in this place."

Still glowering at Tarl, The Wolf warrior did as bid. However, Tarl remained on his feet, ignoring Loc's command.

"Sit," Galan growled at his brother, "before I knock you down."

Reluctantly, Tarl took his place at the table, although with ill-grace. He knew that Galan did not make idle threats.

Now that the fight had ended, conversation resumed within the tent, the roar of voices drowning out the storm outside.

Galan watched Tarl for a few moments, noting that Donnel was now speaking to him. Judging by the tautness of his youngest brother's face, and the angry gleam in his eyes as he spat out short sentences, Donnel was tearing strips off his brother for his poor behavior.

Satisfied that Tarl would behave himself now, Galan turned his attention back to his bride. She met his gaze; her eyes were dark, her lips slightly parted. If the fight had bothered her, she did not show it.

Tea had not spoken a word to him all night.

He did not know what to make of her. Her silence hinted that she was not happy about this match, and yet every time their gazes met the heat between them made him catch his breath. The look in her eyes now made him forget all else around them. Lust robbed him of his appetite, made him lose his taste for mead.

The only thing I want to feast on is her.

At this point of the evening, oatcakes dripping with honey were passed around the table. The sweets were typical of handfasting and supposed to ensure a fertile and happy marriage.

As tradition dictated, Galan fed Tea a morsel of cake. Her gaze held his as she took a bite and chewed slowly, her lips glistening with honey.

However, his heart nearly stopped when she reached up and took hold of his wrist. She kept his hand raised as she licked honey from his fingers. Her tongue slid over his skin, setting it alight.

Around them the table went silent.

The only sound was the snap and crackle of the fire pit and the roar of the storm beyond the tent.

Galan's groin stiffened so suddenly in reaction that he almost groaned. He paid no attention to the revelers watching them, forgot they were surrounded by kin and warriors. His whole world shrank to this sensual, raven-haired beauty. She licked his fingers as if they lay alone together in the furs, their limbs entwined.

It was more than he could stand.

Galan leaped to his feet, scooped Tea into his arms, and carried her from the tent. Catcalls, hoots, and lewd comments followed them, but he cared not.

He could think about nothing but the beautiful woman in his arms and what he intended to do to her once they were alone.

Tea huddled against her new husband's broad chest as he strode through the encampment toward their tent. The rain battered them in icy needles, and the wind howled like a wailing woman. Tea did not mind. Her head spun, and she could still taste the honey she had licked off Galan's fingers. Her belly fluttered with excitement at the feel of his strong arms around her.

Hunger consumed her, but it was not for more venison or honeyed oat-cakes. Instead, it was for this man.

The feeling of strangeness had increased as the evening progressed. She now felt as if she had stepped out of herself, as if a different woman—a lusty fairy maid—had taken over.

At the back of her mind, an angry voice heckled her. It told her she was a traitor to her family, that a true woman of The Wolf would have brought a knife to the ceremony and slit Galan mac Muin's throat. Her conscience had been quite vocal earlier, during the handfasting and at the beginning of the feasting, but then as the night went on, she found herself ignoring it.

Wildness had taken over. She had forgotten her kin sitting nearby and her brother's warriors watching her from across the fire pit. She had barely noticed, or cared about, the fight between Galan's brother and one of Loc's men. The world had shrunk to her and Galan. The impulse to lick honey off his fingers had risen unbidden, and the look on his face when she had done so nearly unraveled the last vestiges of her self-control.

She ached for him.

He carried her into a tent that sat near The Wishing Pool. The leather flap covering the entrance fell closed, sealing them inside a warm, dry space. Outside, the rain lashed and the wind shrieked, yet in here a lump of peat burned on a brazier, and a pile of furs had been placed in the center of the space, ready for the newly wedded couple.

Galan set her down before him, his arms going around her torso. His hands slid over her bare midriff to the supple leather binding around her breasts. Tea, who stood with her back to Galan, leaned into him and let out a low groan.

In response he muttered an oath and buried his face in her hair.

Deftly, he unfastened the binding and freed her breasts. His hands cupped them, feeling their fullness, before his fingers slid to her aching nipples. Tea groaned once more and leaned farther back against him, angling her hips so that she was pressed hard against his pelvis.

It was Galan's turn to groan. He swept aside the curtain of hair that flowed over her shoulders, his lips trailing up her neck to the shell of her ear.

Tea's groan turned to a cry, and she melted against him. If he had not been holding her up, she would have fallen. Every nerve ending in her body felt as if it was on fire.

Galan's hands slid down from her breasts to her waist. There, he unbuckled her heavy gilded belt and unlaced her skirt. The folds of plaid tumbled to her feet, pooling around her ankles. Then he pulled her back against him once more, and Tea stifled a gasp when she felt his shaft, thick and hot, pressed up against her buttocks. Wild excitement reared up within her.

They had not spoken since entering the tent and had not moved from just inside the entrance. Things were moving so fast that Tea felt out of breath.

Slowly, she rotated her hips, pressing against his shaft. Galan's answering groan caused a flush of pleasure to flower across her breast.

A heartbeat later he bent her forward and entered her from behind.

She gasped at how big he was—Forcus was her only experience of men, and his manhood had been far smaller. Instead, Galan stretched her, filling her completely. She was so wet that he slid into her like a hot blade through tallow. Pleasure thrummed through Tea; her body began to sing like a harp the moment he entered her.

The groan she let out then was so loud and animal, she did not even recognize it as her own. Shuddering, her

legs gave way under her, and she sank to the ground.
Galan lowered himself to the floor of the tent with her.

On all fours now, she gripped the edge of the furs while her husband—this stranger, a man she had not known until this afternoon—rode her in slow, deep thrusts.

Tea stretched on the furs and slowly awoke. Her limbs felt loose and languorous, and she felt a few moments of incredible well-being.

Then, like a crashing wave, reality intruded. Confused memories of the night before obliterated her fragile state. She could not remember everything that had happened. The memories were foggy, out of focus. There had been lucid moments, yes. She had known what she was doing, yet she had been unable to stop herself.

Galan had spent the long night loving her body, showing her the many ways that a man and woman could pleasure each other. Mortification flooded over Tea when she remembered how she had responded to him, how she had groaned and writhed under his touch, and how eagerly she had touched him and given him pleasure.

Her enemy.

Tea pushed herself up into a sitting position and groaned. Her head hurt; it felt as if an iron band had been fastened around her forehead and was slowly tightening. Not only that, but she felt bilious. Her stomach churned, and she felt as if she would vomit.

Shaking, she climbed off the furs and scrambled for her clothing. Mercifully, she was alone in the tent. Galan had disappeared for the moment. She dressed as quickly as she was able: hands shaking, nausea rolling over her in waves, sweat beading on her skin.

What's wrong with me?

She felt as if she had been poisoned. Her belly was griping terribly. She needed to find a private place where she could put herself back together again—a place where she could come to terms with what she had done.

She finished dressing and turned to leave, only to find Galan standing in the entrance to the tent. He bore a tray of fresh bread, goat's cheese, and a jug of milk. Dressed in nothing but plaid breeches, the sight of him brought memories of the night before. She had kissed and licked her way across every inch of that broad, tattooed chest. As if reading her mind, he gave her a slow, sensual smile.

"Good morning." His voice was low and deep, gliding over her skin like honey. Yet this morning Tea was immune to his charms. Without uttering a word, she flew across the tent, pushed past him, and ran outside.

It was shortly after dawn. The sun was rising over the edge of the hills to the east, although the Black Cuillins that reared overhead in a looming dark wall still lay in shadow. The storm had spent itself overnight and moved on, leaving the air fresh and crisp. The waters of the pools sparkled in the dawn light, but Tea paid the beauty of the setting no mind. Instead, she sprinted through the encampment and ran behind a lichen-encrusted boulder.

There, she fell to her knees and threw up the contents of her stomach.

Never had she felt so wretched, both physically and emotionally. Never had she felt so ashamed.

She had been bid to wed Galan mac Muin, not to practically mate with him at the table. She wanted to blame him for last night, but he had merely acted like a man. He had taken a woman to the furs who had been more than willing; it had been their wedding night after all.

She had been planning to fight him, to suffer their physical union as a duty but take no pleasure from it.

Instead, she had groaned, whimpered, and cried out for more. She had given herself to him completely.

Mortification flooded through her.

How will I face him?

"Tea ... are you well?"

Galan's voice, directly behind her, caused Tea to scramble to her feet. She wiped her mouth with the back of her hand and turned to find Galan standing a few feet away, watching her.

"No," she answered honestly, her voice a low growl. "After spending the night with you—I'm far from well."

Chapter Seven

The Cold Light of Day

GALAN'S GAZE NARROWED, although his mouth quirked in wry amusement. "You seemed to enjoy yourself."

His masculine arrogance riled her. "I wasn't of my right mind," Tea snarled, balling her fists by her sides.

Galan's amusement faded. "What?"

"My sister prepared me a potion to calm my nerves so I could go through with this farce of a handfasting," she told him, biting out each word. "The woman you wedded wouldn't have cared if she was handfasting a hog—or mating one."

Galan's body stiffened, and his face went stony. When he spoke, his voice was calm and deathly cold. "So you don't recall last night?"

Heat rushed through Tea at his words. She remembered more than she wanted to, although she was not about to admit that to him. Instead, she shook her head. "I do not remember much."

Galan's lip curled, and he gave her a look that made her squirm. He folded his arms across his broad chest and regarded her under lowered lids. "I think you're lying."

Anger flared in Tea's breast. "I don't want this marriage." She stepped up to him, raising her chin to meet his gaze squarely. Not for the first time, she was glad of her height. She did not like the thought of a man looming over her. "When my brother told me I had to wed you, I considered throwing myself off the cliffs into the sea."

Galan held her gaze, his calm infuriating. She was trying to bait him, but he refused to be drawn into it. "Such hate, such venom, Tea," he murmured. "Do you not want peace, like your brother?"

"My brother is a coward," she snarled. "I will never forgive what your people have done to mine—or forget."

Galan mac Muin stepped back from her then, deliberately distancing himself from her bitter words. He continued to hold her stare but gave a regretful shake of his head. "Perhaps it would have been better if you had thrown yourself to your death. For now you are wedded, and there is nothing you can do about it."

With that, he turned and walked away.

Tea watched him go, rage and loathing churning within her so violently that her bile rose once more. Retching she turned, fell to her knees, and was sick again.

Galan strode back toward the camp.

In just a few moments everything had changed. He had just spent an unforgettable night with his bride, experiencing pleasure he had never known existed. Tea had been everything he desired in a woman, and the way she had given herself to him, her reactions as he took her again and again, had left him floating three feet off the ground at dawn.

Only to come crashing violently back to earth a short time later.

Had a changeling come while he went to fetch them food and drink, and spirited his wife away, leaving a nasty, barbed-tongued shrew in her place?

He could not believe that she had spoken the truth, that she had taken some potion that had made her submit to him. Yet if he thought back to the ceremony, he remembered thinking she resembled a warm corpse. Her gaze had been unfocused as if she was not even there. He had thought she had merely overindulged in strong drink, but the reality was far different. The bride who feasted and drank next to him later had been very different to the woman who had just cursed him. She had barely said a word to him all evening, but whenever their gazes had met, he had seen her desire for him. And then when she had—

Stop it.

It was lies, all lies. Tea hated him. The venom in her eyes had been a slap in the face after what they had shared together. It should not have bothered him—for this was no love match—but it did.

Galan ducked inside his tent. He halted there, his gaze going to the pile of furs where the two of them had lain entangled.

It had been a mistake to return here.

The sight of the rumpled furs reminded him that, despite one night of intimacy, he and Tea were still strangers to each other.

Inhaling deeply and cursing himself for even caring, Galan left the tent.

Tarl was waiting for him. Hair rumpled from sleep, his face creased into a grin, his brother gave him a wink. "I was wondering when you'd emerge. Managed to drag yourself away then?"

Galan gave him a sour look. "You're too late—we've both been up for a while."

Tarl raised an eyebrow. "So where's your lusty bride?"

"Not so lusty this morning. We've just argued."

Tarl barked out a laugh and folded his arms across his chest. "What is it with you and women? She seemed keen on you last night—what did you say to enrage her?"

"I didn't have to say anything. Her brother forced her to wed me."

Tarl's smile faded. "That makes no sense. We all saw the pair of you at the feast. I thought you were going to take her then and there on the table. You both looked as if you'd found your other half."

Galan brushed past him. He was in no mood to discuss this. "Appearances are deceiving—you were wrong."

Tea stood by her pony, waiting while The Eagle and Wolf warriors finished packing up the encampment. It was late afternoon and the air was chilled. She wore a thick woolen mantle and had deliberately pulled the hood up to warn off any who were foolish enough to approach her.

Tea had kept away from everyone over the long morning, shunning company—even her sister's. She had been terribly ill after her confrontation with Galan and remained behind the boulder for a while till her stomach quietened. Even now queasiness lingered, and her skull throbbed as if a gnome with a hammer had taken up residence inside it.

Later she had sat pale and sullen at Galan's side, while The Eagle and The Wolf feasted together once more. During this meal Galan had ignored her—focusing his attention on Loc, seated to his left. The two men discussed the new peace between their tribes and their own plans to rebuild the villages and forts within their territories, which had been lately decimated by war. The

pair also talked of trade between the two tribes—
something that had not occurred in many years.

Tea had barely taken in a word. All she had been able
to think about was how she had shamed herself, shamed
the memory of both her parents.

The shadows were growing long by the time both
tribes packed up camp and readied themselves to leave.
Neither would reach home by nightfall—instead, they
would have to make camp in the open. However, Loc had
insisted on the delay, for there were many things he and
Galan had to discuss before they parted ways.

Tea was still brooding, waiting for her husband and
his band to finish their preparations for departure, when
Eithni drew near.

Dressed in a heavy fur cloak ready for travelling, her
sister's face was tense, her brow furrowed. She stopped
before Tea, peering under the shadowed recesses of her
sister's hood.

"Tea, are you well?"

Grinding her jaw, Tea took a deep steadying breath.
"Not particularly."

"I told you not to drink last night," Eithni murmured.
"I wish you had listened to me."

Tea's gaze narrowed. "It was only some wine and a
cup or two of mead. What does it matter?"

Eithni's expression tightened, her shoulders sagging
slightly. "I'm sorry, Tea—this is all my fault."

Tea's frown deepened. "Excuse me?"

Eithni looked pained. "There was more in that draft
besides All-Heal," she began hesitantly. "Loc told me to
prepare a love potion, something that would make you
see Galan in a different light. I added crushed apple
blossom, chamomile, and mugwort to the tincture."

"You did what?"

Her sister dropped her gaze. "I know you don't want
to hear it," she said quietly, "but you make a handsome
couple. I think he will treat you well."

Tea clamped her jaw shut. She did not want to shout
at her sister, did not want the last words they shared to
be angry ones. She had no idea when she would see
Eithni again, so she swallowed her outrage and held her
tongue.

Yet the fact remained—both her brother and sister
had conspired against her.

"You drugged me," she hissed. "I made a fool of
myself because of you."

Loc approached her then. His lean face was somber
as he stepped up next to Eithni. Tea went rigid. Although
she had managed to rein in her temper when speaking to
her sister, she was not sure she could manage the same
with her brother. Eithni would never have betrayed her
of her own accord—this was his fault. One word, just one
inflammatory word, and she would explode.

Sensing her mood, Loc gave her a wary look. The
three of them had been close growing up. Until now, Loc
had been his sisters' protector, defender. Now he was
Tea's betrayer.

"I know what you did." She spat the words at him,
fisting her hands at her sides to stop herself from lashing
out. "How could you?"

"And I'm sorry for it," he replied, although his tone
told her otherwise. "But too much was at stake. I couldn't
have you ruin things. Understand that I'm doing this so
that our children, and our children's children, may grow
up secure and happy— without the threat of war."

Tea stared at him, rage rendering her momentarily
speechless. A few feet behind Loc, she spotted Forcus
and her cousin, Wid. Her cousin looked worried as he
watched her, whereas Forcus's expression was one of
schooled neutrality. If he was sad to see her go, he did
not show it. Suddenly, she wished she had agreed to run
away with him. Forcus would never have betrayed her as
her brother and sister had.

Despite Tea's fury, a hollow sense of loneliness settled upon her. Despair swiftly followed on its heels. Betrayed, isolated, and now wedded to a man she despised—she had never felt so alone.

Chapter Eight

The Journey South

TEA REFUSED TO hug her brother and sister goodbye. It was all she could do not to scream abuse at them. Instead, she stepped back from Loc and Eithni and pulled her hood low over her face, making it clear she did not want to be touched. Eithni's eyes glittered with tears; she knew what she had done had ruined their relationship.

Loc said nothing, although his face was sterner than she had ever seen it. He knew he had just sacrificed his sister for peace—and she hoped his conscience never let him forget it.

Tea turned away and mounted the shaggy dun mare Galan had saddled for her.

The Eagle company moved off, and a sense of relief settled over Tea. She wanted to be away from Loc and Eithni; the sight of them made her still delicate stomach roil. Instead, she focused her attention on managing her pony. The mare tugged at the bit and swished her tail moodily. Her furry ears were back, as if she picked up on the turmoil churning within her rider.

Giving the mare a sharp nip with her knees, urging her forward, Tea guided the pony down the steep, pebbly path, leaving the Lochans of the Fair Folk behind.

Soon after, they reached the river valley below and set off south with the forbidding outline of the Black Cuillins rearing up at their back. The ponies wove their way over rock-studded hills. They picked their way down pebbly slopes before splashing through crystalline creeks. The woody scent of heather filled the crisp air.

Once her mare had settled down, Tea's thoughts turned inward. There was a certain solace in travelling, on focusing on the journey. It was a welcome distraction. She rode alongside a stone-faced, silent Galan at the head of the column of riders. Their journey would take them the rest of the day and most of the next morning, before they reached the fort on the south-western peninsula of The Winged Isle.

She did not glance at Galan as they rode but was acutely aware of him next to her. Although Tea was loath to admit it, The Eagle chieftain was a man of incredible presence. The moment she had set eyes on him, she had seen he was someone who dominated a space purely by stepping within it. He appeared to be a man of few words, and her viciousness had caused him to withdraw further from her—Tea was grateful for that.

He was a different kind of man to her brother. Although Galan and Loc were of similar ages, her new husband appeared a more serious, commanding figure than The Wolf chieftain. It seemed as if Loc was still proving himself to the men and women he led, whereas Galan gave the impression—by the way he carried himself and spoke to his warriors—of needing to prove nothing.

After a while the party stopped briefly at the bottom of a bare, windswept valley, where a silvery creek bubbled over the rocks. Here they watered their ponies, and Donnel's wife handed out hard bread buns studded with walnuts. Tea did not touch her bread; her sensitive stomach clenched at the thought of food. Although her nausea had started to abate and her aching head had eased, she still felt in a delicate state.

Instead of eating, she sipped at a skin of water and leaned against her irascible pony for company. The mare flattened her ears back and snaked her head round, trying to nip Tea on the arm, only to receive a slap across the nose for her trouble.

Depressed, Tea stepped away from her mount, her gaze scanning the empty valley before her. She had never travelled this far from home; this landscape was unknown to her. Mercifully, sensing her black mood, Galan and his kin did not approach Tea. She perched on a moss-covered rock and drew her mantle close about her. It was exposed here; the wind whistled down the valley and chilled her cheeks. The bitter season was on its way.

The thought depressed Tea even further—moons and moons trapped indoors with Galan and his kin.

How will I bear it?

Galan urged his pony up the incline, loosening the reins to let it find its path. The stocky stallion carried his weight easily. It was a hardy creature and hardly seemed fatigued.

Unlike its rider. Weariness pulled down upon Galan with every step. He had hardly slept the night before, and the discussions with Loc had drained him further.

Stealing a glance at the hooded figure riding beside him, Galan wondered if Tea would ever thaw. Still, despite her clear dislike for him now, he did not regret the night before.

For one night he had known a rare moment of abandon. It made him realize how serious and controlled his life had been till now. The eldest son, he had always carried the weight of responsibility like a heavy cloak.

He had watched his father slowly grow embittered over the years as feuding with their northern neighbors escalated. As he grew older, Muin had obsessed about his enemies and the wrongs he perceived they had done him.

The day they buried Muin mac Uerd, Galan had made his father a silent promise.

This hate ends with you.

Now that he and Loc had made the first step toward lasting peace, Galan intended to make good on his word. He and Tea had got off to a rough start, but he would make the best of things.

A chief does not marry for love.

He was doing this for his people—so that his brothers, his cousins, and those living in the lands around Dun Ringill could live in peace and prosper.

Tea watched dusk settle over the land in a soft, dark blanket. The wind whipped her hair into her eyes, making them water as she struggled to unsaddle her pony. Around her she caught snatches of conversation, bursts of laughter, and the flapping of goat hide—The Eagle company was making camp for the night.

Rounded jade hills reared up either side of the camp, with the shadow of dark, craggy mountains to the northwest—the Black Cuillins were gradually diminishing in size. Tea glanced up at the sky, her gaze narrowing. It would be another stormy night.

She removed her mare's saddle and began to rub the pony down with a twist of heather. Presently, the rich smell of burning peat drifted through the camp. Galan's men had lit lumps of peat in a fire pit at the center of the ring of tents.

Leaving her mare with one of the warriors, who was fastening hobbles around the ponies' front legs to prevent them wandering off in the night, Tea reluctantly made her way into the center of the camp. The ground was spongy underfoot, still damp from last night's rain.

The peat threw out a great heat, and Tea extended her chilled fingers over it in an effort to thaw them. She had been standing there a few moments when a small dark-haired figure approached her.

"Greetings, Tea. I'm Luana—your new sister-by-marriage."

Tea turned and fixed her gaze upon the pregnant woman she had seen at Galan's youngest brother's side. Part of her wanted to snarl at the woman, to send her scurrying away, but the moment she met Luana's sea-blue gaze, the cutting words she had been about to utter died.

Luana's face held such gentleness, such calm, that Tea's animosity could find no outlet. She nodded curtly and received a warm smile in response.

"The men have readied your tent. I can take you there if you want?"

Truly, Tea had no wish to leave the warmth of the burning peat; the pungent scent of its smoke calmed her.

"Worry not," Luana said, with another gentle smile, "We have lit a fire in your tent too."

Tea followed the woman to the largest tent in the circle, entering it to find a brazier with a lump of peat burning in the center. A slit in the roof let out the smoke, and someone had placed a pile of furs a few feet away from the brazier. The sides of the tent billowed and snapped, and a gust followed the women inside, making the peat glow red.

Once inside, Luana turned to Tea. Her smile had faded, although her expression was still welcoming. "I will bring you some supper and water to wash with," she said softly. "You must be exhausted."

"Thank you." They were the first words Tea had spoken since leaving the Lochans of the Fair Folk, but she could not continue being rude to Luana. Frankly, she felt embarrassed that this heavily pregnant woman was waiting upon her. Her sister-by-marriage looked drained; her pretty face was drawn, and she had dark smudges under her eyes. "I should fetch my own supper and water," she said, surprising herself as she uttered the words. "It's you who should be resting."

Luana shook her head, flashing Tea another warm smile. "My back hurts after riding all afternoon. It's good to move around a little." She gestured to the furs. "Make yourself comfortable—I'll be back soon."

As soon as Luana departed, Tea shrugged off her heavy mantle and removed her leather foot wrappings. A few drafts gusted in through gaps in the tent's stitching, but the peat had warmed the interior nicely. Gathering two of the four furs, Tea carried them over to the other side of the brazier. With a sigh, she sank down onto their softness.

Luana returned presently, laden down with a heavy tray. Tea leaped to her feet and relieved the smaller woman of her burden. "You should have asked someone for help," she scolded. "This was too heavy for you."

"I'm stronger than I look," Luana replied, chagrined.

Tea gave her a narrow-eyed look. "How far along are you with child?"

"Seven moons."

Tea carried the tray across to her side of the brazier and set it down. "I'm surprised your husband let you come on this journey. You should be resting."

Luana made a soft scoffing sound. "I insisted he bring me—this handfasting was too important to miss."

Tea turned to face her sister-by-marriage, and found Luana watching her. The air inside the tent suddenly grew heavy. Tea realized that Luana was gathering her courage to speak on a more difficult subject.

"I know you are not happy about this match," she said finally, "and I understand why, but I am glad you are with us nonetheless."

Luana's words came as a surprise to Tea. She had expected hostility, not a warm welcome. She was so taken aback that it took her a few moments to gather her wits and respond.

"My brother forced this upon me." Her voice sounded harsh and bitter, especially after Luana's softly spoken words, and Tea almost winced at the sound of them. "I will never accept Dun Ringill as my home."

Luana's face sagged a little at this, her disappointment clear. When she spoke, sadness tinged her voice. "Never is a long time, Tea. I hope you prove yourself wrong."

Chapter Nine

Opposite Sides of the Fire

GALAN DELAYED ENTERING the tent for as long as possible. He ate a light supper with his brothers by the outdoor fire pit, watching the lumps of peat burn bright in the darkness. The seeking wind had a raw edge to it.

"Another storm is coming," Donnel announced, peering up at the dark sky. "I can smell it on the wind."

Tarl laughed. "All I can smell is burning peat."

"We should reach the fort before it does," Galan replied, moodily staring into the fire. He felt his brothers' gazes upon him.

"What happened?" Donnel asked finally. "After watching you at the feast, I thought you'd both be all smiles today—yet you look as if you just wedded The Hag herself."

Galan threw him an irritated look. He'd already warned Tarl off this subject; clearly the two brothers had not spoken.

"Aye—you should have seen his face this morning," Tarl added ignoring his elder brother's frown. "I think the lass wore him out. Maybe she needs a man with greater stamina."

Donnel roared with laughter at this. "Are you offering?"

"Shut your mouths … both of you," Galan growled, his patience snapping. "It appears my new wife doesn't remember much of last night. Her sister made her a draft, a special potion, so that she could go through with our handfasting."

He glanced up to see Tarl and Donnel staring at him. At least his admission had wiped the smirks off their faces.

"Surely she remembers the handfast?" Tarl asked.

"Aye, and the rest of it too—although she denies it. She wants nothing more to do with me now that the effects of that potion have worn off."

Tarl's mouth twisted. "Sounds like female mischief to me. Just throw her down on her back and teach her who rules."

In spite of his foul mood, a smile tugged at the edge of Galan's mouth. His brother had no idea how he longed to do just that; only, such an act would make her hate him even more. For this union to work, he needed to go softly.

Donnel snorted at Tarl's comment. "Your knowledge of women astounds me," he said. "No wonder none of them will warm your furs."

Tarl laughed. "Marriage has turned you soft, brother." He punched Donnel's shoulder. "I don't need them to warm my furs—I'm too busy riding them."

Donnel punched him back. "One day you'll tire of just riding them—you'll want a woman to share your life with, to have your children, to grow old with."

Tarl smirked. "That day is long off."

Despite himself, Galan smiled at his brothers' banter. Since becoming chief, he had lost his sense of humor— his brothers reminded him that he was still young. Tarl and Donnel grounded him.

However, it grew late, and eventually his brothers made their excuses and retreated to their tents. Galan stood alone beside the smoking fire.

He did not want to face her.

Before arriving at the Lochans of the Fair Folk, he had wondered what his bride would be like—none of his imaginings had brought him to this eventuality. He hated to admit as much, but Tea, daughter of Domech mac Bred, had completely unbalanced him. His usual calm, unwavering sense of purpose had started to falter, and he felt strangely lost.

Remember why you agreed to wed her. This union must forge lasting peace.

He turned from the fire and strode toward the tent he and Tea shared. Enough. He could not shy away from his duty. He needed to mend things with his bride, to approach her gently like a skittish pony and build her trust.

Tea lay on her side, with her back to the glowing brazier, when she heard Galan enter. She had been dozing, teetering between wakefulness and an exhausted slumber, when a gust of cold air warned her of his presence.

Instantly, her entire body went rigid.

Under the furs her hand went to the sheathed knife she always wore at her waist—one she used for skinning and de-boning animals or chopping vegetables. She had climbed into the furs fully-clothed, unlike her usual habit of sleeping naked.

Galan's heavy tread stopped behind her, and she felt the weight of his gaze settle upon her.

"Tea," he spoke her name softly, his powerful voice a low rumble. "Are you awake?"

Tea ignored him, feigning sleep.

"I know you're awake—you're not breathing," he continued, a faint edge of amusement creeping into his voice. "You're a poor mummer."

Irritation surged through Tea. She rolled over and fixed him in a hard glare.

He met her gaze, his own steady, before favoring her with a slow smile. "That's better."

"What do you want?"

"We have not spoken all day—it's time to break the silence between us."

"I have nothing to say to a Dun Ringill dog."

Galan gave a heavy sigh and shrugged off his cloak before unbuckling the leather vest that covered his strong torso. "Your insults become repetitive, wife. Surely you have better names for me than that."

Stinking pig turd. Maggot spawn. The insults rose within Tea, but she choked them back. He was deliberately baiting her, and she would not give him what he wanted.

Galan's clothes fell to the ground, leaving him stark naked before her. Tea wanted to look away; the sight of him—powerful, tattooed, and virile—made her loins melt. Once again it was a test, and she would not satisfy him. Men liked to assert their dominance over women, but she was not easily cowed. Still, she made sure she kept her eyes on his upper torso—far from his manhood.

However, Galan was not looking at her as he stood by the glowing brazier. Instead, his gaze went to the two remaining furs on the other side of the tent. His face was serious when he glanced back at her.

A dark eyebrow quirked. "So that's how it's to be? A husband cannot share the furs with his wife?"

The heat in his gaze caused Tea's pulse to race, and she resisted the urge to clutch the furs to her breast in protection. Forcing down her sudden nervousness, she raised her chin and narrowed her gaze. "I won't have you near me."

He cocked his head, infuriatingly calm. "You didn't seem to feel that way last night."

Anger surged, hot and wild within her. "I told you I was not myself last night," she replied through gritted teeth. "I took—"

"So you say." He raised a hand, cutting her off mid-sentence. "But, I think you are just making excuses. The woman I plowed last night is still there—you remember more than you admit."

Galan strode round to the other side of the brazier, moving with unselfconscious male arrogance. "I'll let you have your way for now, Tea. You are tired, upset, and missing your kin. However, I won't let you risk peace for my tribe. Tonight you can sleep apart from me—but once we reach Dun Ringill, you and I will share the same furs." He fixed her with a challenging stare that made her body feel hot while her temper nearly boiled over. "Naked."

With that, he climbed into the furs and turned away from her.

Tea stared at his broad back, her fingers fastening around the bone hilt of her knife. Just two strides and she could reach him, before plunging it between his shoulder blades.

She would have killed him too, yet something held her in check. Perhaps the fact he had his back to her kept her from stabbing him. Tea preferred to face her enemy if she was to take his life. Or was it the memories of the night before that still tormented her? He was right, she remembered more than she let on, although she would never say so to him.

Galan's conceit and dominance turned her vision crimson. If he tried to force himself on her, she would make him regret it.

On the other side of the brazier, Galan stared at the flapping side of the tent and waited for sleep to claim him. Despite his exhaustion, sleep was slow arriving tonight. He could feel Tea's gaze stabbing into him, her hate emanating across the tent like the glow from a burning forge.

I could have dealt with that better.

He had planned to treat her softly and attempt to win her trust, but her manner had goaded him. She was so haughty, such a savage beauty. He had enjoyed angering her: seeing the rage flare in those deep-blue eyes and watching her high cheekbones flush.

She will never soften toward you at this rate.

Galan inhaled deeply before letting his breath escape slowly. Tomorrow, he would start again.

Chapter Ten

The Mark of The Eagle

DUN RINGILL SAT high on the edge of a dark lake; the stacked stone fort perched upon a grassy, windswept knoll commanding a view west over Loch Slapin.

As they approached, Tea noted how different the fort was to Dun Ardtreck. Tea's home nestled upon a craggy cliff, surrounded by sharp rocks—an austere and isolated spot that caught the prevailing north-west wind. Yet the land on the south-western edge of The Winged Isle was softer, easier to farm and till. Scattered herds of sheep, goats, and stocky, long-haired cattle grazed on the gently curved hillside. Tea also noted terraces of vegetable plots protected from the elements by wattle fences.

The company rode by a number of villages on the way in, past squat roundhouses made of timber and stone with conical thatched or sod roofs. Smoke rose from the dwellings, drifting south with the breeze. The isle's harsh climate meant that folk dug out the ground first, creating a living space surrounded by alcoves, before building a roof over it. Such homes protected them from strong winds and the chill of the bitter months. The villages consisted of tightly packed clusters of roundhouses, wattle animal enclosures, and cone-roofed store houses. Animal skins hung outside, curing in the sun.

The smell of smoking herrings reached Tea as she rode in through the gate in the outer defense wall.

It was just after midday and folk emerged from their dwellings as the company rode in, brushing the crumbs of their noon meal off their tunics and leggings. Recognizing their chief, they called out, hailing him. Next to Tea, Galan raised an arm in greeting.

Tea felt his gaze shift to her. It was the first time Galan had looked her way since they had set off that morning. "These are your people now, Tea," he said. "Greet them as their leader."

Gritting her teeth, Tea glanced across at him. She had no wish to hail these folk, for she barely suffered being among them. She was about to defy him—but when she met Galan's storm-grey eyes, her words of scorn caught in her throat. She had expected to see a stern expression upon his face, but his look was almost pleading. Did it matter so much to him?

Irritated, she looked away before raising a hand to the crowd of men, women, and children who now clustered around the entrance to the fort. She felt their gazes, curious and wary, upon her as she rode under the massive stone arch and into the yard beyond.

Tea swung down from her mare and took in her surroundings. Unlike Dun Ardtreck, which was shaped like an enormous beehive and perched high upon a platform above the rest of the fort, Dun Ringill was a squat and broad structure. There was more space here; a wide yard ringed the base of stacked stone. Fowl pecked at grain nearby, and the children ran, shrieking as they chased each other around the base of the high stone wall ringing the fort.

Galan stepped up close to her, his gaze seeking hers. "This is your home, Tea." His voice, as often, was low yet commanding. "My people will accept you if you pay them the same courtesy."

Rage clawed its way up her throat. Either he was dense-headed or stubborn as a boar, for he already knew her feelings on the subject. Meeting his gaze, she saw Galan was no fool. Although she had only known him two days, she had already assessed him as an intelligent, deep-thinking man. She hated him for that too—it was easier to despise a man she thought stupid.

"This will never be my home," she snarled, before she turned away to see to her mare.

Dun Ringill held a great feast that night, in honor of the chief and his bride.

Tea sat at the chieftain's table next to Galan and wished she could disappear. The feasters sat at long tables around a central hearth in a wide, cavernous space. Oil-filled cressets studded the stone walls, casting a gilded light over the interior. High, smoke-blackened beams reached overhead, and alcoves draped in furs and tapestries had been set into the walls.

A harpist played upon a wooden dais behind them, the strains lifting up and echoing against the stone. The music was beautiful, but it reminded her of Eithni. Her sister was a talented harpist. Tea had spent many a long evening playing knucklebones with her brother or cousin while listening to Eithni's playing. Tea clenched her jaw, her fingers tightening around the cup of wine she held.

Eithni and Loc's deceit still felt like a knife-blade to the back.

Contrary to Tea's black mood, the people of Dun Ringill appeared in high spirits this afternoon. Mead, ale, and wine flowed, and they passed around the drinking horn.

When the food arrived at the table, Tea could see they had spent days preparing it while Galan and his party had been away. Lads carried in spit-roasted haunches of venison, while women carried roast puffin, braised onions, boiled eggs rolled in flaked sea-salt, and barley bread with fresh butter.

The smell and sight of the venison, usually Tea's favorite meat, made her feel queasy. It reminded her of her handfasting feast and of the spectacle she had made of herself. Nonetheless, her appetite had returned, and although she avoided the venison, she managed to eat some of the meal, including the crab-apple and bramble tarts served with thick cream that the women brought out later.

As the feast dragged on, Tea started to feel uncomfortable. Few of the people looked her way, and when they did she found their gazes hard and assessing. Their chief's handfasting was an opportunity to feast and drink, yet she sensed the good cheer was a thin veneer. Like her own people, they did not trust the enemy. She was a Wolf woman, and many at these tables would have lost kin in skirmishes between the two tribes.

Galan might have welcomed her, but she noted the cool looks his brothers favored her with. More than once she saw Tarl and Donnel look her way before speaking together in low voices. Tarl especially looked at her with insolence, and his laughter after Donnel murmured something to him made her hackles raise. She knew he was laughing at her.

Next to Tea, Galan refilled her bronze cup with sloe wine. "Is my feasting hall pleasing to your eye, wife?"

Tea stiffened at being addressed as his woman, something he did not plan on letting her forget. "Aye," she admitted grudgingly. "It is a well-proportioned space."

Galan smiled while, next to him, his brother Tarl raised an eyebrow. "You approve of something at last?"

Tea favored Tarl with a dark look. "I give credit where it's due."

"How generous of you."

Tea stiffened. She did not like Tarl or the brazen way he was looking at her. "This union was not my choice, so forgive me if I don't sit here beaming," she ground out.

Tarl held her gaze for a moment, before a smile split his handsome face. "You've got a handful there, brother." He winked at Galan before taking a deep draft from his cup.

"Aye," Galan replied, casting his brother a quelling look, "but there's no need to poke the adder with a stick."

Tarl threw back his head and laughed, as did Donnel seated next to him. However, Luana, who sat to her husband's left, did not share their mirth. Instead, her gaze met Tea's, and she gave her a sympathetic smile.

Tea was too incensed to return it. Her fingers curled around the edge of the table, gripping hard until they started to ache. She hated the men for laughing at her expense.

The Reaper take you all.

The feasting and drinking stretched out until late. It was a cold, windy night, and drafts pushed in through tiny gaps in the stone, causing the embers in the great hearth to pulse.

One by one, folk rose from the table and staggered off to their furs. Many who lived within the hall bedded down for the night on the rush-strewn floor—the higher ranking warriors closest to the fire, while the younger, untested men and women slept closer to the drafts. Others, members of the chieftain's family, retired to their alcoves.

Reluctantly, Tea followed Galan to their recess. Her husband carried a ewer of wine and two cups as he led the way across the floor. Their alcove was large, hidden from view behind a heavy tapestry. Unlike many of the niches, which were barely large enough to stand up in, this one was a decent-sized, windowless chamber. Two stone cressets illuminated the space, and there was room for a low table and a row of wicker baskets where Tea could store her clothing.

A mound of soft seal fur dominated the space.

Tea's throat closed—the moment she had been dreading all day had come.

The tapestry thudded shut behind them, sealing her and Galan inside their alcove. She watched Galan set the ewer and cups down on the low table, before he turned to her.

"Will you have some wine?"

Tea shook her head. After the handfasting she was wary of drinking too much again. "I'm not thirsty."

His mouth quirked into a half-smile. "Undress then, and let us go retire for the night."

Stomach in knots, Tea stepped back from him, unfastening her long plaid skirt and removing the leather vest she wore. Underneath, she wore a sleeveless linen tunic that reached her knees. Leaving it on, she moved toward the furs.

"Tea." Galan's voice stopped her. She turned to find him standing naked a few feet away, his clothing dropped carelessly at his feet. "Naked."

She stiffened. "I'd prefer to wear a tunic at night."

"And I'd prefer you were naked."

Tea stared at him, deliberately keeping her gaze fixed upon his face and not at his nude body. She lifted her chin, stubbornness rising within her. "Will you force yourself on me, Galan? I won't lie with you willingly."

He approached, stalking across the alcove toward her. Tea took a few steps backward till she found herself pressed up against the damp stone wall. He moved close, so close she could feel the heat of his body reaching out to her. She inhaled the warm, male musk of his body and felt her senses reel. Her loins melted, completely betraying her.

The Mother protect her, the effect this man had on her body was frightening. Just his nearness was enough to turn her will to porridge. She had to be strong, to remind herself who he was.

"Do you think me that kind of man?" he said quietly. "I would never take you against your will."

She lowered her gaze slightly, for looking into his eyes when they stood so close was too intense for her to bear.

"Take off your tunic and come to the furs," he said softly. "I will not touch you—I promise."

He stepped back from her, leaving a gulf of chill air between them. Shivering, Tea watched him walk over to the furs. She could not help but admire the muscular column of his back, the firmness of his buttocks, and the length of his legs. He was a beautiful man.

Yet he used her attraction to him like a weapon. He would use it to break down her defenses, till she melted, helpless in his arms. She could not let that happen.

Tea stripped off her tunic and dropped it to her feet. She stood there, naked, aware that her breasts thrust out proudly, her nipples rock-hard from cold and arousal. Galan stood by the furs and was about to climb into them; however, his gaze rested on her a moment, hot and hungry, raking down her body.

Tea's breathing quickened, and she found herself doing the same to him. When she saw his shaft, hard and swollen against his belly, her body ached with need. She remembered how he had felt inside her on the night of their handfasting—how he had taken her to the brink and over it. How he had stopped time for her.

Stop this—now.

Tea forced her gaze up so that she met his eye.

"So, you're not like your father then?" she asked.

His gaze narrowed, and she saw the desire on his face cool slightly. "What?"

"Not a man to ravish a woman."

His expression tightened. "What are you talking about?"

Tea drew herself up, scorn obliterating the lust she had been struggling against. "Your father raped my mother—don't dare deny it."

He reeled back as if she had struck him. The shock on his face was so real that she almost believed he had no idea about the event that had ripped her family apart. Heedless, Tea pressed on, taking a step forward to show she was not afraid of him, or of any man.

"Ten summers ago he attacked her party while they were travelling home from Dun Skudiburgh. He raped her before slitting her throat and mutilating her."

Galan stepped forward, eyes blazing. "He did not. Who told you such lies?"

Tea's face twisted. She loathed him for denying it, for not owning the truth. It was the act of a coward.

"He scored his mark—the mark of your people into her flesh," she spat, gesturing to the eagle tattoo that covered Galan's right bicep. "So that my father would know who had defiled and murdered his wife."

The look of horror on Galan's face made her shiver with hatred. He had accused her of being a poor mummer—but he was the best she had ever seen. She could almost believe her words had upset him.

"It's a lie," he finally rasped. "Someone must have done it to breed hatred between our peoples." His gaze, dark with hurt, met hers. "And they have succeeded well. How do you even know my father did it?"

"It's common knowledge," she snarled. "My brother betrayed both my mother and father's memory with this handfasting. But I will never accept it."

Trembling with the force of her rage, she climbed into the furs and turned away so that her back was facing him. She waited, her body as tense as a bowstring, for him to deny the truth once more—but he did not.

Neither did he climb into the furs beside her.

A tense silence filled the alcove, and she heard the faint rasp of his breathing above the thundering of her own heart. Then she heard him move, followed by the rustle of him pulling on his clothes.

An odd mix of elation and despair consumed her when the tapestry thudded shut, leaving her alone in the alcove. She should have been pleased her attack had hit home like a knife-thrust to the guts.

Instead, she just felt empty inside.

Chapter Eleven

In Search of Answers

GALAN STOOD UPON the walls of Dun Ringill and looked west over the glistening waters of Loch Slapin. The moon was out, casting its friendly face over the sleeping isle and turning the lake into beaten silver. It was a breathtaking sight, but Galan was blind to it.

Grief twisted his gut. He was in turmoil.

He could not believe his father to be the beast that Tea described—he would not. His parents had been happy together. To Galan's eyes, his father had always seemed devoted to his wife and had never appeared to covet another woman.

They were lies—but lies his wife believed.

Despair settled over Galan's broad shoulders like a stone mantle. This was his fault—he had been a fool to hope for peace, to believe he could end the blood feud between Dun Ardtreck and Dun Ringill. The Wolf and The Eagle could never be friends. There was so much hate between them, too much blood spilled over the years. There were too many who nursed hate in their breasts like a canker.

It cannot be the truth.

Loc, like his sister, must have thought that Galan knew of this incident. The new Wolf chieftain was a brave man indeed to try and forge peace under such circumstances. Galan's throat constricted—Loc must have wanted peace very much to sacrifice his sister to the enemy he saw responsible for the rape and murder of his own mother.

Galan's fists clenched at his sides. *I won't believe it—not without proof.*

Someone must have hated his family very much to have carved an eagle into Fina's flesh as a message for her husband.

Galan was determined not to let this be; such accusations could not lie.

Tomorrow, I will get answers.

He knew exactly whom to ask.

A windy dawn greeted Dun Ringill. It whipped the dark surface of the lake into frothy peaks and gusted across the exposed hilltop, blowing straw, fowl feathers, and dust into Galan's face as he strode out of the fort and into the village below.

Folk called out to him and waved as he passed, but Galan did not slow his step. He had not been able to sleep the night before. Eventually, the night's chill had forced him indoors, but he did not return to his alcove. Instead, he had sat by the hearth in the center of his feasting hall, surrounded by slumbering bodies. He had spent the night brooding, and by the time the sun rose over the hills to the east, his mood was black.

This morning he would have answers.

The hovel he sought sat on the outskirts of the village, just yards from the stone defensive wall that ringed the fort. The dwelling was smaller than most, and its thatch roof had been patched in many places. Galan walked past a messy vegetable patch and small fowl coop, stepping through a rambling growth of herbs, before he reached the door to the dwelling. The scent of baking griddle bread and the stronger aroma of burning peat wafted out.

Outside the door, Galan paused. He had not been to see the bandruí in a while. He had glimpsed her briefly at his father's burial: a slight, cloaked figure at the back of the crowd. Muin had relied heavily on Ruith over the years, following her divinations and insights, especially after the loss of his wife. Yet Galan had never felt entirely comfortable in the seer's presence, and he hesitated now on the threshold of her home.

"I know you're there, Galan mac Muin," a husky female voice greeted him through the wattle door. "Come inside ... I won't bite."

Frowning, Galan pulled the door open and stepped into the hovel, squinting as his eyes got used to the dim light.

The bandruí squatted next to the fire pit, tending a wheel of bread she was toasting on an iron griddle. She wore a dark long-sleeved tunic, and her greying hair, braided into many plaits, hung around her face. Ruith was nearing her sixtieth winter, but Galan could see she had once been a beauty. She had high cheekbones, piercing dark-blue eyes, and a proud stance.

I wonder if Tea will look like her when she ages, he thought suddenly before catching himself. He did not want to think of his wife now. He needed to focus.

"Good morning, Ruith," he greeted the seer.

She motioned to the stool on the opposite side of the fire pit. "Sit down."

He did as bid, not taking offense at the familiar way the bandruí spoke to him. It was her manner. Ruith was not like other folk; she was a part of the soil, the air, and the grass. She was Dun Ringill's conduit to the gods and the world beyond.

The seer met his eye as he settled himself upon a stool, her mouth curving into a smile. "I saw you ride in with your new woman yesterday."

Galan inhaled slowly, fighting the growing tension in his chest. This was why he had never felt comfortable with Ruith; he preferred plain speech. The seer rarely spoke about things directly.

"She hates me," he admitted finally after a long pause. "I thought it was because of the blood feud between our peoples, but last night I discovered there is more to it than that."

Ruith met his eye across the fire. She flipped the wheel of bread over so it could cook on the other side. "Go on."

"She accuses my father of raping and murdering her mother."

The bandruí's gaze widened at this, and relief crashed over Galan in a great wave. The seer did not know of this tale—it had to be a lie.

"When was this?" she asked.

"Ten years ago, I believe." Galan paused here, thinking back. He would have been around fifteen at the time, yet he could not remember any incident that would have implicated his father.

"What did she say exactly?" Ruith asked finally.

Galan told her, word for word, what Tea had spat at him. When he spoke of the mark of The Eagle being engraved into the dead woman's flesh, the bandruí's gaze narrowed. She removed the bread from the griddle and placed another wheel of dough on to cook.

"Your father knew Fina," she said when the silence had stretched out so long that Galan had begun to think she would never reply. "They met when they were very young at a gathering of the tribes. She was from the northern tip of the isle, from Dun Skudiburgh." The seer paused here, her gaze meeting Galan's. "Muin spoke to me of her once—they bonded at the gathering. He'd hoped to wed her, but the feuding between our tribes made their union impossible."

Galan stared at her. He had not come here expecting this. He had wanted assurance that his father and Tea's mother had never met, not that they had once been lovers. Bitterness soured his mouth.

"So you think he could have murdered her?"

The bandruí raised a finely arched eyebrow. "You've come here looking for guarantees I can't give, Galan. I knew your father well, but I cannot account for all his actions."

Galan inhaled deeply, fighting his growing frustration. "Then, knowing him as you did, do you think he was capable of it?"

Ruith cocked her head. "Your father was proud and could be brutal at times. I think he regretted losing Fina. I know not if he secretly raged over it."

Galan clenched his jaw before answering. "You can't help me, can you?"

The seer flipped the second wheel of bread off the hot plate and rose to her feet, dusting flour from her hands.

"I can cast the bones for you? Perhaps then you will get your answer."

Galan shook his head, rising to his feet with her. "No, I'll leave you now—thank you for your time."

Ruith had known his father better than anyone— better even than his mother had. After his mother's death, Galan had wondered if they had been lovers, such was their closeness. So if the seer could not be sure that his father was innocent of this atrocity, he could not cast Tea's words aside as lies. The bones would be no further help to him.

Ruith watched the chieftain leave. Her gaze slid over his tall, broad-shouldered form in frank admiration.

Galan wore plaid breeches this morning and a leather tunic, leaving his muscular arms bare. His long dark hair spilled down his back; its color and sheen made her think of a selkie—creatures that lived as seals in the sea but took human form on land. Male selkies were thought to be incredibly handsome in their human form, with great powers of seduction over women.

For a brief moment Ruith wished she was a young woman again. She sensed he was a man who knew how to please a woman in the furs; his father had been such a man too. Galan's wife was a fortunate woman indeed—although she clearly thought otherwise.

Ruith knew Galan's worth; she had watched him grow from infant, to child, and then into a man. Out of the three sons, Galan reminded her of Muin the least. He had far more of his mother in him—a silent strength and a deep wisdom. Muin had ever been of a more reactive temperament, far more like Tarl. He had gone at life like a bull, whereas his eldest son was watchful, farsighted.

Ruith let out a gentle sigh. Muin. She missed him. They had been friends for many years, and then after his wife's death, he had found solace in her furs. The nights now felt cold and lonely without him.

Pushing aside thoughts of her dead lover, the seer's attention shifted back to the young Eagle chieftain. She had not been surprised when Galan had accepted the Wolf chief's peace offering. He was a warrior who knew that leadership was about more than war. Ruith was pleased Galan had chosen peace, although she knew many at Dun Ringill did not share her relief. Folk here had suffered because of the People of The Wolf; it would take them a while to forget.

What will come of this union?

Curious, Ruith drew the leather bag containing her 'telling bones' from her skirt and poured them out onto her palm; the pieces of bone, inscribed with the symbols of her people, rattled as she weighed them in her hand

and squatted once more beside the hearth. Thinking upon Galan and his wife—a woman of the People of The Wolf—she then cast the bones on the dirt floor. The light was dim inside her hovel, so Ruith had to climb down on stiff knees to read them properly.

The two bones depicting The Wolf and The Eagle had fallen close to each other—a good sign. Perhaps this handfasting would bring peace after all ... yet some of the other bones worried her. The Bent Arrow upon a Crescent Moon had fallen directly above the symbols of the two tribes, and up against it, the mark of the Serpent.

The seer sat back on her heels, her gaze narrowing. She was glad Galan had not seen these bones, for her divination boded ill.

Her reading spoke of death and betrayal.

Galan left the bandruí's hovel with a heavy heart and strode up the incline back toward the squat shape of the fort. He had been sure Ruith would set his mind at ease, but she had only raised more questions.

Father knew Fina. Doubt niggled at him. He did not want to believe Tea, but the bandruí had sown the seed now, and it began to germinate. He would not speak to his brothers of this; they must never know. If Tea did speak the truth, he would have to learn to live with it. However, his hopes that she would one day thaw toward him had shattered. She thought she had good reason to hate him.

Galan had almost reached the entrance to the fort when he spied Donnel approaching. His youngest brother's face was unusually serious this morning, his muscular frame tense with purpose. The wind ruffled his short dark hair as he waved to Galan.

"I've been looking for you."

Galan stopped. "Why—is something wrong?"

Donnel shook his head. "Not sure—guards at the defense have spotted riders approaching from the south-east."

Galan went still. "How many?"

"Thirty ... at least."

"Cruthini?"

Donnel nodded. "I think so—they do not look foreign."

Galan relaxed slightly. The invaders who lived south of the great wall were a threat to their lands, but they had never ventured this far north. But even if the riders were Cruthini, folk of the lands north of the wall, he had good reason to be wary. "Gather the men," he ordered, turning on his heel toward the stables. "We'll ride out to meet them."

Chapter Twelve

The Campaign

THE EAGLE WARRIORS entered the fort. Their voices rose high into the rafters, echoing off the stone and shattering the scene of domestic peace within.

Tea rose from her place by the hearth, the flax basket she had been weaving clutched in her hands. Next to her Luana also got to her feet. The young woman's delicate features scrunched in discomfort as she massaged her lower back.

"This babe kicks," she muttered.

Tea glanced at her, casting Luana a look of sympathy. The two women had barely spoken that morning, although Luana seemed to be content to work in silence. For her part, Tea was in a black mood and did not welcome company. She had not seen Galan since their confrontation the night before; her belly clenched in dread at the thought of having to speak with him again. However, she put aside her own concerns for the moment as her gaze settled upon Luana's face. The young woman had looked drained ever since returning from the handfasting.

"You should rest," she observed.

Luana waved her away. "There's too much to be done."

Tea spied Galan then. Tall, dark, and stern, he strode into the wide space, followed by his brothers. He saw Tea and walked to her. The intensity of his gaze speared her, and she nearly wilted under the force of it. Then, remembering who she was—the daughter of warriors who stared down their foes—she held his eye, tilting her chin imperiously.

Galan's gaze narrowed, and he shifted it to Luana.

"We have visitors." Galan greeted his sister-by-marriage, ignoring Tea completely. "They will eat with us at noon. Can you make sure we have enough to feed them?"

Luana nodded. "Who are they?"

"Warriors of this isle, and Cruthini from across the water. They're gathering fighters for a campaign to the south."

Tea watched the newcomers with fascination as they took their places at the long tables that formed a square around the great hearth. Most of the warriors were male, although there was a handful of women amongst them.

The warriors were lightly clad. Many of them left their limbs bare, showing off their tribal markings. The women wore leather bindings across their breasts, their hair pulled back from their faces in elaborate braids.

All of them, men and women alike, bore the blue painted symbols of their people. Tea spied the mark of The Stag on a handful of them, as well as tattoos of The Boar; it appeared this group had already visited two of the tribes living upon The Winged Isle. The People of The Stag were her mother's people, a tribe that inhabited the east and far northern coast of The Winged Isle. The People of The Boar occupied the isle's south and south-eastern corners. Of Tea's own people—The Wolf—she saw none. She imagined the group would travel to Dun Ardtreck next.

Seated next to Galan, Tea helped herself to some boar stew, before her gaze returned to the warriors once more.

The sight of the fierce women caused bitterness and longing for war to well within her. She too could fight. Many of the warrior women were tall and strong, as she was, and easily matched their menfolk in combat ability. Tea's father and brother had taught her how to fight with her fists; and how to use an axe, spear, and sword. They had offered the same to Eithni, but Tea's gentle younger sister had declined; her gifts lay with healing the sick and injured, not with warfare. However, despite her father's eagerness to teach Tea how to fight, Domech had never allowed her to accompany him on any of the skirmishes against their enemies.

You're too valuable, lass, he had told her, his eyes glistening with emotion. *I lost your mother. I will not lose you too.*

Tea was deep in thought, brooding upon the past, when Galan's voice roused her. He was questioning the leader of the band: a huge man named Wurgest with dense black hair and beard, and wild blue eyes. Wurgest bore the mark of The Boar on his right bicep.

"How many warriors have you gathered?" Galan asked.

"At least two-hundred of our own people wait on the shores of the mainland," Wurgest replied in between huge mouthfuls of stew. "The Scotti and Atecotti are also gathering and travelling south as we speak."

Galan's dark eyebrows shot up. "They will join you?"

Wurgest nodded, his intense gaze spearing Galan. "Aye, there's even word of the Saxones readying themselves to the south. The time has come to fight back against the Caesars."

Listening to this, Tea felt a thrill of excitement. Yet Galan's strong-featured face gave nothing away. She could not tell if this news pleased him or not.

"Why now?" he asked. "Have you news from beyond the wall?"

Wurgest grinned. "Aye. The great empire is weakening … rotting from the inside out. A few winters back they fought amongst themselves, and since then the mood at their garrison has turned sour. The cruel general who leads them, Catena, is hated. There are deserters and rebels willing to join with us."

"And when will you move against them?" Galan asked.

Wurgest's grin widened, making him look half-mad. "Mid-winter."

"I will go with you."

To Galan's right, Tarl spoke up. Tea watched Galan's brother with interest. She did not like Tarl's cockiness, but today his face was serious, and his eyes gleamed as he held Wurgest's gaze. "I will bring Eagle warriors to aid you."

"Tarl." Galan's voice cracked across the table like a whip. "You forget yourself."

Blinking, as if suddenly remembering his brother sat next to him, Tarl turned to Galan. His expression hardened. "Don't try to stop me, Galan," he warned. "Or any of us who wish to join the campaign. Unlike you, I still have balls."

Tea's breath caught at this insult.

She had noticed Tarl's attitude toward her had bordered on insolence, but she had not realized he resented his elder brother.

Galan leaned forward, his gaze snaring his brother's. Tea had to admit, his self-restraint impressed her. Tarl had just insulted him in front of kin, warriors, and guests. A more volatile man would have lashed out.

"I still have my balls, brother," Galan growled, his face like hewn stone, his eyes narrowed. "Would you like to see them?"

A stunned silence followed, before Tarl's mouth quirked. Wurgest threw back his head and roared with laughter, shattering the tension at the table.

Galan shifted his attention to The Boar warrior. "I decide who joins with you," he rumbled. "I can spare twenty spears, and my brother will lead them."

The big warrior nodded, still grinning. "A generous offer—thank you, Galan."

"I want to go too."

Tea had spoken without even realizing it. Desperation had welled up in her upon hearing Galan offer his warriors to the war band. The chance to escape this marriage, to fight for The Winged Isle, was too enticing, and she could not still her tongue.

Galan inclined his head toward her. "You cannot, Tea."

She narrowed her gaze. "I can fight as well as any of them—my kin taught me well."

A smile crinkled the corners of Galan's eyes, the austerity in his face softening. "I'm sure they did, but the answer is still the same. Your purpose, to forge peace between our tribes, is just as noble as Tarl's."

His words kindled rage in Tea's breast. Her heart started to thud against her ribs, and she was aware that every eye at the table now rested upon her. Fuming, she glared at him. "In your eyes, perhaps. But I'm better suited to warfare," she challenged. "I'm no peace-weaver."

"She speaks true," Tarl agreed with a grin. He gave Tea an appraising look that made her want to lash out at him. "Worry not, Galan—I'll look out for your fiery wife while we're away."

"She stays here," Galan replied, his tone almost bored now. He picked up his bronze cup and raised it to his lips. "And that's the end of it."

Tea fisted her hands under the table, fuming at his dominance. However, both Tarl and Wurgest were still grinning, clearly enjoying the show she had put on for them. To Tarl's left, Donnel was observing the conversation with cool interest. He met his brother's eye when Tarl turned to him.

"Will you join us, brother?"

Donnel's chiseled features tightened. "I would, but someone has to stay behind to guard the fort."

"Galan and his warriors will be enough to defend it," Tarl countered. "I'd feel better knowing one of you was fighting at my side."

Next to Donnel, Luana had gone the color of porridge. Her eyes were huge upon her delicate face as she watched her husband. Tea saw her alarm, her naked fear.

"My wife is heavy with child," Donnel replied finally. He looked ill at ease as he said the words, as if he knew he was making an excuse and a weak one at that. Scorn rose within Tea at his words—men did not use their wives as a shield.

"And she will be taken care of here," Tarl answered, the look on his face mirroring Tea's own thoughts. "She needs no coddling from you."

Donnel's mouth thinned, and his eyes hardened. The mood between the two brothers suddenly felt charged.

Galan broke the silence between them. "Let Donnel make his own decisions. You have no woman or children here—nothing to bind you. Don't judge your brother for not being as eager as you to die in battle."

"I'm as eager as any of you to fight," Donnel growled, "but my responsibility, for now, lies here."

Tarl rolled his eyes in response before downing the dregs of ale from his cup. He then refilled it from the ewer in front of them before holding it aloft at Wurgest. He met the warrior's gaze and favored him with a wolfish grin. "Fear not, at least one of Muin's sons will join you."

Galan stood upon the wall outside Dun Ringill and watched the war band leave. They were riding north, to gather more warriors from Dun Ardtreck. Donnel stood beside him, his lean frame taut, his face stern. Galan could feel the tension emanating off him, could sense his inner conflict.

It was a still, bright morning. The misty green of the surrounding hills, and the deep-blue of the loch at his back, stood out against a smoky sky. The sun glinted off the iron spear-tips and the polished bosses of the warriors' square shields. Tarl rode at the head of The Eagle band, a proud figure clad in leather, a deer-skin cloak hanging from his broad shoulders. As he rode off, he glanced back at them—two lone silhouettes upon the stacked stone wall—and raised a hand in farewell. He was too far away for Galan to make out his expression, although he imagined Tarl was grinning at them, as always.

"It's better this way," Galan mused aloud. "Tarl is restless. He thirsts for battle, for glory, and will not settle until he finds it."

Next to him Donnel snorted. "He thinks me craven."

Galan glanced over at Donnel, frowning. Donnel met his gaze, his own troubled. "He thinks the same of me," Galan replied, "but that doesn't make it the truth."

Donnel's features tightened. "We had words last night. He doesn't understand why I can't go—why I can't leave Luana."

"I do," Galan replied. "All three of us have seen battle, have killed. You have nothing to prove. Tarl too would think differently if he had a woman he loved."

Donnel held his gaze for a few moments, before his mouth curved into a smile. "What's your excuse then?"

"For what?"

"Not going with them. If I had a bride that cold I'd be happy to leave her."

Now it was Galan's turn to snort. He did not disagree with Donnel about Tea; her outburst yesterday had angered him, although he had been careful not to let her—or anyone else—see it. They had not spoken since. "What, and leave Dun Ringill undefended? We've only just negotiated a fragile peace with The Wolf—we still need to be wary of The Stag and The Boar."

Donnel frowned. "You think they will attack us?"

Galan shrugged, casting a glance back at the departing riders. They were crossing the last hill before the north-western horizon swallowed them. He was not sure of anything, least of all his own feelings on a host of matters, but he did not share his thoughts with Donnel. "I know not," he said quietly, his gaze still resting upon the point where the warriors had disappeared, "but The Boar have grown bold of late, sending hunting parties deep into our territory without asking for permission. With war coming to these lands, we must keep our defenses strong."

Chapter Thirteen

Gateway

TEA PEERED DOWN into the glittering water. Holding her breath, she watched a winged shape glide through the shoals toward her.

Slamming down her spear, she pinned the flounder to the pebbles with the sharp tip. Checking she had speared the flatfish properly, Tea lifted it out of the water and waded to the pebbly bank, where a basket of mussels, dab, and flounder sat. It had been a good morning's fishing.

Tea deposited her flounder—the biggest she had seen in a while—into the basket and stretched her aching back, letting her gaze travel over her surroundings.

Even though it galled her to admit it, the fort's location was a breathtaking one. Loch Slapin was impossibly blue this morning, framed by softly rounded mountains. Beneath the fort there was a stony beach, and it was here she had gone out to collect shellfish and try her luck at spearfishing.

Women's work inside the fort bored her. Although she liked Luana, she had no wish to spend her mornings preparing the noon meal and her afternoons weaving, sewing, and spinning. Like the other warrior women, she preferred to be outdoors, where she felt free, with the wind in her face.

Her basket was now full and her feet numb from wading through the ice-cold water of the loch, or she would have remained out here longer. The women working indoors would want this fish for a stew.

Reluctantly, Tea picked up her basket. Carrying it in one hand, and her ash spear in the other, she made her way along the pebbly shore, to where a row of steps had been cut into the hillside.

Beyond the walls, she spied mounds of twigs and branches. Folk were readying themselves for the night's celebration of Gateway. Many days had passed since Tarl had ridden south with the warriors, and now the night that marked the passage from summer to winter was upon them.

Reaching the village above, she took the path through the scattering of roundhouses. She deliberately slowed her step as she approached the wall leading into the fort itself. The sun felt good on her face, and she had no wish to re-enter the dark, smoky interior on such a beautiful morning.

She had nearly reached the stone arch that led into the yard, when she passed a group of lads. They were young, of no more than ten years, but they watched her with hard, knowing eyes.

"There she is," one of the boys cried out. "The Wolf-bitch!"

"Her people killed my da," one of his friends added, fisting his grimy hands and advancing toward her. "Let's get her!"

Tea stopped in her tracks and spun toward them. Then she raised her spear in fighting stance. "Alright then," she growled, taking a menacing step toward the lads. "Which one of you wants a spear in the guts first?"

Her aggression made them halt. Tea did not want to frighten children, but she knew a mob could be dangerous. There were five of them, and they looked wiry. She could not let them think they could intimidate her.

The lads glowered at her. The one whose father had fallen stood a few feet in front of his friends, his eyes hard beyond his years. Although she understood his hate, the lad's venom reminded Tea of her status at Dun Ringill. She struggled to think of this fort as her home, and despite Galan's assurances, some folk here did not welcome her.

Tea thrust her spear at them. "Get back to your chores," she snarled.

Muttering insults, they backed off. However, before he joined his friends the fatherless lad spat on the ground, making his feelings clear. Tea watched him slope off and told herself she would need to be warier in future.

She needed to remember the enemy surrounded her.

Turning, she entered the fort and carried her basket of fish into the feasting hall. Luana was there, kneading dough for the bread they would serve with the noon meal. She spied Tea and raised a floury hand in greeting. Next to her, Deri—a young woman who had recently wed Cal, one of Galan's trusted warriors—peeled onions for the fish stew.

Deri, short and plump with a mane of beautiful dark-brown hair, looked up from chopping onions. Her green eyes were watering. "Did you catch anything?"

"Aye." Tea placed the basket in front of her. "Take a look at the size of that flounder."

Deri did as bid, her eyes widening. "What a monster!"

Despite her bleak mood, Tea found herself smiling. She was becoming fond of both Luana and Deri. It was hard to dislike either of them. Deri's sparkling smile and joyous laughter brought a little sunlight to her days, and

Luana bore herself with noble serenity. Sometimes, Tea would find herself observing Luana and questioning her own character. Few women railed against the world like Tea did—and sometimes her fire threatened to consume her. Tea envied Luana her peace.

"Will you help us with the baking this afternoon?" Luana asked. "We've got a mountain of apple cakes and walnut tarts to prepare for the Gateway offerings."

The thought of being stuck inside on such a beautiful day needled Tea, but she found herself nodding. Gateway was an important celebration to all who lived upon The Winged Isle. She would need to play her part in the preparations.

Today in Dun Ardtreck, there would be excitement in the air. Women would be sewing costumes for the night's guising for the children. Many folk would dress as brownies, selkies, and wulvers—men with wolves' heads—in the evening, before going out to prowl the gloaming.

Thinking of Dun Ardtreck brought back many memories, and Tea found herself wondering about Loc and Eithni. Did they miss her? The passing of time had caused her fury to ebb slightly. It no longer raged like a wildfire, but instead smoldered in the pit of her belly. Nonetheless, she had not forgiven either of them.

She was not sure she ever would.

"Does something ail you this morning?"

Tea glanced up to find Luana watching her. Tea frowned, irritated that the young woman could read her so well. "Nothing."

Luana gave her a sly look. "You haven't given in to Galan yet then?"

Tea scowled. "I don't know what you mean. He leaves me be."

Luana's eyebrows lifted. "After the heat I saw between the two of you at your handfasting that surprises me. You two virtually set fire to the table."

Tea looked away and started removing the fish from the basket. "I wasn't myself that night," she muttered. "I don't know what came over me."

Luana gave a soft laugh. "I do."

Tea glanced her way, still scowling. "What's that then?"

"It's called lust."

Tea snorted before reaching for the knife at her waist. She then began to descale the large flounder. "Lust can be overcome," she growled.

"Not in my experience it can't," Luana replied, amusement in her voice. "Lust unattended just tends to grow in strength until you are forced to give in to it or go mad from wanting."

"For the love of the gods." Tea slapped the fish down on the table. "I've never heard such rot."

Luana and Deri's laughter, musical and light, lifted high above them.

"What's all this merriment?"

Tea turned to find Donnel striding toward them. Dressed in plaid breeches and a leather tunic, his short dark hair mussed from being outdoors in the wind, Tea had to admit he was an incredible looking man. His attractiveness was different to Galan's though—for her husband had a brooding sensuality, an aura of contained power that both his brothers lacked.

Annoyed at herself for thinking of Galan so, Tea gave Donnel a sour look and turned back to descaling her fish.

"We were just talking of men," Luana told him with an impish smile.

Donnel grinned before sauntering over to his wife. He enfolded her in his arms. "And what of them?"

"Nothing of consequence," Tea replied, casting Luana a warning look.

Her sister-by-marriage winked at her and reached up to stroke her husband's face. "Some conversations are best left between women, my love."

Dusk fell over Dun Ringill and men lit great fires outside the walls. Wrapped in a thick fur mantle, Tea joined the crowd and watched the flames leap high into the sky. Tonight, the veil between this world and the next was at its thinnest. The souls of the dead walked among them, and the fires helped purify the night of any that might wish them harm.

Tea watched the men, women, and children, all wearing their guises, dance around the fire—grotesque silhouettes against the golden firelight. There was a darker aspect to this night, for it was sacred to The Hag and The Reaper. It heralded the coming of darkness.

She was so intent on watching the celebrations, her thoughts turned inward, that she did not notice the tall, muscular figure that stopped next to her. It was only when Galan spoke that she realized he stood barely more than a hand span from her.

"Are you enjoying the festivities?"

She glanced up and found him staring at her. Like Tea, Galan wore a thick fur mantle to ward off the chill; it made his shoulders seem even broader than usual.

"It is pleasant enough," she replied quietly. She was in an introspective mood this eve and did not wish to fight him. They went to their furs together each night, naked, although in cold silence, and awoke the same way. There were no words, no eye contact, and no ease. The tension between them was beginning to exhaust Tea. Her new life was draining her. She wondered how she would be a year from now—little more than a bitter, empty husk?

"Does it remind you of your kin?" he asked, drawing Tea from her brooding.

Tea nodded. "We light our fire on the hill beneath the broch."

"I've always enjoyed this night," Galan admitted. "I used to guise myself as a wulver when I was a lad." His mouth curved into a smile at the memory. "Frightened my poor mother half to death."

Tea resisted the urge to smile at the thought of this big, stern man running wild around the fort, pretending to be a wolf. Still, this was the first time Galan had mentioned his mother, and Tea wondered about her.

"When did she die?"

"Five winters ago." Galan looked away from her, his gaze shifting to the dancing flames of the Gateway fire. "It was sudden. She went to bed with a terrible pain in her head and was dead by morning."

Tea watched him for a moment. Despite that she hated being here, that she had never wanted this marriage, she found herself studying her husband. In many ways, he was a mystery. Tarl and Donnel were both much easier to read—Galan wore a shield around him that made it difficult to gauge his thoughts.

"Were you close to her?"

Galan glanced back at her, and she saw a flicker of surprise in his eyes. His mouth quirked. "Not really—I was too interested in pleasing my father, in being the warrior *he* was. Folk tell me we were alike in character though, my mother and I. My brothers take after father—whereas I have her quietness."

Tea held his gaze for a moment, aware suddenly of the heat of the fire caressing her face. He was looking at her in that hungry way he had on the eve of their handfasting: a look that made breathing difficult, one that robbed her of appetite and made her acutely aware of him too.

She should not have let her guard down with him, for Galan mac Muin had the ability to strip her naked with one heated look. She should have remembered that, but she had spent her time here trying to block him out. She had almost forgotten the attraction that burned between them. She now felt the force of his will, his desire that she submit to him. He wanted her to accept her new life, to accept him.

I will not.

Heart hammering, Tea tore her gaze from his and turned back to watch the revelers.

Leaving the fires to burn bright, the folk of Dun Ringill wandered indoors. They had left offerings outside the entrance to the great stone fort: cakes, breads, and jugs of mead for the dead. It was the last part of the Gateway ritual, before they sat down to a feast.

Three hoggets had spent the afternoon spit-roasting over open fires outdoors, and lads now carried them in for the feasters. Roast turnip, mashed carrots, and braised onions sat on large platters on the tables, and the aroma of roast hogget hung heavily on the air, making Tea's belly rumble. She had been so busy today, she had barely had time to eat.

Indoors, there was plenty to keep her busy. She helped pour warmed sloe wine and made sure food had been set out on all the tables. The women had spent days getting ready for this feast.

Eventually, Tea took her place on Galan's left at the chieftain's table. Taking a sip of wine, she gave a sigh of pleasure as the warm, spicy liquid ran down her throat and warmed her belly. The wine was delicious.

Next to her Galan sliced a choice piece of the hogget shank and placed it upon the wooden platter they shared. It had been strange, getting used to dining off the same plate as one another, but it was what a husband and wife did. She noted that Galan placed the best bits of meat and roast vegetables on her side of the plate, as he had since she had arrived at Dun Ringill, and she felt a stab of annoyance.

Why does he have to be so good to me?

She did not deserve his kindness or his consideration. She was merely a wife he had wedded to secure peace. It would have made it easier to hate him if he was cruel or thoughtless. However, his wordless gestures made her feel confused, upset, and angry. His kindness made her want to lash out at him.

Instead, she took a large gulp of sloe wine and welcomed the numbness it brought.

Chapter Fourteen

Between Man and Wife

GALAN LAY UPON the furs and watched his wife undress. He had deliberately avoided doing so of late, for the hostility between them had been too great. She had wounded him with her accusation against his father; the charge still haunted him. He had not spoken of it to Tarl before his departure, and he would not say a word to Donnel either.

He could not bear to taint their father's memory so. Yet if it were true ...

The sight of Tea's nakedness drew his thoughts back to more pleasant things. She was magnificent: tall and strong, hard and soft in all the right places. Her assertion that she could fight did not surprise him. One look at her long, finely-muscled limbs told him that she would be an agile, resilient fighter. However, the lush curve of her buttocks and her large, high breasts told another story.

Under the cover of furs, he felt his cock harden. She was a goddess in human form. He remembered every moment of their handfasting night: how her skin felt under his, the tight heat that wrapped around him as he took her, and how the column of her neck stretched back as she groaned her pleasure.

Stop it.

Galan tore his gaze away, just as Tea turned toward the furs. He stared up at the stone ceiling of their alcove and willed his erection to subside. His wife was not willing; there would be no coupling tonight or any night soon.

He felt the furs shift as Tea climbed in next to him. He glanced over at her, knowing that—as always—she would be facing away from him. The light of the one cresset still burning on the wall cast a soft, burnished light over the smooth skin of her shoulder. His gaze slid down to the blue tattoo of a wolf's head upon her upper-arm. It had been finely done, by an artist of skill.

"Tea," he said gently, not wishing to startle her. "You are welcome to keep up your warrior training here. If you wish to have a partner for swordplay, we can spar together."

There was a moment's silence before Tea responded. "I would like that ... thank you."

Galan lay there, watching her for a short while longer, gathering his thoughts before speaking again. "Tea," he repeated her name, continuing in the same tone he used with a nervous pony. "I wish to know more about you."

As expected, he saw her body tense. He had seen her discomfort at dusk, when they had spoken outdoors, and at supper. She was on her guard against him; he had to find a way to lower her defenses, for her to realize he was not the enemy.

"What do you wish to know?" she asked finally, her tone wary.

"Tell me of your childhood. What was it like to grow up at Dun Ardtreck? I've heard it is a great stone broch— far grander than this fort."

"It is an impressive structure," she admitted. "Higher than this building. There are alcoves around the walls like Dun Ringill, and a great central hearth, but there are also two levels above, where the chieftain and his kin sleep. The broch sits high on the cliff, looking north and west over the sea. On a clear day it seems you can see forever.”

She paused here, and silence stretched out between them for a few moments. Galan had thought she would say no more, when Tea continued. “I grew up clambering over the cliffs and getting into trouble with my brother. We would often involve our sister, Eithni, in our mischief, although she was different to us and preferred quieter games.”

“You miss your sister.”

Tea hesitated a moment before replying. “I should … but I am angry with her.”

His gaze narrowed. “Why?”

She looked away, making it clear she did not wish to discuss her siblings with him. “It doesn’t matter.”

“In the spring, if you wish it, we can send for her. She can stay with us under mid-summer if your brother allows it.”

Tea turned to face him. Her expression was guarded, her eyes—the color of the sky just before nightfall—wary. “Why are you so kind to me?”

Galan gave a soft laugh. “What a question—did you really expect me to treat you roughly?”

“You are the son of Muin mac Uerd,” she replied softly. “I expected a different sort of man.”

The lingering smile faded from Galan’s lips. She had brought the conversation full-circle to the shadow that was never far from his thoughts.

“I went to see our bandruí after you told me what happened to your mother,” he admitted.

Tea raised a dark eyebrow but said nothing.

“The seer was close to my father,” he explained. “I wanted to see if she knew of the crime you accused him of.”

"It wasn't an accusation," she said, her voice hardening. "It was the truth."

"Did any of your tribe see my father kill your mother?"

She stared at him, her gaze narrowing. However, eventually, she shook her head.

"Then you have no proof."

"The sign carved into her flesh is proof enough for me."

Galan's own gaze narrowed. "Not for me."

She glared at him then, and Galan had the sinking feeling they had retreated back to where they had been days ago—hostile, untrusting enemies. Yet she did not turn away from him as he expected. Instead, her dark-blue gaze bored into him in wordless challenge.

"What did the bandruí tell you," she asked finally.

Galan broke eye contact with her and looked up at the ceiling. He suddenly regretted being so open with her; Tea would use his words as weapons.

"She said that Muin and Fina knew each other."

He heard Tea's sharp intake of breath. Glancing in her direction he saw she had sat up, clutching the furs to her breasts. "They did?"

"They met at a gathering of the tribes many years ago, when they were both unwed. It seems my father fell in love with Fina, but the feuding between our tribes made their union impossible."

Tea stared at him. Her face had gone pale, except for a flush of color upon her high cheekbones. "There's the proof you wanted," she said tightly. "He was angry that my mother wed another, and he exacted his revenge."

"So many years later?" Galan countered, his own ire rising. "You mean to say he carried hate with him for years while he wed another and sired three sons, before taking his reckoning? Do you have any idea how far-fetched that sounds?"

She looked down her aquiline nose at him. "Men have killed for less."

He sat up, his gaze drawing level with hers. The scent of her reached him there, the sweet perfume of rosemary and lavender from her hair mixed with a woman's musk that sent his pulse racing. Pushing the distraction aside, he frowned.

"My father loved my mother. He was never the same after he lost her. Your mother was just a lad's fantasy … a first love that's quickly forgotten."

"You don't know that," she countered. "You say you need proof he did it, but I need proof to the contrary. You said it yourself earlier this evening, your father was a hero in your eyes."

Galan stared at her, aware that his pulse now beat rapidly in his throat. He was not quick to anger, but this woman knew just how to rile him. She wielded words like boning knives. He had wanted to have a quiet conversation with her, to know the woman beneath the wall of ice, yet all he had succeeded in doing was making her even more resentful toward him.

Inhaling deeply, he drew back from her. "Then we will both continue to be at odds with each other," he said with a shake of his head. "I do not want to fight with you, Tea."

He saw that the use of her name caused Tea's pupils to dilate slightly. However, her lips thinned, and she shook her head. "We are enemies," she said, her words faltering slightly.

Galan's mouth curved into a humorless smile. "No, we are man and wife. It is a bitter irony that while our tribes are now at peace, you and I are at war."

Tea admired the falcon perched upon Galan's arm.

The bird, whose name was Lann—'blade'—had a majestic profile, cream and grey markings on its head, and a mackerel patterning on its back and wings. Tea was fond of birds of prey—she and her father had always hunted with hawks and falcons in the hills around Dun Ardtreck.

Lann's talons dug into Galan's leather glove, its beady-eyed gaze sweeping the valley below in search of prey. Around them spread out a rumpled landscape of soft, shadowy green knolls and hillocks.

"That's it for today." Galan reached out and stroked the falcon's back with his free hand—an act of trust, for like its name implied, the bird's hooked beak could have flayed his hand open. "You did well, Lann."

Indeed, the falcon had brought down three grouse and a rook, making it a successful morning's hunt. The dead birds were tied behind Tea and Galan's saddles. Tea rode her ill-tempered dun mare, while Galan sat astride his black stallion, Faileas. Behind them one of Galan's men, Ru, and his brother Donnel rode a discreet distance away.

Galan turned his attention from the falcon to Tea then, his gaze seeking hers. "Did you enjoy the hunt, wife?"

Tea nodded. Despite that she loved hunting, she had done her best to look unimpressed when Galan had suggested it. Nonetheless, the ride east of Dun Ringill—a rolling landscape framed by smoky, sculpted mountains—had been exhilarating.

The temperatures had dropped, a warning that now that Gateway had passed the bitter weather would soon come. The cold did not bother Tea though—she loved the taste of the air and the feel of the wind on her face.

"Let's get home," Donnel called out to them, reining his pony around. "We'll be late for the noon meal."

"Always thinking of your belly," Galan replied, grinning. "Very well—let's go."

They turned their ponies west and rode into the wind in the direction of Dun Ringill. Galan and Tea led the way, cantering side-by-side, with Cal and Donnel bringing up the rear.

Tea and Galan did not speak on the way home; ever since their conversation on the night of Gateway, tension had settled between them once more. Tea now believed he had not known about the atrocity his father had committed—yet his stubborn refusal to accept it as truth outraged her.

The party of four rode into Dun Ringill as the sun reached its zenith above. Galan shouted out a greeting to the men guarding the outer wall, and they waved back. In the village beyond, two women were hanging up goat-skins to cure outside their roundhouse.

"Good day, my chief!" One of the women, young with a pretty face and curling dark hair, called out to Galan.

Tea watched her husband favor the girl with a wide smile. "Good day to you too, Leia."

Tea glanced away—irritated that watching Galan flirt with a woman would even bother her.

The four riders entered the fort and were unsaddling their ponies when Luana came out to meet them.

The young woman was now so heavy with child that she could not walk without waddling. Her belly was getting so big that it was starting to make her chores difficult.

Donnel stepped away from his pony and pulled his wife into his arms. Tea watched them embrace. Donnel kissed his wife passionately, not caring that the others looked on. When they drew apart, his eyes shone with adoration.

Envy lanced through Tea like a newly-whetted blade, catching her off-guard. She would never know what it felt like to have a husband look at her like that, never know the security and love of being held in a man's arms.

Throat constricting, Tea looked away from the lovers. Some scenes were too difficult to watch.

Chapter Fifteen

The Red Hill

TEA RAISED THE wooden sword, flexing her hands around its hilt, her gaze meeting Galan's. In her left hand she carried a rectangular shield made of pine, covered in leather with an iron-boss.

"Are you sure you want to fight me?"

His answering cocky grin made Tea grit her teeth.

"Afraid you'll hurt me, wife?" His look was sultry, which angered her further.

Tea glared at him. *The Warrior willing, I'll wipe that smirk off your face.*

She had initially been surprised, and pleased, when he had suggested they practice swordplay together. She had not lifted a weapon since her arrival at Dun Ringill nearly two months earlier and missed sparring. However, now that Galan stood before her, clad only in plaid breeches, his bare chest gleaming in the watery morning sun, she wished she had declined his offer. Better to practice with someone else—someone less distracting.

They circled each other, swords and shields raised, legs slightly apart. Tea had donned plaid leggings and a woolen tunic, girded at the waist with a thick leather belt. She had removed the soft leather wrappings she usually wore outdoors, preferring to fight barefoot. They stood in the warriors' fighting enclosure behind the fort. Galan's trusted warriors—Ru, Namet, Lutrin, and Cal—watched them, naked interest on their faces.

Tea ignored them all. Galan was observing her, waiting for her to attack first. His approach did not surprise her. Despite his known prowess as a warrior, he would not be the type to start a fight. He liked to take the measure of his opponent first, to locate their weaknesses and let them tire before he took them down.

Aware that she was being scrutinized, Tea clenched her jaw once more. This was her chance to vent the rage that had simmered within her, to unleash the warrior woman.

Snarling a curse, she leaped for him.

The rhythmic thud of wooden sword-blades colliding rang out across the arena. Tea attacked and parried, circling her opponent with calm determination, warding off his strikes with her shield.

He was good—better even than her brother. A match even for Forcus, who had always been her father's best swordsman. She had thought his size would go against him, for a lighter-built man could move faster, but Galan made sword-fighting look easy. He expended only as little energy as necessary, all the while watching his opponent and biding his time.

Thud. Clack. Clack. Thud.

Tea side-stepped the thrust of Galan's sword, feeling the draft of the wooden blade as it skimmed past her flank. Galan's reach was longer than hers. She skipped back and struck at him in a wide arc—their blades joining for a moment, before Tea twisted away and dodged out of reach.

Cheers of approval rose from the sidelines. The crowd had grown as the fight progressed, although neither Tea nor Galan had noticed it.

The joy of the fight sang in Tea's blood as she engaged Galan once more. He too was grinning. A faint sheen of sweat now covered his broad chest, while Tea had started to pant with effort. He was both stronger and fitter than her; if this fight turned into a test of endurance he would surely win it.

They circled each other once more, Tea leading the attacks, although Galan's parries and feints grew gradually more aggressive.

Then he suddenly attacked, swift and silent as a bird of prey.

Tea leaped backward to avoid him, but she was too slow. Galan knocked her sword from her grip and sent it spinning across the enclosure. Tea staggered back and fell on her rump as the watching crowd hooted and cheered.

His chest heaving with exertion, Galan stepped up and looked down at her.

"You weren't boasting about your skill with a sword," he said, his mouth curving into a smile. "I'd happily fight with you at my side."

Despite that her defeat stung, his words pleased Tea. She had never bested Forcus in a fight, and Galan was easily his equal, if not better. She was proud to have held her own against him for so long.

"I'd better get back to work then," she replied, fighting a smile of her own. "I've got baskets to weave."

He shook his head. "Enough of that—you've done nothing but toil since coming here. It's time you explored your new home. How about we take a ride together? I'd like to show you Beinn na Caillich. It's not a long journey—we can take food with us and make an afternoon of it."

Tea gazed up at him. The fight had eased the tension between them and allowed her to give her anger a target. She felt oddly relaxed and calm in the aftermath. She did not want to spend time alone with Galan, for he was too easy to like, but his offer tempted her. She had indeed toiled since coming here; it had been her means of escaping her new life and husband.

The thought of visiting Beinn na Caillich, the 'Red Hill' to the north-east of Dun Ringill, excited her, and she found herself nodding. "Aye, I'd like that."

Galan's smile widened, and he reached down to help her up. With all eyes upon them, it would have seemed rude to brush aside his offer of help; even so Tea hesitated before taking his hand.

She had not touched him since coming here.

Their hands clasped together, and the strength and warmth of his fingers as they closed around hers made Tea's breath catch in her throat.

May her mother and father forgive her, but her body and soul hungered for this man. It was only her iron will that kept her from succumbing to the attraction that pulsed between them.

Galan pulled Tea to her feet. "Come then," he said still smiling, although she saw his grey eyes had darkened with arousal. "Let's ready the ponies."

They rode out of Dun Ringill a short while later, upon two sturdy stallions—one black, the other chestnut—with a brisk easterly wind in their faces. Tea was relieved that Galan had not given her that cantankerous mare she had ridden here on. The chestnut stallion was fiery but much more manageable, and he kept up easily with Galan's feather-footed black pony, Faileas.

Together, they thundered over velvet-green moorland, a wild sky above them. The air tasted wonderful, like a fresh mountain stream. As when they had gone out hunting, Tea felt joy rise in her breast. It was as if a great weight had lifted from her shoulders; she had not realized that her anger and resentment had become such a burden. They had been such constant companions that she felt as if she was missing a limb without them.

She had not yet accepted her fate, to live here as Galan mac Muin's wife, but today she did not fight it either. Suddenly, the world around her had color again.

Their journey took them north-east over the rise and fall of many hills and through clear streams that trickled over granite pebbles. The 'Hill of the Hag', merely a stain against the cloud-streaked blue sky at first, gradually drew closer. It was a magnificent sight, a huge mount rising up from moorland. Tea had to admit that the hill did appear to have a red hue, no doubt from the short, seared grass that covered its smoothly rounded sides.

They rode up an incline, crossing a burn before making their way up the hill's steep, boulder-strewn face. Scree covered the ground and clumps of red-gold grass poked out amongst it. After a while they were both forced to dismount and lead their ponies. However, as they climbed higher, the space between the boulders narrowed, and it became impossible to take the ponies any further.

Galan turned to Tea. The pair of them had barely spoken during the journey here; it had been an easy silence, but now Tea felt herself tense as her husband favored her with his full attention. "I've the hunger of a wolf," he announced. "Let's eat here."

Smiling, Tea turned and retrieved the meal she had brought from her leather saddle bag. Luana had been generous, giving her huge slabs of fresh bread and pats of butter, boiled eggs, and slices of a cake studded with hazelnuts and dripping with honey.

She sat down next to Galan, perched on the edge of a boulder, and handed him some food upon an oiled cloth.

The fresh air had also given her an appetite, and she found her belly rumbling as she peeled an egg.

They ate in companionable silence, each admiring the view. From here they had a vast panorama over The Winged Isle.

The view to the west was desolate: a savage series of rudely formed mountains of discolored black and red, almost as if they had been ravaged by fire. Among them was Beia-an-ghrianan, Mountain of the Sun, a sacred spot for the people of this isle—followed by the serrated tops of Bla Bheinn, the clustered heights of Quillin, and the soaring peak of Cuchuillin. The deep recesses between these alps were narrow vales where herds of deer roamed.

To the south-west, in the direction they had come, Tea caught sight of the glittering blue of Loch Slapin. She had never seen the isle from this height, and the sight of it took her breath away.

"What do you think?" Galan asked, helping himself to another slab of bread. "Worth the trip?"

Tea nodded. "Aye. It's magical up here."

"I'd hoped you'd like it."

The sincerity in his voice made Tea's breathing quicken. He wanted to please her and did not try to hide it. The realization made her panic slightly. She did not want him to care, yet despite all her attempts to hurt him, he still made an effort with her.

She looked down at the slice of hazelnut and honey cake and fought a sense of shame. "You have a thick-skin, Galan mac Muin. Most men would loathe me after how I've treated you."

He laughed, a low rumble that made her skin prickle with need. "Nothing worthwhile is easily gotten."

Tea raised her head and looked at him. He was watching her, his gaze intense. "Really, you believe that?"

He gave her a slow smile. "Aye—I do."

Slightly flustered, she picked up her slice of cake and took a bite. It was delicious, infused with sweet honey perfumed of heather. The taste of it almost made her groan with pleasure.

"Gods … Luana is a talented cook."

"One of the many reasons Donnel wed her, I'm sure." Galan was grinning now. His gaze devoured her as she took another bite. Tea was aware of his stare and found herself growing hot under it. Yet she pretended not to notice—this cake was too good not to finish. However, when she licked the honey off her fingers, she became aware that Galan had gone very still next to her.

Tea froze, suddenly recalling the evening of their handfasting; how she had licked honey off his fingers at the feast—and the events that had unfolded quickly afterward.

Luana—the conniving minx. She had packed this honeyed sweet deliberately.

Tea met Galan's gaze, her heart suddenly thrumming hard against her ribs. Wordlessly, he stretched out a hand and took one of hers. He then brought her fingers to his mouth and began to lick them.

The feel of his tongue, warm and smooth, gliding over her skin made Tea stifle a gasp. Why did this feel so good? Then when he drew one her fingers into his mouth and sucked it gently, she let out a soft moan of need.

The sound shocked her—and it caused an instant reaction. With a muttered curse, Galan pulled her against him, scattering the remnants of the meal at their feet.

His kiss was hard, wild, and hungry, and she matched it. This was the first kiss they had shared—for they had not done so during their handfasting night. That night, their mating had been too frenzied, too desperate.

They devoured each other. Tea tangled her hands in his hair, the strands fine and soft like spider silk. She drank in the taste of him. With a deep groan, Galan pulled her up onto his lap so that she sat astride him. His hands slid down the length of her back—his touch firm, possessive—to cup her buttocks. He pulled Tea against him so that she sat in the cradle of his hips, her breasts crushed against the hard wall of his chest.

Despite the layers of clothing they wore, she could feel his shaft pressing against her lower belly. Excitement pulsed between her thighs at the memory of what he had felt like inside her.

It would be so easy to reach down and unlace his breaches, to take his shaft in her hands, to stroke him. It would be even easier to strip off her tunic and let him feast on her breasts. However, if she did that there would be no going back. Only the fact that she wore breeches, and not skirts that could easily be hitched up around her hips baring her naked lower torso to him, prevented Galan from taking her easily.

As his hands slid round to her front, fumbling for the edge of her leather tunic so he could rip it from her, Tea pulled away.

Panting, she pushed against his chest so that their bodies were no longer pressed together. It was impossible to think straight when this man was near her, and when he kissed and touched her, her thoughts dissolved like mist under the hot sun.

"Galan," she gasped. "No ... please."

He gazed up at her. "What's wrong?" His voice was thick, his eyes glazed. "Am I too rough with you?"

She shook her head, fighting the urge to melt into his arms once more. Yet it was not her attraction to him she fought, but the feelings that he roused in her. A wave of tenderness, of soul-longing crashed over her, bringing tears to her eyes. Breathing hard, she climbed off him and tried to master it.

"Tea ... what's wrong?"

"Nothing."

Liar. Everything was wrong. She was not supposed to want this man, yet animal attraction she could deal with—mating was a union of bodies, not hearts. But Galan did something to her. Just a short time in his company, and he had stripped away the walls she had spent years building. He was good to her, he listened to her, and worse still, he wished to know her.

Tea turned away from him, blinking as tears blurred her vision. It was too much to bear.

"Tea?"

"I'm fine," she choked out the words. "Let's go home."

Chapter Sixteen

The Birth

DUSK WAS SETTLING in a grey cloak over the land when Galan and Tea rode back into Dun Ringill. Galan's warriors had lit torches on the defensive walls, golden beacons beckoning them home.

It had been a tense return journey. The easy camaraderie they had enjoyed earlier that day had gone after the kiss they had shared. When Tea would not answer Galan's concerns, he retreated. The man who rode beside her now was the same cold stranger she had enjoyed hating on her first days here.

Only now she knew that was not the real man.

It had been an effort to choke back the tears, but she had forced herself to. She could not weep in front of Galan, could not tell him the real reason for her upset. He would not understand. Who would understand such foolish fears?

Tea hardly understood them herself.

All she knew was that she would not love; she would not let anyone in. If you cared, you risked loss—better to turn your heart to stone.

She was considering this decision, and reflecting on the lonely existence before her, when they rode through the gate into the fort. Dismounting in front of the stables, they led their ponies into their stalls and began the process of unsaddling and rubbing down.

Each of them kept their silence for a while, but it was eventually Galan who broke it.

"Whatever I did to upset you, I'm sorry for it," he said, regarding her over the withers of his stallion. The braziers at the entrance to the stable cast long shadows over the stalls, illuminating Galan's strong, proud face in gold.

Tea met his gaze, stifling a wince at the confused look on his face. She could not let him blame himself.

"You did nothing wrong, Galan," she said huskily. "It's me. I can't give you what you seek."

He opened his mouth to answer her but was forestalled by Donnel, who strode into the stables.

Excitement danced in Donnel's eyes, his body tense with purpose. His gaze darted between Galan and Tea, barely noting the tension between them. "You're back!"

Galan glanced his brother's way, his expression darkening. Donnel's appearance had shattered a delicate moment between man and wife. "What is it?" he snapped.

"It's Luana—the babe is coming a month early."

Tea threw down the twist of straw she had been using to rub down her stallion. She shifted focus, her thoughts leaving Galan and fixing upon her sister-by-marriage. If the babe was coming early, Luana would be upset.

"I must go to her," she announced before striding from the stall. "Luana will need me."

"Move around if you want to." Tea rubbed Luana's lower back soothingly. "It will help the cramps."

Luana's pretty face scrunched in discomfort, but she did as Tea bid, pacing around the alcove, her bare feet crunching on fresh rushes. "I'm exhausted already," she said, her voice breathy with pain. "My feet feel as if they're filled with wet sand. My ankles have been swollen since dawn."

Tea watched her, a frown furrowing her brow. For the first time since leaving Dun Ardtreck, she wished Eithni was here. Although she was young, her sister had already brought a number of healthy babes into the world. Tea had assisted her at some of the births and knew what to do to help—yet she lacked Eithni's confidence, her healer's touch.

Luana's pregnancy had concerned her; she had not carried the babe easily and had complained of fatigue and 'heaviness' for a while now. Dun Ringill's midwife, a middle-aged woman named Alia, had been summoned. Tea hoped she would take control of the situation and soothe Luana's fears.

"It's too soon," Luana gasped, clutching her lower back as she took short, pained steps around the small space. "What if the babe is harmed?"

"Many children are born early," Tea assured her with more confidence than she felt. "There's nothing to worry about."

At that moment the hanging of stitched goat-skin that shielded them from the open space beyond drew aside. A short, heavyset woman with dark braided hair and flushed cheeks entered.

"Now," she clucked, bustling over to Luana. "Why the worried face?"

"The babe has come too soon," the young woman groaned, doubling over as a contraction seized her. "It's not right. I don't feel right."

"Nonsense." Alia cast Tea a stern look, as if she blamed her for Luana's agitation. "Women give birth to healthy babes every day, and you will too."

Luana attempted a smile of gratitude that turned into a wince as the contractions returned.

Satisfied she had calmed Luana sufficiently, Alia glanced back in Tea's direction. "Get me hot water and fresh linen. The babe will be coming soon."

Donnel and Luana's son was born as the moon reached its zenith that night. Talor mac Donnel was a tiny babe, so small he fitted into his father's cupped hands. He was a red-faced infant, who squawked like an angry fowl.

Donnel's eyes glistened with tears as he cradled his son in his arms. Exhausted, her delicately featured face pale against the dark furs, Luana gave her husband a wan smile. "He will be handsome, like his father."

Donnel smiled. "And hopefully wise, like his mother."

Looking on, Tea's eyes misted. It was a tender scene, and one for them to share in private. Satisfied her work was done, Alia had gone off to her fur by the fire. Tea needed to leave them now too.

She edged back to the hanging and slipped beyond it. The fire in the great hearth had burned down to embers, and a chill lay in the air. Tea shivered and padded over to the alcove she shared with Galan. Like her, he had stayed awake until the babe had been delivered, and he was waiting for her when she entered. He propped himself up on one elbow, regarding her sleepily.

"All is well?"

"Aye, Luana just needs to rest."

No sooner had she spoken, when Donnel's shout rang out through the stone fort, followed by an infant's wail. "Alia!"

Tea started, her hand going to her throat. Whirling, she pushed back through the hanging, aware of movement behind her as Galan sprang from the furs.

She reached Donnel's alcove to find Luana in convulsions. Donnel gripped the crying babe under one arm, while he tried to still his wife with the other.

Tea rushed forward and plucked wailing Talor from him. A moment later Alia stumbled into the alcove, her eyes wide.

"The Mother preserve us," she gasped. "She has the birthing sickness."

The birthing sickness? Tea clutched Talor to her breast, terror washing over her. She had never heard of it.

"What's wrong with her?" Galan demanded from over Tea's shoulder.

"Don't just stand there gawping, woman," Donnel snarled at the midwife. "Do something!"

Face ashen, Alia rushed to Luana's side. She grabbed a scrap of linen, dipped it into the bowl of water beside her, and tried to mop Luana's face. However, the convulsing woman paid her no heed; her head was now jerking from side to side.

"There are poisons in her body," the midwife muttered, her eyes bulging as she tried to keep Luana from hitting her in the face. "They are devouring her."

"Can you stop them?" Galan now stood next to Tea, his face revealing the same horror she felt.

Alia's eyes gleamed with tears as she shook her head. "There's nothing anyone can do. When the birthing sickness hits, the woman will die."

Donnel's roar of rage echoed through the alcove. "Save her!"

"I can't." Tears now ran down the midwife's face. She grasped hold of Luana's convulsing shoulders and tried to pin her to the bed.

Tea, Galan, and Donnel watched, horrified, as
Luana's body went rigid, her eyes rolling back in her
head. A heartbeat later she slumped, lifeless, in the
midwife's arms.

Chapter Seventeen

Lament for Luana

THEY BURIED LUANA—daughter of Cern, wife of Donnel—in a cairn of stone upon a hillock east of the fort. The day was cold, the air damp with the promise of coming snow. A biting north-westerly wind buffeted the mourners as they carried the body up the hillside to its final resting place.

Tea walked behind Galan and his brother, each step leaden. She wore a heavy fur cloak, yet it could not warm the chill within her. In her twenty winters she had seen far too much death.

The loss of Luana seemed so cruel, and the injustice of it left a bitter taste in her mouth. In her arms, she carried a small creature with a fluff of downy black hair, wrapped in fur to ward off the chill. Next to Tea walked Mael, Luana's elder sister. She too carried a babe, although her daughter was nearly three moons older than Talor. She still had plenty of milk, so she would raise her nephew.

Grief mottled and lined Mael's pretty face, making her look much older. Her slender shoulders shook as she silently wept. Tea deeply felt her grief, reflecting on how she would react to losing Eithni in the same way; it did not even bear thinking about. Her own eyes burned with tears, and it was with great effort that she kept her grief at bay.

The light was fading, the pale sun disappearing to the west. Night would soon settle on Dun Ringill and the deep loch behind it. Tea, Mael, and Deri had spent the day preparing Luana for her burial: cleaning her body and dressing her in a beautiful woolen robe edged in sable fur. Mael had sobbed as she had brushed out her sister's thick dark hair.

Now the time had come to bid Luana goodbye, to send her forth to meet her ancestors.

The procession of mourners reached the stacked-stone cairn and waited as the men—Galan and Donnel among them—slid Luana's bier into the tomb. By rights, it should have been Mael to sing her sister's final lament, yet she was now bent double with sobs, so that her husband was forced to take her daughter from her lest she accidentally hurt her.

Tea inhaled deeply. She would sing it; she owed Luana that much.

Her voice, low and strident but with a slight quaver, rang out across the hillside. It lifted and fell in grief as Tea sang of beauty, kindness, and a gentle spirit taken too soon. The lament had an intensity, a passion that stilled all that heard it.

Even Donnel, who flanked the entrance to Luana's cairn, lost his expression of contained fury as she sang. Instead, he bowed his head at its haunting vehemence. Tea sang on, watching as tears streamed down Donnel's proud face. She was singing this for him, for her father ... for all men who had lost a woman they loved.

When the final strains of the lament died away, Tea felt wrung out. Blinking back the tears that blurred her vision, she swayed slightly on her feet. She did not resist when Galan put an arm around her shoulders to steady her.

The light dimmed further and the mourners turned back toward the fort. They walked slowly, cloaked somber figures in the gloaming. A light supper of broth and bread awaited inside, but Tea did not join them.

Instead, she took a lantern—an oil filled clay vessel that guttered in the wind—and carried it down to the water's edge. Seated on a flat stone, with the bulk of the fort looming above her, Tea looked out across the loch. The dark waters gleamed from the reflected fires of Dun Ringill above.

Tea drew her cloak close and stared sightlessly into the distance.

Luana was dead. Never again would she tease Tea about Galan or sit spinning by the hearth gossiping with Deri. Nor would she see her son grow to a man or watch her husband age. The Reaper had taken her too young, for no purpose at all but to cause suffering.

Tea picked up a smooth stone and hurled it into the gleaming loch, hearing the hollow sound of it falling in deep water. Then she picked up another and threw that, and another; she hurled stones until her arm ached.

Breathing heavily she slumped on her stone seat. The injustice of it choked her. The Reaper always chose the kindest, the best, and left the others behind. Luana had deserved a long and happy life.

The gods are so cruel, she thought bitterly.

"Tea."

A man's voice behind her made Tea turn. Even in the darkness, she recognized Galan's height and breadth.

"May I join you?"

Her first instinct was to rail at him, to send him away from her as she had during her first days at Dun Ringill. But although fury filled her over Luana's loss, she felt no anger toward her husband.

None of this was his fault.

Wordlessly, she nodded.

Galan stepped forward and sat down on a boulder next to her. They sat so close that their thighs were almost touching. Tea could feel the heat of his body next to hers. His nearness calmed her a little and gave her a sense of comfort. Galan had such a peace, a strength about him.

"I can't believe she's gone," Tea eventually whispered. "It doesn't seem real."

"No one can believe it," Galan replied. "Least of all, Donnel."

It was true, Galan's brother was far from accepting of his wife's death. The only moment when he had shown the grief that tore him up inside was during Tea's lament. The rest of the time, he raged. His fury at losing Luana burned like a wintry fire. When the midwife had confirmed Luana dead, he had stormed from the alcove and proceeded to tear the hall beyond to pieces with his bare hands. Dogs, children, men, and women alike fled as he smashed stools, snapped distaffs, crushed pottery underfoot, and upended tables. Finally, it had taken Galan and three others to bring him down, pinning him to the rushes as he bellowed and cursed.

Once dawn broke, his rage had burned inward. He had sat, unmoving by the hearth, staring into the flames as the folk of Dun Ringill set about repairing the damage he had wrought.

"Do you worry about him?" Tea asked Galan finally. She remembered her father's grief over her mother. Donnel's reaction reminded her of him.

"There is little point in that," Galan replied wearily. "He will grow to accept his loss ... in time."

Tea's mouth compressed. "My father never did."

Silence stretched between them then. The muted sounds of the fort—the rise and fall of voices, and the wail of an infant—reached them. Sadness filled Tea at the sound. "It's not right that Talor will grow up without a mother."

"Mael will look after him."

"It's not the same. Luana would have been a wonderful mother."

Galan sighed. "You must stop this, Tea."

She stiffened, turning to him in the darkness. "Stop what?"

"Tormenting yourself, railing against fate. Sometimes I look at you, and I see a woman who would bend the world to her will if she could."

"And what's wrong with that?"

"It's impossible. You'll only kill yourself trying."

Her throat constricted. "I can't be like you," she choked out the words. "You're so accepting of everything. Don't you ever get angry? Don't you ever rage at the injustice of it all?"

She felt his intense gaze on her face. His own features were partly thrown into shadow by the flickering lantern, yet she sensed she had struck a nerve.

"We don't all have the luxury of giving our impulses free rein," he replied, the tightness of his voice the only hint that she had offended him.

"So I'm supposed to tell myself that Luana's death was right ... to just accept it?" She heard the scorn in her voice but was not sorry for it. His fair-mindedness made her want to lash out.

"No," he replied, his voice strained now. "Grief and loss must be felt, just don't let them poison your heart."

"It's too late for that," she snapped. "There's nothing left of it to poison."

"Don't say that," he replied, his voice suddenly hard. He leaned forward, his hand fastening around her forearm. "You're too young, too strong to give up."

His touch, the heat of his skin against hers, caused Tea's anger to ebb. In its place sorrow bubbled up.

"There's been so much death," she gasped, "so much pain. I just want it to stop."

A sob rose within her, and then suddenly tears spilled over like a bursting dam. She doubled over, her shoulders shaking with the force of her grief. She had been holding it back all day, trying to remain strong while others wailed and sobbed, but she could not do it any longer.

Wordlessly, Galan gathered her up in his arms and pulled her against him. The gesture swept away the last vestiges of restraint within Tea. She sank against him, buried her head against his chest, and wept as if her heart would break.

Chapter Eighteen

Donnel's Departure

THE DAY AFTER Luana's burial it began to snow. Pristine white flakes floated down from a scree-colored sky and settled over the land, covering it in a thick white crust. Days passed, and as mid-winter approached, the snow continued to fall, obscuring Luana's cairn in a blanket of white.

Life moved indoors. The air inside the fort often felt close with the smell of peat smoke, wet wool, dogs, and stale sweat.

Like she had in her first days at Dun Ringill, Tea threw herself into a flurry of industry. Not wanting to remain inside, Tea braved the cold. Wrapped up in furs, she went fishing, collected shellfish, went hunting with Galan, and helped look after the ponies and livestock within the fort.

She dreaded going indoors, for every time she stepped inside the feasting hall she was reminded of Luana's absence. How often had she come indoors to see her friend kneading bread at one of the long tables or adding finishing-touches to a stew bubbling over the hearth? The fort seemed a joyless place without her.

Life without her sister-by-marriage felt cold indeed. It was not that the other women were unpleasant, but that Tea felt very different to them. Deri was cheerful company, but she was not Luana—no one could replace her.

One afternoon Tea came in from feeding the fowl that lived in the yard outside, a basket of warm eggs under one arm. It was freezing outdoors; even her short time out in the swirling snow had left her hands and feet numb with cold. Teeth chattering, Tea hurried over to the glowing hearth and tried to ignore the squealing of two lads nearby who were being reprimanded by their mother.

She was just helping herself to a cup of warmed ale, when Galan entered the fort.

Snowflakes dusted his dark hair and had settled upon the fur mantle about his shoulders. Spotting Tea, he raised a hand in greeting, and she did likewise. As always, the sight of him caused her belly to flutter in excitement.

Ever since the night of Luana's burial, when he had held her in his arms while she wept, the tension between them had eased. She had appreciated the comfort he had given her, and how he had asked nothing in return. They still slept back-to-back upon their bed of furs but now would often talk together for a while after retiring for the night. They had become friends, and Tea was beginning to know the man beneath the role of chieftain—a deep-thinking man with a dry sense of humor.

Tea reached for a second wooden cup. "Warmed ale?" she asked Galan. "You look like you could do with some."

"Aye," he replied with a smile. "I've just been out helping repair the southern walls. It's bitter out there."

She poured a large cup of steaming ale and passed it to him. Galan took a sip and gave a sigh of pleasure.

At that moment Donnel entered the fort. Like Galan, he wore a snow-dusted mantle, yet the sight of him gave Tea a pang of misgiving. She had always liked Donnel before—preferring him to Tarl—but Luana's death had changed him. His handsome face had turned austere, and he wore a perpetual scowl. His muscular frame was taut and his shoulders tense. He strode across to the hearth and thrust out his hands over the burning peat.

"Some warmed ale, Donnel?" Tea asked.

He screwed up his face as if she had just offered him dog piss and shook his head.

"Have you been to see Mael of late," Galan asked his brother. "I dropped in to see her earlier. Your son thrives."

Donnel shrugged in response, his gaze never leaving the dancing flames in the hearth. "I care not," he said finally.

"Talor is your son," Galan replied evenly. "Surely you wish to see him grow."

Donnel looked up, fixing his brother in a gimlet stare. "He took Luana away from me. I don't need a constant reminder."

"But a part of Luana lives on through him," Tea spoke up. It was hard to see Donnel so bitter, a painful reminder of her own behavior. "He has her eyes."

"Still your tongue," Donnel snarled. "I've no wish to hear your opinion Wolf-bitch."

"Donnel!" Galan cut in, his voice snapping like a whip. "Show some respect when you speak to my wife."

Donnel regarded them both, his gaze flint-hard. His mouth then curled as if he found the sight of both of them distasteful. "I didn't come in here to share an ale or argue," he growled. "I'm leaving—riding south to join Tarl and the others."

Galan's face went hard at this news. "It's too late, they'll be too far away by now."

Donnel shook his head. "There's still time. Tarl told me that they would be gathering warriors until after mid-winter before they ride to the wall."

Galan's gaze met his. "Is this what Luana would have wanted?"

Donnel's face twisted. "She's not here to have a say in the matter."

"Then you shouldn't go. Don't throw your life away—think of your son."

Donnel shook his head. "I only care about fighting. If I die helping to defeat the oppressors, I'll be content."

"Talor won't be," Galan replied. "Do you really want to leave him without a father?"

Tea glanced between the two men; it was clear that Galan was fighting a losing battle. Donnel had no intention of changing his mind. Every objection Galan raised only made his resolve stronger.

"He won't even remember me," Donnel said finally. "I should have done as Tarl asked and ridden south with the others. I would have been spared watching my wife die in agony. I want the world to pay. I will spill the blood of the Caesars till the earth is stained red. I will make the gods weep for taking her from me."

Donnel departed the following morning. The snow fell silently in thick flurries as Galan watched him saddle his pony, a heavy-set grey stallion that their father had gifted his youngest son five years earlier. The stallion would carry him as far as the village of Kyleakin, on the south-eastern coast of the isle. There he would have to travel by boat across the narrow channel to the mainland and find another mount to continue his journey.

Tea stood a few feet behind Galan, silently looking on while Donnel made his final preparations. She had deliberately stepped back to give the brothers some time alone, and Galan appreciated the gesture.

He stepped forward and passed Donnel a leather bag filled with freshly baked bread; boiled eggs; salted pork; a wedge of cheese; and small, sweet apples. "Tea has packed this for you," he said quietly. "It should sustain you for a couple of days at least."

Donnel turned and took the bag from him, nodding his thanks.

Now that his brother had made his decision, a little of his hostility toward the world had eased. He had found an outlet for his rage and was merely impatient to be away.

"Here." Galan handed him a sword, sheathed in a leather scabbard inscribed with the swirling symbols of their people. "You earned one of these years ago."

Donnel's eyebrows raised. "I've a spear and an axe."

"And now you've a blade as well."

Donnel inclined his head slightly, his gaze narrowing. "But this is your sword."

"I've asked the smith to make me another—this one is for you."

Donnel took the sword and buckled it around his hips. "Thank you, Galan."

"We'll make offerings for you at Mid-Winter Fire," Galan replied, "for you and Tarl both."

Donnel favored him with a wry smile. "You think we need it?"

Galan's mouth twisted. "No matter how skilled he is, a warrior needs The Reaper on his side."

Donnel tied the bag of food behind his saddle and slung his shield over his back before turning once more to his brother. For the first time since Luana's death, Galan saw Donnel's expression soften.

"I've been difficult to live with of late," Donnel admitted quietly, "and I'm sorry for it. Grief has brought me low."

"None of us judge you for that," Galan replied. "I know how much you loved her."

Donnel's eyes shone as his gaze met Galan's. Then, wordlessly, the two brothers hugged.

"May the Warrior ride with you into battle at the wall," Galan said, feigning a heartiness he did not feel.

"And may the Mother bless you and Tea both," Donnel replied, casting a speculative look in Tea's direction. "I know it was not a match either of you would have chosen—and I still doubt it will bring lasting peace—but it could be the making of you both."

With that, Donnel turned and took hold of the reins, guiding his stallion out of the stall into the yard beyond. The pony's hooves sank up to its fetlocks in snow. Galan walked out behind him and watched Donnel mount. Eager to be off, the beast tossed its head, jangling its bit.

Donnel rode out of the yard, through the stone arch, and down the slippery path leading to the defensive walls. Galan and Tea followed him, their boots crunching in the snow. It was a still morning, and the snow fell silent and thick. Reaching the outer wall, Galan climbed the icy steps, taking Tea's hand as he did so to prevent her from slipping. Standing side-by-side, they watched Donnel ride out of the fort.

Like Tarl, nearly three months earlier, Donnel twisted in the saddle and waved when he was around a furlong distant from them. He had pulled up the fur-lined hood of his cloak, partially obscuring his face.

Galan raised his hand in farewell and remained there, watching, until pony and rider disappeared over the brow of the hills to the east.

Only then did Tea speak. "Don't blame yourself—you couldn't have prevented him from going."

"Aye," Galan replied, his voice bleak. He saw the wisdom of her words, but that did not ease the ache in the center of his chest. The weight of responsibility had never felt heavier; he almost felt smothered by it. He tore his gaze from the snowy horizon and looked at her. "I could lose them both."

He watched her expression soften and studied her finely-boned, proud face as she stared up at him. They both knew there was no response she could make that could ease his fears, and so she remained silent. Even so, he saw understanding and compassion in her eyes.

Chapter Nineteen

Collecting Drualus

THE SNOW REMAINED as the winter solstice approached, covering the world in an ermine crust. The water in the troughs outside the fort froze solid, and snow drifts solidified into gleaming mountains of ice outside the defensive walls.

Tea found herself looking forward to Mid-Winter Fire. This festival had always been the one she enjoyed the most, for it was when the dark half of the year relinquished to the light half. The morning after the Long Night, the sun would climb just a little higher in the sky and remain a little longer. Light and warmth would creep back into the world.

On the Long Night they celebrated the rebirth of the Oak King, the giver of life who would warm the frozen earth. In the days leading up to the festival, Tea helped bake loaves of sweet bread studded with nuts and damsons, and honey oat-cakes. Men and women journeyed to the woodland north of Dun Ringill and brought home baskets filled with oaken branches.

They also dragged back a large bough of oak, which
would burn in the fort's great hearth. The people of The
Winged Isle believed that at this time of the year, the sun
stood still for twelve days. During this time they would
keep the log lit to conquer the darkness, banish evil
spirits, and bring good fortune for the coming year.

On the day of the Long Night, Tea accompanied a
group of women into the woods to gather drualus, holly,
ivy, and boughs of pine for Mid-Winter Fire. The nearest
woodland was a morning's walk from the fort, so the
group dressed warmly in heavy mantles and fur feet
wrappings. They trudged through the deep snow, baskets
under the arms. It was a gelid morning, although the sky
was clear, and so their voices were full of good cheer.

The bandruí of Dun Ringill accompanied them.
Walking a few yards behind Ruith, Tea observed the seer
with interest. She was a small, wiry woman with thick
greying hair braided into plaits. Despite her advancing
years, she held herself straight and proud as she walked.

The bandruí led them deep into the woods, to the
places where drualus grew upon ancient oaks. While the
rest of the women went in search of the other seasonal
plants, Tea helped Ruith cut the drualus. As she worked,
the bandruí murmured words of blessing. Oaks were
sacred, and the drualus that grew upon it like a parasite
was a symbol of life in the dark winter months.

Ruith stepped back from her task, glancing across at
where Tea now held a basket full of evergreen leaves
with woody stems, and waxy, white berries.

"It is good to see color in your face and light in your
eyes," the seer said. Her directness took Tea aback. She
had not thought Ruith had paid her any attention since
her arrival here. Today was the first time the two women
had actually spoken.

Seeing her consternation, the bandruí smiled. "I saw
you the day you rode in," she said by way of explanation.
"All I remember is an ashen face and wild eyes—you

looked formidable. I feared our chief might have his throat slit one night while he slept.”

Tea grimaced. “I considered it.”

“But something prevented you?”

Tea nodded, looking away from Ruith’s intense gaze. “I can’t harm Galan.” She glanced back at the bandruí, to see that she was smiling. “He told me that he came to you about me.”

Ruith nodded, her smile fading. “He came looking for answers, but I fear he left me less happy than when he arrived.”

The two women moved over to the second oak in the mossy clearing, and Ruith climbed up to reach the drualus that grew higher up in its branches. She climbed with impressive agility and confidence, bracing herself against two boughs while she began cutting the plant and dropping it down to Tea.

“He told me about his father and my mother,” Tea said eventually. “That Muin had wished to wed my mother all those years ago.”

Ruith looked down at her. “*All those years ago* ... so says the young woman. Seems only yesterday to me.”

Tea tried to smile but failed; she had little sense of humor where the subject of Muin was concerned. “Was he embittered?”

The bandruí sighed. “I remember he returned from that gathering elated at the prospect of having Fina as his wife. A few moons later, when he realized she’d wed another, he was angry, yet I don’t remember his disappointment lasting long. If he felt resentment, he hid it well.”

Ruith paused here as she turned her attention to her task. When she slid back down to the ground, her expression was introspective. “Muin was very happy with Galaith, Galan’s mother. After her death Muin and I became lovers.”

Tea listened with interest. She was still unconvinced, yet like most folk, she respected a seer's opinion. Besides, her time here had softened her view of Galan's people. She had treated them all with contempt since her arrival, but for the most part they had accepted her. Luana's death had made something shift within her—had made her see the world differently.

Ruith met Tea's eye once more, her expression serious. "Muin hated the People of The Wolf, but it was a loathing born of years of feuding, one passed down to him through his father and his father's father before that. I never sensed there was more to it than that."

Their task of gathering drualus complete, the two women started walking back through the trees in the direction of Dun Ringill. The pale winter sun shone down through the skeleton trees, although there was hardly any heat in it.

"Do you still hate Galan?" Ruith asked, a twinkle in her eye. "In your place, I'd find him very hard to resist."

The seer's comment reminded Tea of Luana—of her attempts to make Tea see Galan in a better light. Those honey oatcakes she had packed for them that day had been yet another attempt to thaw the ice between them. The memory of Luana's kindness, just a short while before her death, made Tea's throat constrict.

Tea looked away from the bandruí, as if the frozen ground had suddenly become fascinating. "He is hard to resist," she admitted quietly.

Ruith gave a soft laugh. "You make that sound like such a terrible thing. Do you know how many women can't abide the sight of their husband?"

Tea glanced up. "How I wish that was the case between us. For the sake of my people, for my parents' memory, I wanted to despise him."

The bandruí inclined her head slightly. "It's for the sake of both our people that Galan wed you—to bring peace to our corner of The Winged Isle. Why do you continue to fight your attraction to him?"

Tea sighed, forcing a wan smile. "I don't rightly know. I suppose I fear that once I cross that line, there'll be no going back. Dun Ringill will finally be my home."

Ruith smiled. "It already is, Tea." She then reached into her basket and withdrew a sprig of drualus. "I bless this plant with life, love, and happiness for you both—wear it in your hair tonight."

Tea took the drualus, her stomach fluttering in sudden nervousness at what the seer was promising. "Very well," she murmured. "I shall."

At dusk the folk of Dun Ringill lit two bonfires of oak just outside the defensive walls. Tea and the other women brought steaming iron pots of spiced cider outdoors to toast the Long Night. They would also share the drink with the crops and trees in the fields outside the fort, to encourage a bountiful crop for the following summer.

The women had done an admirable job of decorating the fort, both inside and out, with holly, ivy, drualus, and boughs of pine. The latter filled the interior of the fort with its pungent resin-scent. A great oaken log now burned in the hearth, before it would smolder for the coming days.

Cheeks reddened from being outdoors in the cold, folk packed inside the feasting hall. They took their places at the long tables around the hearth, their chilled fingers wrapped around steaming cups of spiced cider.

Men brought in spit-roasted pigs that had been stuffed with apples, dried damsons, and nuts; placing one on each table. There were also roasted turnips, carrots, and onions, and large tureens of braised kale—

all of which were served with fresh loaves of caraway bread.

After she had finished pouring cider for all who sat at the chieftain's table, Tea took her place next to Galan. It was the first time she had seen him all day, for the preparations for the Long Night had occupied them both. Galan looked dangerously attractive tonight, clad in fine doe-skin breeches, a studded belt, and a dark leather vest that left his muscular arms bare. The sight of him made Tea's pulse quicken.

Meeting her eye, Galan smiled. "It's a fine feast."

"You have many good cooks here at Dun Ringill," she replied with an answering smile. "Deri prepared most of this—I cannot take credit for it."

Galan carved some pork, placing it upon the dish they shared before spooning out some stuffing. Despite the excitement his very nearness elicited, the aroma of the roast meat and stuffing made Tea's mouth water. Feasts such as these were special events indeed, and to be savored, for there were still many moons of cold weather before them.

At the table opposite, Tea spied Ruith. A revered member of the community, the bandruí was always invited to feasts inside the fort. The seer laughed at something the man next to her said, flicking her braids flirtatiously. Watching her, Tea fought a smile. She liked Ruith's spirit and zest for life.

She raised her cup to her lips and took a sip of warmed cider before glancing at Galan. He was watching her under lowered lids, a heated look that made her breathing grow shallow.

"You look lovely this evening," he murmured. "You have drualus in your hair."

Tea found herself smiling. "Aye—Ruith gave it to me."

He raised a dark eyebrow. "Have you been spending time with the bandruí?"

Tea nodded. "We collected drualus together today." Her smile widened when she saw his discomfort. "What is it?"

"I've never been comfortable around the seer," he admitted, casting a reproachful glance in Ruith's direction. "She has a look that devours a man."

Tea laughed, realizing as she did so that it was the first time she had let mirth overtake her since coming to Dun Ringill. "She certainly thinks you're attractive—she told me so."

Galan grinned at that. "What else did she say?"

Tea gave him a coy look. "Men shouldn't know what women say amongst themselves."

His eyes gleamed. "Really? Now I'm curious."

Tea looked away and pretended to be interested in her meal. However, the heat of Galan's stare made her feel stripped bare. She took another sip of cider and let its spiced warmth calm her. His nearness made her feel as if she was sitting right next to the burning oaken log in the hearth. His thigh sat just a hair's breadth from hers on the bench. Her heart skipped a beat when she felt him shift closer, and his leg pressed against hers.

Heart pounding, Tea looked up and helped herself to a piece of roast turnip.

How am I going to get through tonight without bursting into flames?

Across the room Ruith caught her eye. Perhaps seeing Tea's struggle to contain her desire for the man sitting next to her, the bandruí winked before favoring her with a wicked smile.

Chapter Twenty

Mid-Winter Fire

THE FEASTING OF the Long Night passed with agonizing slowness. Although the food was delicious—especially the apple and prune pudding served with thick cream that was served as a sweet—Galan had no appetite for it.

All he could think about was Tea.

He had not been exaggerating earlier—she had truly never looked lovelier than tonight. She wore a simple, high-necked tunic of jade green, edged in gold thread, and that same heavy circlet about her throat that she had worn for their handfasting. The tunic showed off the full swell of her breasts. It left her long, shapely arms bare, and upon her left bicep she wore a golden arm ring. Her hair, which she usually wore braided, she had brushed out before piling it high on her head, the drualus woven amongst it. This hair-style showed off the long column of her neck, including her nape.

Galan had ached to kiss her there all night.

Once the feasters had eaten their fill, more spiced cider was mulled, and a harpist began to play. Men and women rose to their feet, pushed two of the tables to one side and began to dance.

Watching them, Galan was aware only of the feel of Tea's thigh against his. Struggling to calm his breathing, he reached over and took her hand in his. Her skin was warm, her fingers slender and strong. Wordlessly, he laced his fingers through hers before stroking her palm with the pad of his thumb. He heard Tea's sharp intake of breath next to him and felt a thrill of victory.

He was beginning to think he was the only one who was suffering, that she was sitting next to him in cool oblivion. However, that gasp told him it was not so.

Galan looked over at her, their gazes meeting. As always, he drowned in the storm-blue of her eyes.

Around them the crowd of revelers cheered as a man with a bone whistle joined the harpist. An exuberant tune echoed high into the rafters, accompanied by laughter, as one of the men dancing spun his woman around, her hair flying like a flag behind her.

Galan was oblivious to it all. His thumb continued its gentle caress across Tea's palm as he watched her. He saw Tea part her lips slightly, a gentle sigh escaping her. Suddenly, it was as if they were alone in the cavernous space. She too paid the dancers and revelers no heed.

"Galan," she murmured his name like a caress.

He tried to smile and failed. His longing for her felt like a blade in his groin. His heart thundered like a galloping pony.

"Yes, Tea."

She swallowed; the smooth skin of her cheeks burnished by the flames of the hearth, mulled cider, and arousal. "I don't want to fight this anymore ... I can't."

Her words made his breathing still, made hope flare in his breast. They were the words he had been waiting for since their handfasting. To hear them made the wait worth it. He would not let this moment pass unnoticed—he had to act now before she changed her mind.

"Come," he murmured, rising to his feet.

Tea glanced at him, her gaze widening. "But the dancing?"

His gaze held hers. "No one will care if we leave."

It was true, the crowd were too busy clapping and cheering for the dancers. Few of them—save Ruith, who missed nothing—noticed the chieftain rise to his feet and lead his wife away from the table.

Tea's body felt molten, her limbs boneless, as she stepped into the chieftain's alcove. Galan stepped in behind her, the heavy fur hanging swishing shut. Beyond, the music and cheering echoed through the fort, yet she barely noticed it.

Instead, she turned and reached for her husband.

Two steps brought her hard up against him, and then her arms were locked around his neck, her mouth attacking his.

Galan gave a deep groan, pulling her hard against him. His hands were everywhere. He unfastened her hair so it fell in heavy waves around her shoulders, and tore at the flimsy material of her tunic so that it fell from her body, pooling around her ankles. Likewise, Tea ripped at his clothing, untying the leather vest and tearing it from him, her hands fumbling with the laces on his doe-skin breeches.

She pushed the breeches down over his hips, his shaft springing free. She stroked the length of him, before she wrapped her fingers around his girth. Tea's breathing caught in her throat.

He's magnificent, beautiful.

His mouth still devouring hers, Galan scooped her up against him and closed the gap between the edge of the alcove and the pile of furs—the place where they had lain side-by-side night after night without touching.

Tonight, all that would change.

They collapsed on the furs, limbs and tongues tangling. Galan tore his mouth from hers, only to kiss and lick his way down the length of her body. Tea gasped at the heat of his mouth, the aching pleasure as he took each of her swollen nipples into his mouth and suckled her. Her hands raked over his skin, marveling at its velvet softness over the hardness of muscle. How long had she longed for this? How long had she fought that longing?

"Tea," he groaned as he parted her thighs. "I'm going to spend all night showing you how beautiful you are—but right now I can't wait. I have to be inside you."

Her breathing caught in her throat. She wanted him so much, she could not bear to wait a moment longer. In answer, she spread her legs wide and wrapped them around his hips, angling herself up to him.

Galan entered her in one smooth, deep thrust; he was so big and hard that she cried out. Her body started to shudder uncontrollably. Waves of pleasure crashed over her. Tea started to sob and gasp his name.

In response, he grabbed hold of her wrists, pinned them together and held them over her head so that her breasts thrust up to him. Then he plowed her, slow and hard.

Tea felt as if she was flying, as if together they had left the mortal world behind and were soaring like falcons high above the earth. Nothing mattered but this moment—the past and future ceased to exist.

Rearing over her, his skin flushed with pleasure, his lips swollen from the violence of their kisses, Galan threw back his head and let out a low, throaty groan. Tea dug her heels into his buttocks and thrust her hips up to meet him.

His groan turned into a hoarse cry, and she watched him give himself up to her.

Galan propped himself up on an elbow and stared down at Tea. Unspeaking, he drank her in.

She looked up at him, her eyes wide, her face soft. The light from the cressets that burned on the walls caressed her nakedness, and Galan found his gaze slipping from her face, down her long, smooth limbs, and over the flare and curve of her hips to the lushness of those delicious breasts.

He would never tire of admiring his wife's body—she was divine.

When his gaze travelled back up to meet Tea's, he found she was smiling.

"What is it?" he asked.

"Nothing," she replied gently. "I'm just thinking, that's all."

He reached out and stroked her cheek with the back of his hand. "Thinking about what?"

"About how things change." Her gaze flicked away. "I don't know what I believe in anymore."

Galan stared down at her for a moment before replying. "Believe in us," he murmured.

Tea's eyes glittered with emotion. "I'm sorry for being so foul toward you—I'm surprised you didn't beat me for my insolence?"

He grinned. "I don't think I'd dare ever try."

"I mean it—you are a good man ... only you never bargained on getting a shrew."

Galan shook his head. "I didn't—I got a proud, beautiful woman whose trust I needed to win." He reached down and took her hand in his, cupping it tenderly.

"I wish to believe that my father is innocent of killing your mother," he said after a few moments, "but I have to accept that it could have happened. It's not something that's easy to bear." He gently squeezed her hand. "Please believe me when I tell you that I and my brothers had nothing to do with her death. None of us would ever stoop so low. I would never harm you or yours."

Tea nodded, her eyes shining with unshed tears. "I realize that now."

Chapter Twenty-one

No Other Woman

IN THE DAYS following the Long Night, the snow finally melted away and the earth thawed. The oaken log in the hearth smoldered for twelve days, until finally nothing but embers and ash remained. Once the snow had cleared, leaving the earth soft and muddy, a chill mist settled over The Winged Isle.

Mists like this were commonplace, especially in the winter. Tea knew this weather well, although she, like most folk, disliked it when the mantle of mist descended, as it would linger for many days, obscuring the friendly face of the sun and chilling all to the bone.

Yet the mist did not bother Tea this year. Tempests could have raged, and she would have hardly noticed— such was her newfound joy with Galan.

Since Mid-Winter Fire, a warmth had burned within her that had nothing to do with the festivities. She and Galan spent much time together. They would rise late from their furs, often waking early but lingering in the warmth of their bed together, pleasuring each other. They would talk while the rest of the household roused the peat in the great hearth and warmed the cavernous space.

Some mornings they would ride out with Galan's men to secure the south and eastern borders of The Eagle territory. The People of The Boar, their closest neighbors, had been seen hunting in the vales to the east earlier in the year, and Galan wanted to make sure they were not taking further liberties. However, the scouting parties found nothing suspicious. Other mornings they would spar together with swords or staffs, oversee the repairs on the defensive walls, or take Lann out for a hunt so that the falcon could stretch his wings.

In the afternoons, more often than not, Galan would come looking for her and together they would ride out alone upon their two stallions: his black, hers chestnut.

The thick mist made visibility difficult, but Galan knew this landscape very well, and he led the way over the hills, or along the edge of the loch, with confidence. They rode side-by-side, their knees almost touching.

These were magical days for Tea. She slowly let her guard down. Galan was patient with her; he did not question her about her family and did not bring up the wounds of the past that could risk driving a wedge between them. Their trust was still fragile, still too new, and they both understood that they had to tread carefully or risk destroying the bridge they had built.

One afternoon Tea and Galan left the walls of Dun Ringill and headed west along the shore of Loch Slapin. The mist had cleared slightly, leaving long, slender wisps, like crone's hair, drifting along the tops of the green hills.

To the north rose the dark shadows of the Black Cuillins, those mountains that would forever remind Tea of her wedding day. Only, now that she and Galan had formed a bond, she no longer looked upon that night with shame or anger but instead recognized it for it was—the first step on the path to a new life.

They reached the coast—the point where the waters of the lake met the sea—where surf crashed against the rocks below, sending up a thick spindrift. Under the lee of a hill, they climbed down from their ponies and perched upon a rocky outcrop. The wind raked through their hair, and the cry of gulls echoed down the cliff-face from where they wheeled overhead. It was a lonely spot, but a beautiful place to be alone with her husband.

The afternoon was chill, but they neither cared nor noticed as Tea perched on Galan's lap and wrapped her arms about his neck. The pair gazed out to sea, enjoying the solitude and the closeness.

"I've never been this happy," Galan whispered in her ear, his breath tickling her skin. "I knew the moment I saw you that there could be no other woman."

She glanced down, expecting to see a teasing smile, but instead saw that he was serious. Galan could be that way—when he spoke of things that mattered his gaze was piercing. It snared hers and held her fast.

"Really?" she murmured. "Surely not—I was so sullen that day."

He inclined his head slightly. "You were magnificent. You captivated me the moment you stepped out of that tent and walked down toward the edge of the pool. I thought one of the fairy folk had taken human form."

She laughed, the sound whipped away by the wind. "Now, you're teasing."

He shook his head. "Not at all. I always knew it would be like that for me—that there would only ever be one woman. That one woman is you, Tea."

She studied him for a few moments, her humor fading. "You're a constant surprise," she said finally. "I thought you so intimidating when we first met, so serious."

A wistful smile tugged at his mouth. "I can be like that sometimes—I take my role as chief seriously. It sometimes feels like a cage."

Tea reached out and stroked his cheek, feeling the rasp of stubble along his chin. "I used to think we were opposites, but now I see we're actually alike, you and me."

His gaze widened. "How so?"

"We're both loyal to those we love, maybe too much so. We're both protectors." She smiled into his eyes. "I think, together, there's nothing we couldn't achieve."

He reached up and trailed his fingertips along the line of her jaw. His grey eyes turned that smoky shade she was coming to know well, the color that told her he was pleased. She shivered with pleasure under the lightness of his touch.

Wordlessly, she leant down and kissed him. The gesture was initially chaste, but as soon as their lips touched, heat ignited between them, and a moment later she was sitting astride him. They shared a deep, sensual kiss that sent her pulse racing and ignited a melting sensation deep in her belly.

"Tea," he groaned into her mouth. "My wife."

She gave an answering groan, her hands sliding down his chest over the leather vest he wore, to the bulge at his groin. Deftly, she unlaced his breeches and freed his manhood. It sat stiff and proud against his belly, straining toward her as she reached out and stroked it.

Galan inhaled sharply. "Gods, your hand is cold."

Tea laughed. "I know somewhere much warmer."

She hiked up her skirts so that the heavy plaid bunched around her hips. Often, Tea changed into leggings before going out for a ride, but today she wore heavy skirts with nothing underneath. To keep the chill wind from them both, she pulled her thick fur mantle about them.

Raising herself up, she settled upon his shaft, sliding down until he was buried to the root inside her. She groaned. He was large and this position brought him deep—so much so that the pleasure that pulsed through her lower belly was almost edged with pain as he pressed against her womb.

Head bowed, she buried her face in his neck. She gasped as he took hold of her hips and started to move her against him. The pleasure grew in waves, till it was almost unbearable. Suddenly, her body felt as if it did not belong to her. She bucked against him and let out a cry.

Galan gently bit her neck, his teeth trailing down to the hollow of her shoulder, where he nipped her. His hands slid under her skirts, cupping her buttocks. He then pulled her hard against him, penetrating her deeper still.

Tea cried out again, arching back as she climaxed.

The wind whipped her cry away, as she gave herself up to the pleasure that crashed through her like surf on the beach below. When Galan finally reached his own climax, their cries soared high, mingling with those of the wheeling gulls above.

Afterward Tea lay limp against his chest, her heart thundering, her limbs boneless. The depth of pleasure he could arouse in her never ceased to amaze her. Finally, when the wind's teeth began to bite through the fur mantle into their exposed skin, they rose from their rocky seat and made their way back to the ponies.

Tea mounted, adjusting her skirts so that they covered her legs, protecting her from the cold. Feeling Galan's gaze upon her, she glanced up to find him watching her, a sensual smile on his lips, hunger in his eyes.

"What is it?"

"You've bewitched me woman," he growled. "I want to throw you down on the grass and take you again."

The crudeness of his words made heat pulse between Tea's thighs. She loved this dominant, wild side to him. If they had not been on horseback, she did not doubt his word, and she would have taken delight in every moment of it. However, it was getting late. The shadows were lengthening and the light dimming. Days were short this time of year; it hardly seemed any time at all between dawn and dusk. A warm hearth and a hot supper awaited in Dun Ringill.

She grinned at him before winking. "I'll bet I can get home before you."

He raised a dark eyebrow. "You'll never outrun Faileas," he replied, patting his stallion's furry neck. As if knowing he was speaking of it, his black stallion tossed its head and side-stepped.

"We'll see about that."

She turned her chestnut pony, a muscular stallion with a white blaze, and took off north down the rocky path. Bent low over his neck, the pony's mane flicking in her face, Tea felt a wave of exhilaration. She grinned when she heard the thunder of hooves behind her and knew that Galan had given chase.

Ruith was picking some greens for supper from her garden when the chieftain and his wife returned from their afternoon ride. They were late home this eve, for dusk had almost settled. Galan's warriors had already lit the braziers on the wall around the fort, and the chill of the coming night caused an ache in the bandruí's bones.

She straightened up, a handful of kale in one hand, and waved to them with the other as they thundered through the stone archway. They were both smiling, their faces flushed with cold and happiness.

Spying her, both Galan and Tea waved. As they neared, Ruith smiled at their obvious joy. They made a handsome couple, both tall and dark, with proud bearing. Galan, whose face had grown so austere of late, looked young and breathtakingly attractive, while Tea was radiant. Her hair had come loose of its braids and rippled over her shoulders in thick dark curls, and her eyes were dancing.

"Evening, Ruith!" Tea called out. "Will you join us for a mulled cider by the fire later?"

"Aye," the bandruí replied. "As soon as I've had supper, I'll join you."

She watched the chief and his wife ride past, her gaze following them as they headed for the fort's walls. It warmed her heart to see a couple in love. It was as the bones had foreseen. The Eagle and The Wolf would be united.

Ruith's smile faded then as she remembered the other, less pleasant messages, the bones had left her.

Death and betrayal.

She wanted to believe the bones had lied to her, that they were mistaken, but Ruith had been a seer since she was fourteen winters old, and her divinations were rarely wrong. Misgiving settled upon her, as she turned back to her hovel and went inside to make supper.

Chapter Twenty-two

Raiders

TEA STEPPED OUT of the fort and blinked as a stiff breeze feathered her face, blowing strands of hair in her eyes. She made her way across the muddy ground toward the squat dwellings beyond. It was the first time the sun had shown its face in many days, and Tea found herself smiling.

Beyond the walls of Dun Ringill, she spied the rippling waters of Loch Slapin. White crests, like the manes of galloping ponies, raced across the surface of the lake.

She wandered down through the settlement, walking amongst the stone roundhouses with sod roofs, making for one of the large homes in the center of the settlement. This was the home of Mael and her husband Maphan. They had taken in Donnel's son, Talor, and were raising him as their own.

Mael was well overdue a visit, and Tea was looking forward to seeing how Luana and Donnel's son was growing.

Waving to some of the folk of the fort, who knew her well by now, Tea felt a sense of belonging. She had never thought after leaving Dun Ardtreck that Dun Ringill could ever be her home—but how wrong she'd been. Now, four months on, this place felt more like home than Dun Ardtreck ever had. It was odd, the tricks that life played on you. She would never have imagined she could be happy here.

Tea reached Mael's roundhouse and knocked on the timber door, calling out. "Mael, are you at home. It's me—Tea."

"Tea!" A woman's voice called out from within. "Come in!"

Tea opened the door and ducked inside, squinting as her eyes adjusted to the dimmer light. Mael's home was a lovely one. More spacious than most, the roundhouse had a dirt-packed floor and alcoves around the sides—a large one for husband and wife, and smaller ones for the children. A stone-lined fire pit burned in the center of the space.

Tea spied Mael's daughter in one alcove and Talor in the other. The two babes were both awake, gurgling and waving their arms around, their chubby hands grasping at the woolen hangings that Mael had suspended over them.

The aroma of mutton stew filled the home. An iron pot sat simmering over the fire pit.

Mael beamed. "I'm so glad you've visited."

Tea smiled back, guilt trickling over her. She had been so taken up with Galan over the past days, she'd had little thought for anyone or anything else. She barely knew Mael, but she could see that the young woman possessed the same kindness and gentle spirit as her elder sister. She had that same gift for making one feel welcome in her presence.

"Please sit down." Mael gestured to a stool by the hearth.

"Thank you." Tea handed her the basket she had brought before taking a seat. "We baked some sweet buns, with walnuts and dried currants in them," she said with a smile. "I thought you could do with a treat."

Mael's gaze shone. "That's very kind of you. I was just about to warm some milk and honey. Would you like some?"

"Aye," Tea replied. She watched Mael bustle about pouring fresh goat's milk into a pan with a drizzle of heather honey. After heating it, she retrieved two wooden cups and filled them. Tea accepted her cup gratefully, wrapping her fingers around its warmth.

"How's Talor?" she asked, glancing over at the gurgling infant. She could see that he had managed to tangle his fingers in the wool.

Mael smiled, her expression tender. "He's a lovely wee lad. He has a gentle nature and hardly cries." Mael's smile faded then. "But sometimes I wonder if he isn't a little sad ... as if he knows what he has lost."

Tea felt a pang of grief at these words. On a rational level, she knew that Talor was too young to grasp that he had lost his mother and father; but on another level, she too believed that the infant had been affected by the grief surrounding him.

"You can hold him if you like," Mael offered, putting down her cup.

"I'd like that," Tea replied.

Mael went over and retrieved the little bundle, wrapped in seal fur. She brought him over and placed him in Tea's arms. Tea's gaze settled upon him, and she found herself smiling. He had a serene, beautiful face that was definitely a mix of both parents. He had his mother's eyes already, you could see that, but you could also see the beautiful lines of Donnel's face.

"He will be a heartbreaker, like his father," Mael observed.

Noting the trace of bitterness in her voice, Tea glanced up. "Are you angry with Donnel?"

Mael sighed, looking away. "I don't blame him for his grief, for I know Maphan would be the same if he lost me," she admitted. "Yet I'm angry that he showed no interest in Talor before he left. If he meets his end in the south, it would be such a shame for his son."

Tea was silent a moment. She agreed with Mael, but at the same time, being of a passionate disposition herself, she knew what grief could do to people, and how it could change them. The pain she had seen in Donnel had been so raw it risked destroying him. Going away had been his only choice.

"He'll be back," she said, with more conviction than she actually felt.

Mael managed a wan smile and their gazes met across the fire. "For Talor's sake, I hope so."

Tea was introspective later as she left Mael's roundhouse and wandered back through the village to the high walls surrounding the fort. She had enjoyed her visit, but her conversation with Mael had left her out of sorts.

Mention of Donnel made her wonder what was happening across the water to the south. Had the tribes gathered as planned? Had they attacked the wall? The Winged Isle sat far from the worries of the rest of the world, and yet she sensed the shadow of forces beyond their control, creeping toward the shores of her island.

The aroma of roasting goat caught Tea's attention then, drawing her from her thoughts. It was nearing noon, and the cooking smells wafted out of the fort, carried on a strong breeze.

Tea quickened her step; she had lingered a little too long at Mael's. She made her way up the stone stairs and through the stone archway into the wide space beyond.

Inside, women were making the final preparations for the noon meal.

Deri was tending the roast goat, basting the meat and adding the final seasonings, while two other women were setting out wheels of cheese and long loaves of fresh bread on the tables.

Tea crossed the space, her feet crunching on rushes, to Deri, before she placed her empty basket on the table.

"How are Mael and the lad?" Deri asked.

"Very well," Tea replied with a smile. "Talor thrives—and is starting to look very much like his father."

Deri grinned and was about to reply, when her gaze shifted over Tea's shoulder, to where Galan had entered the fort. Tea turned and smiled at him, waiting while he approached. As always, the sight of him made it difficult for her to think upon anything else.

Reaching Tea, Galan pulled her into his arms and kissed her passionately, not caring who looked on. Tea returned his embrace, coiling her arms about his neck. They were both breathless when they parted.

"It's a beautiful morning out," Galan said, smiling into her eyes. "Finally, some sun."

"Aye," Tea replied. "I'm looking forward to this afternoon's ride. I thought we could return to Beinn na Caillich." Their last trip to the Red Hill had been marred by her reaction to their kiss; Tea was eager to give them more pleasant memories of that breathtaking spot.

Galan's smile widened. "Yes, we'll do that."

Warriors started entering the fort and taking their places for the noon meal. Soon they were all seated at the long tables and helping themselves to roast goat. The clatter of wooden dishes, spoons, and iron knives caused a din, drowning out the rumble of conversation. Ruith had joined them today. Dressed in a high-necked tunic made of thick wool, she squeezed in at the end of a table, next to a heavy-set warrior who was taking up the space of two men.

Tea was just taking her seat upon the bench next to Galan when a man appeared in the entrance to the fort.

She did not recognize him.

Dressed in mud-splattered leathers, his dark hair wild, his foot wrappings caked in dirt, he looked as if he had run through peat bogs to reach them. Observing the man, Tea supposed he must belong to one of the many settlements around Dun Ringill, for the People of The Eagle occupied a number of villages upon the peninsula.

Galan spied the newcomer immediately and rose to his feet. "Mund, welcome," he called out, before his gaze narrowed. "What brings you here?"

The man staggered across the rushes toward them, clearly close to collapse. "Raiders!" Mund gasped, his breath ragged. He stopped before the chieftain's table and bent double to recover his breath.

Conversation died, as did the thump and clatter of food being served at the long tables.

Galan went still. "Where?"

Mund looked up, his cheeks flushed, eyes wild. "North and west. They've attacked, pillaged, and burned two villages already—and have started on the third."

Gasps followed this news. Tea glanced across at Galan and saw his face had turned to stone. When he spoke, his voice was hard, emotionless. "Who are they?"

Mund's gaze flicked from Galan to Tea then. Their gazes met, and Tea saw hatred flare in the man's dark eyes. She stiffened, her stomach clenching. She knew that look, for she had given Galan the same one shortly after their first meeting. Suddenly, she knew what the man would say next. A chill feathered over her skin, and she gripped the edge of the table.

If only she could make time stand still; in a few moments the peace she had just begun to enjoy would be shattered.

Mund shifted his attention back to Galan.

"It's The Wolf, My Chief," he said, his words ringing out across the fort. "Loc mac Domech has broken the peace."

Chapter Twenty-three

Peace Breaker

TENSION RIPPLED THROUGH the hall as soon as Mund had spoken. Tea sat, frozen, next to Galan. She felt unable to look in his direction, unable to tear her gaze from Mund's accusing stare.

It has to be a lie.

Her mind churned and scampered, like a rat chasing its tail, as she tried to take it in.

It makes no sense.

Their tribes had made peace—Loc had been as committed to it as Galan, perhaps even more so. Surely, Mund was mistaken.

She could not, would not, accept this news as truth.

Galan was silent for a few moments, marshalling his thoughts, his reaction. When he did speak, his voice was calm and soft. Iron cloaked in velvet. Tea sensed his anger that boiled just beneath the surface.

Tea glanced at him then and saw that he had shifted his gaze to meet hers. Unlike the warmth of just moments earlier, his eyes were now like pieces of hard flint.

"Your brother betrayed us," he accused her.

She shook her head, denying his words. "It can't be so. Loc wants peace. This man must be mistaken—there are two other tribes on this island, it must have been them."

"It wasn't," Mund cut in. "I saw the men at close quarters—none of them bore the mark of The Stag or The Boar. It was a wolf's head tattooed and painted over their bodies."

Tea's chest constricted, and her head started to spin. Suddenly, she felt as she had when she had first come to Dun Ringill—as if she stood in the enemy camp. Cold, hard stares dug into her in silent accusation.

They blame me, she thought, nausea stealing over her. She turned back to Galan, her gaze seeking his. However, he would not look at her.

"Galan, please," she murmured. "This sounds like treachery. Someone wants to rekindle the old feud."

"And they've succeeded."

Galan swung away, dismissing her, his gaze now sweeping over his four warriors who sat around him. Cal and Lutrin's faces were rock-hewn, whereas Ru and Namet were staring at Tea as if she were a serpent coiled in their midst. "Ready your ponies and gather your weapons," Galan ordered. "We ride out."

With that, he stepped away from the table and strode toward the door. A heartbeat later his warriors leaped to their feet and followed him.

Tea hurried through the fort, toward the stable complex. She had to speak to Galan. She had to make him understand that Loc was not responsible for this. She knew Mund swore that he had seen men bearing her tribe's marks attack his village, but she refused to believe it.

She reached the stables, ignoring the glares of the warriors who were readying their ponies. On her way across the yard, she passed Ru. The warrior cursed her under his breath and spat upon the ground, making his feelings for her clear.

Tea lifted her chin and strode past, refusing to be intimidated. She walked toward where Galan was saddling Faileas in a stall at the far end of the stables.

"Galan, please—can we speak a moment."

He shook his head. "I don't have time, Tea. We're leaving now. Go back into the fort—I've left men there to protect you while I'm gone."

To protect me or keep me prisoner?

Tea ducked under the stallion's neck so that she stood before him. They had slight privacy here, for the stallion's bulk stood between them and Galan's warriors, and a wooden wall rose behind them. However, she was still aware of the muttering, the hard looks, surrounding her. Even Galan's presence did not prevent the men from showing their anger.

"Galan," she said, her voice low. "Surely, you don't believe that Loc would betray you?"

He swung round, his gaze spearing hers. "I don't want to believe it, but Mund knows what he saw. Your brother is a peace breaker. He's made a mockery of our handfasting."

Panic welled up within Tea at these words. "That's not true. You spoke to Loc, you saw what this meant to him. He ruined his relationship with me to forge this peace. He would never go back on it. Those warriors Mund saw could be a rogue band, trying to stir up trouble."

His gaze narrowed further and with a sinking heart Tea realized her words had not changed his mind. If anything, her plea had hardened him against her. He stepped closer to her, however it was not an intimate gesture but a threatening one. "Did you know what he was planning?"

Tea's gaze widened. She drew back as if he had just slapped her. "No, I've just told you what I believe. I've spoken the truth."

"You say that, but I remember how much you hated me after the handfasting. I wanted to believe you could soften toward me, but I was a fool. Did he send you to gather information? You have a lot of freedom here—how am I to know you haven't ridden out to meet one of your brothers' men. How am I to know you haven't already sent word back to him? I stand alone at Dun Ringill with both my brothers gone. It was the ideal time to attack."

Tea stared at him, incredulous. "You think I'm a spy?"

He held her gaze. "I don't want to, but I'm starting to doubt everything between us." His expression was shuttered as he drew back.

Tea watched him, shock rendering her speechless. She could not believe he could be so easily swayed, that he could cast aside the bond that had formed between them, so lightly.

Yet Galan had not finished. A muscle feathered in his jaw as he regarded her. "If I discover that Loc is behind this, there will be reckoning."

With that, he swung round to finish saddling his stallion, signaling that their conversation had ended.

Tea stood upon the walls of Dun Ringill and watched the men depart. Her vision blurred with tears—pain, anger, and confusion wheeled through her, each emotion vying for dominance. She felt as if someone had reached into her chest and yanked her heart out.

It hurt to breathe.

She felt helpless, frustrated. Earlier in the day she had been so happy, and had been looking forward to an afternoon outing with her husband. Now, Galan looked at her as if she was the enemy. A cold stranger had replaced the man she had begun to love.

Rage surged through her then, and she balled her fists at her sides.

I'll throttle Loc if he's behind this.

She watched the warriors ride out of the fort in pairs, upon feather-footed ponies. Leather creaked, pine shields thumped against the men and women's backs, and the ponies' iron bits jangled.

Galan rode up front, flanked either side by Lutrin and Cal. He rode tall and proud, his dark hair pulled back at the nape of his neck, a fur mantle rippling from his shoulders. As Tea watched, Galan urged his stallion into a brisk canter and led the way north, over the edge of the bald hills.

None of the men or women looked back; none saw her standing there.

When the last warrior had disappeared, she remained there a while longer, staring after them.

The wind gusted and blew around her, its chill biting into her flesh. However, she paid it no mind. Still staring into the distance, she came to a decision. Whirling, she descended the steps off the wall and strode back to the stables.

She had little time—the men Galan had left behind would start looking for her soon. She needed to move fast, or they would not let her leave.

The chestnut stallion she usually rode had gone, taken by one of Galan's warriors. The only pony remaining was the ill-tempered dun mare that had carried Tea here four months earlier.

Tea's heart sank at the sight of the crabby beast. It saw her approaching, flattened its ears back, and snaked out its neck, teeth flashing. Tea smacked it hard across the nose before grabbing a saddle and swinging it across the mare's broad back.

"Enough," she muttered. "It's time you and I made a truce—we've got a long ride ahead of us.

No one noticed the cloaked figure upon a heavy-set dun mare that trotted through the stone arch of the fort. The lone rider made their way through the cluster of cone-roofed roundhouses toward the outer perimeter.

No one noticed Tea go except the bandruí of Dun Ringill.

Ruith stood next to her fowl enclosure, a bowl of grain in hand, her gaze following the chieftain's wife as she left the fort.

Tea urged the mare into a fast canter as soon as she passed through the outer wall. The wind gusted this afternoon, and the clouds raced across the sky, obscuring the sun intermittently and casting long shadows across the green hills.

Thinking ahead, she gauged the distance she would need to cover to reach Dun Ardtreck. It was a good day's ride between the two forts, and since it was well after midday now, she would not likely reach her destination until the following morning. That would mean she would need to sleep outdoors tonight. The thought did not bother her. She had been brought up to fend for herself; she just hoped that Galan's men would not come after her.

Tea clenched her jaw. She had brought an ash spear and carried a sharp boning knife at her waist.

Let them come.

Tears blurred Tea's vision then, and she dug her fingers into the mare's spiky mane to stop herself from crying. It was incredible how quickly life could turn, from exhilaration to despair. She thought back to Luana. One moment her friend had been celebrating the birth of her son with her husband, the next she was dead. The wheel could turn in an instant—one moment you were riding high on the favor of the gods, the next they were making sport of your life.

Tea had thought that what had developed between her and Galan was strong, a connection that few couples enjoyed. She had thought they were made for each other, that she had found her other half. Yet it had taken so little for him to believe the worst.

Maybe I'm best back with my own people, she thought bitterly. If Galan could so easily turn on her, she did not belong at his side.

However, that was not the reason she had fled Dun Ringill. She had to know the truth. She had to know what her brother had done and why. If she discovered that he had indeed deliberately broken the peace, Dun Ardtreck would be the best place for her. But if she discovered that her brother's own warriors had gone behind his back, Loc needed to know—and quickly.

There was still hope that peace could be forged once more.

And Galan?

Tea wanted to believe that the sudden rift between them could be mended, but with each passing moment, she started to feel it could not. He had not given her the benefit of the doubt, not even for a moment.

Rage pulsed through her, blotting out the hurt, the pain. She did want to be upset—for it felt like weakness. It was time to start rebuilding the wall that Galan had slowly taken down, piece by piece, during the last few months.

It was time that she turned her heart back to stone.

Chapter Twenty-four

Too Late

GALAN KNOCKED THE man to the ground and thrust the iron blade into his guts. The warrior's wail echoed down the valley, a chilling sound of agony that left Galan cold. He placed a foot on the man's chest and pulled his sword free before slashing it down across his victim's neck. Blood spurted, splattering across Galan's face and clothing.

It was a clean death—cleaner than this raider deserved.

Pivoting on his heel, Galan turned to face the next warrior who sprinted, howling, toward him, axe raised, eyes wild. Galan rushed forward to meet him. The rage, the blood-lust, of battle had descended upon him. He savored it as he engaged the raider.

Galan cut the axe-man down, stabbing him until he fell twitching at his feet, the man's axe sliding from lifeless fingers. Then, dripping with blood—of his enemies rather than his own—Galan straightened up and looked around him.

They had won the skirmish. Broken and bloodied bodies lay scattered round him. Some of them belonged to the villagers who had not managed to escape before Galan and his warriors arrived—the rest belonged to the raiders.

Events this afternoon had moved swiftly.

They had come across this band as the raiders attacked their fourth village of the day. Galan had led his men down the hill in a charge; a convocation of enraged eagles had swept over the village below. Kil was a small settlement, a cluster of hovels around a dirt square, protected by little more than a wooden fence around its perimeter.

The raiders had knocked that fence to the ground. Smoke now stained the darkening sky, rising from the ruined, smoldering shells of the houses. The raiders had set fire to them all before raping the women and killing any of the men who did not manage to flee before them.

All the raiders had now perished—except one.

Cal and Namet dragged a young man toward Galan. Barely out of boyhood, the lad was thin with bulbous blue eyes and a sallow face. He stared at The Eagle chieftain, who stood waiting for him. The raider's eyes grew huge, the pale blue of his irises standing out against the whites of his eyes, as he stared at Galan.

Like the other raiders, the lad wore the mark of the wolf on his right bicep.

Galan's simmering rage boiled once more. Mund had spoken true; The Wolf chief had indeed betrayed them. He stared down at the boy and barely restrained himself from driving his sword into his heart.

He needed to wait—he needed answers first.

Gripping his sword hilt so tightly that his hand ached, Galan strode toward the captive, closing the gap between them. The lad started to tremble as he bore down on him.

"Why?" Galan growled. "We made a peace."

The young man stared back at him, so scared that he seemed to barely register the question. Galan stepped closer to him still, so close he could smell the sour tang of the lad's fear, could see the sweat that coated his skin. "Tell me, why?"

"The feud has begun again," the young man finally managed, each word a gasp.

"We gave you no cause," Galan snarled. "Loc mac Domech gave me his word."

The lad sneered, his body stiffening at the mention of The Wolf chieftain. "Loc mac Domech no longer rules," he spat, lifting his chin in one last show of defiance. "Forcus mac Vist is our chief now."

The light had almost faded when Galan led the way back into Dun Ringill. Sweat lathered his stallion; Faileas's sides were heaving. They had ridden hard to reach the fort by nightfall.

The last rays of sun were now slipping beyond the lines of the hills to the west, turning the sky blood-red.

Galan pulled his stallion up in the stable yard and swung down, his body tense with purpose. Ever since the raider had revealed that Loc no longer ruled Dun Ardtreck, Galan's world had shifted on its axis.

A man Galan had met only briefly at the handfasting, Forcus mac Vist, was now chieftain. The peace had been broken, but in the end it was not Tea's brother who had betrayed him.

Galan needed to see his wife; he had to put things right.

Leaving Faileas with one of his men, who would rub the stallion down and feed him, Galan strode out of the stables and across to the fort. Inside, the inhabitants of the fort were readying themselves for a supper of fowl and vegetable broth. Men were shucking off their heavy cloaks and settling themselves next to the hearth, gratefully accepting cups of ale from their womenfolk.

Galan paid none of them any notice. Instead, his gaze swept over the hall, searching for the statuesque, dark-haired figure of his wife.

He did not see her. Nor did he see Calum or Dirk, the two warriors he had left here to watch over Tea.

Galan spotted Deri, whom he had often seen talking with Tea, pouring out ale for the men. She glanced up, stiffening as she spied him. Galan ignored her.

His focus was entirely on finding Tea.

It could be that after Galan's treatment of her, his wife had taken refuge in their alcove. He did not blame her. He had criticized Tea openly and made her an enemy of his people. Galan had not cared at the time, he had only seen crimson with rage, but now he regretted his behavior.

He strode over to the alcove and drew back the hanging. He expected Tea to be waiting for him, seated upon the furs, her midnight blue gaze burning with outrage, but the alcove was empty. The furs looked as if they had not been lain on all day.

Turning away and letting the hanging drop, Galan's gaze returned to Deri. The young woman approached him, her jade-green gaze wide. She was usually a good-humored lass, but this evening her expression was solemn.

"Where's Tea?" he asked.

Her face tightened. "I've not seen her since the noon meal," she said quietly. "I went looking for her earlier but … I thought she had ridden out with you and your warriors."

"Calum and Dirk—where are they?"

"I haven't seen them all afternoon either."

Galan strode outside, his heart pounding. He went looking for Tea in all the places she might be. First, he went back to the stables, and after that the fighting enclosure where the warriors trained, but he did not find her. Instead, he found Calum and Dirk, lolling on the ground in the empty fighting arena—empty skins of wine scattered around them.

Galan strode over to them. "Where's my wife?"

"Don't know," Calum slurred, peering up at him. "Couldn't find her."

Next to Calum, Dirk let out a loud belch. "You're better off without that bitch anyway."

Fury settled over Galan in a crimson haze. Ignoring Dirk—for he would deal with him later—he bent down and yanked Calum to his feet, holding him up by the collar of his vest so that their gazes were level. "I'll ask you again—where's my wife?"

Sweat beaded on Calum's face. "We went looking for her after you left, to bring her inside like you said." The reek of sloe wine was so heavy on his breath that it made Galan's eyes water. "But she'd left already." He stared blearily up at his chief, before gathering himself up in righteous indignation. "Dirk's right. The treacherous she-wolf has returned to her pack. We're well rid of her."

Galan kneed Calum in the guts before dropping him like a sack of barley at his feet. His gaze swept over the two men cowering on the ground before him. "I decide what's best for this tribe," he said coldly. "Leave Dun Ringill, both of you—now. If I ever set eyes on either of you again, you're dead men."

Seething with rage, Galan strode from the enclosure. He did not want to believe that Tea had run away. Cold sweat now drenched his body, as he made his way to Ruith's hovel.

The bandruí was waiting for him, standing before the door of her dwelling, a heavy fur cloak about her slender shoulders.

"I was wondering when you would think to search here," she greeted him.

Galan took in her cool expression and hard eyes, and felt his last vestiges of hope fade. "She's not here, is she?"

The seer shook her head. "I saw her ride out not long after you, upon a dun pony. She went north-west."

Galan stared at her, his simmering rage boiling over. "Why did you not come to me sooner—she'll be halfway to Dun Ardtreck by now."

The bandruí's dark-blue gaze narrowed. The look she gave him needed no words to clarify its meaning. She had been seated in his feasting hall at noon; she had witnessed what had happened once Mund arrived. She had heard what he had said to Tea, although she had not witnessed his harshness toward his wife in the stables.

The bandruí favored him with another long, hard look that made him feel like a cur. Then, without another word, Ruith turned and went back inside, leaving Galan outside in the gathering dusk.

Darkness settled over the land in an indigo curtain. Tea sat huddled by the small fire that she had lit. Fortunately, she had remembered to bring flints with her; even so, it had taken her an age to get a fire started. She sat on the edge of a valley, just above a small, dark mere. A few clumps of gorse surrounded her, providing a little cover.

To her back rose the giant silhouette of the Black Cuillins. She was close now to the Lochans of the Fair Folk, those mystical pools were she and Galan had wed. The path ran up the hillside behind her, curling over rough, pebbly terrain, past the various pools up to the waterfalls.

Tea had deliberately turned her back to the mountains. She wanted no reminder of that day. It seemed as if she had come full circle—from hate and hurt, to love and hope, and back again. She felt raw on the inside.

She was not hungry this eve, which was just as well for she had brought no food with her. She sat, curled up next to the glowing fire, her fur mantle pulled close. The wind had died at least, although the clear sky meant it would be a cold night.

As she watched the sky, the stars twinkled to life one by one. Eventually, the moon slid into view. Tea observed the cold, silver disc in numb silence. Her skin was icy, and she could not feel her toes, but she did not care. She felt colder still on the inside.

She had ridden for as long as she could until the fading light had made it dangerous to continue. The mare waited a few yards away, tethered to the trunk of a gorse bush so she did not wander off during the night. The pony was still an irascible traveling companion, but Tea found she did not mind; the mare's mood suited her own.

Tea took a deep, shuddering breath and closed her eyes, blocking out the night sky. Somewhere to the south, Galan would be bedding down for the night as well. He might still be out dealing with the raiders or have already returned to Dun Ringill.

Pain knifed through Tea's chest at the thought of his reaction to her absence. What would he do when he discovered her missing?

Would he care? Would he be angry or hurt, or just relieved that an enemy had gone from his life? Would he be sorry?

Tears squeezed out from under Tea's eyelids and dribbled down her cheeks, but she angrily scrubbed them away.

It mattered not. They were enemies again now. It just proved how right she had been all those months ago. You could not end years of feuding with one handfasting—the past could not be cast aside so easily.

Chapter Twenty-five

Homecoming

TEA REACHED DUN Ardtreck late morning. After a cold, still night of clear skies, an equally icy dawn had broken. She had not slept all night, for it had been too cold. As soon as it was light enough to make out her surroundings, she had climbed to her feet; her limbs were stiff and achy, her feet and hands numb, and her teeth chattering.

She had resumed her journey, warming her chilled body against the furry warmth of her pony's back. The ride had taken her over rolling hills and open barren moors that seemed to stretch on forever. She had forgotten what a bleak part of The Winged Isle her people lived in.

The sight of Dun Ardtreck at last, the broch perched upon the cliff silhouetted against a pale blue sky, made her spirits lift. She felt chilled to the marrow, and her belly ached with hunger. She looked forward to taking her place before the hearth and warming her hands over it, and to seeing her kin once more.

Her heart swelled at the thought of seeing Loc and Eithni. She had been so angry with them after her handfasting that she had thrust them both from her thoughts. She had missed them but had hardly realized how much until she saw the familiar bulk of Dun Ardtreck before her once more.

She rode up the lower slopes of the hillside beneath the broch, past the settlement of roundhouses and wattle and daub hovels. There were plenty of folk outdoors, taking care of their morning chores—cutting wood, milking goats, and feeding fowl and geese. Some of the people stopped and stared as she rode past. Tea waved at them, but most of them—folk she had grown up amongst—merely stared at her as if she were a shade. Some of their faces were aghast, while others were bemused. Their reaction disquieted her. She had thought the people of Dun Ardtreck would rejoice at her return.

Perhaps her handfasting had turned them against her. Did they think she had gone to Galan willingly?

Tea clenched her chilled fingers around the leather reins. They would surely hate her if they learned how easily she had succumbed to him.

She urged the mare into a reluctant canter. The pony flattened its ears back and lumbered up the slope, between the cleft created by two large rocks, and toward the great stone arch of Dun Ardtreck.

Two warriors wielding spears guarded the entrance to the fort. Tea recognized them both—Loxa and Pont were young men that Forcus had taken under his wing in the spring to begin their training.

"Tea," Pont greeted her, grinning, while Loxa stared at her brazenly. "Welcome home."

Tea nodded to them and urged her mare through the gateway, reining it in before the steps leading up to the broch. Looking around her, Tea noted how busy it was—there were leather-clad men and women everywhere—

yet the atmosphere was different to when she had left months earlier.

There were no scenes of domesticity in the yard, just warriors practicing at swordplay or sharpening their blades. The smell of hot iron wafted across the yard toward her from the forge, and the clang of a hammer on an anvil echoed through the misty air. It was like a tolling bell, calling warriors to battle.

Dun Ardtreck felt like a fort readying itself for full-scale war.

She recognized many of the men and women, although there were some new faces among them. Most of them looked pleased, albeit surprised, to see her. However, one or two watched her with cold eyes.

Frowning, Tea swung down from the pony and led it through to the stables, noticing that Loxa had hurried up the steps to her right, presumably to alert her brother of her arrival. She would follow him inside soon, but first she had to find someone to see to her pony. In the stables she recognized two of the lads who were mucking out the stalls.

"Tea," one of them gasped, dropping his pitch-fork, his face paling. "What are you doing here?"

She inclined her head, fixing him in a hard stare. "I've returned to my people," she replied firmly, "whom I never should have left."

The two lads continued to stare at her.

Impatient now, Tea frowned. "What is it?" she snapped. "Do you two find it so strange that I should want to return home to my kin?"

"No ... no..." the second lad stammered. "It's just that ..." His gaze met hers. "You don't know, do you?"

Tea went still. Dread seeped through her as if she had stepped up to the neck into a cold loch. Suddenly, she just wanted to turn and flee, run far from here, to where the news that lay upon this lad's lips would never touch her.

Yet, she did not.

Galan urged his stallion up the incline toward the brow of the hill. To the right rose the majesty of the Black Cuillins, their bulk looming overhead and blocking out the blue sky. It was the half-way mark between Dun Ringill and Dun Ardtreck, but he still had a way to go.

Galan did not let himself think about the memories this place evoked. Instead, his entire will was bent upon reaching his destination. Behind him rode Ru, Namet, Lutrin, and Cal—and at their heels followed a band of twenty more warriors.

As he journeyed, Galan wished his brothers rode at his side. He trusted his warriors with his life, but he, Tarl, and Donnel were close. He missed their counsel and wondered if the events of the past day might have played out differently if they been there to advise him.

Pushing these thoughts aside, for they did him no good, Galan stared ahead at where the landscape unfolded like a crumpled hessian blanket of bleak moorland to the north.

The fact remained that his brothers were not here and might never return.

He was the eldest son. He had been made chief, and the decisions were his own to make. He was right to deal with the raiders as he had—swiftly and brutally. They had slaughtered a number of his people and destroyed four villages in doing so. Nonetheless, he had been wrong to jump to conclusions about Loc and Tea. He felt his error even more keenly now, for he realized that Tea did not know of her brother's death.

She would have reached Dun Ardtreck by now; she would have discovered the truth. His chest constricted. The peace he and Loc had worked so hard to weave was now unravelling before his eyes. It was far more fragile than he had realized. All it had taken were a few harsh words, and he had shattered everything he had worked so hard to build. Cruelly, he only had himself to blame.

Fool, he thought bitterly. *If she hates you now, you deserve it.*

Tea stood in the great broch of Dun Ardtreck. The crackle and pop of embers in the hearth seemed loud in the ominous silence.

It felt strange to step back inside this broch. She knew its curved lines, its carvings, as well as the lines of her own palm. Yet today it did not feel like home anymore.

There was a strange atmosphere indoors. Outside, it felt as if warriors were about to march off to battle, whereas indoors there was a breathless tension. Usually, at this time of the morning, as noon approached, men and women filled the broch, with children and dogs getting underfoot as they prepared the main meal of the day.

What few servants and slaves there were in the feasting hall scurried past like frightened mice. They cast Tea nervous looks as they tended the boar stew that bubbled in a heavy iron pot sat over the hearth.

After speaking to the lads in the stables, Tea had stumbled blindly up the stairs into the broch. Inside, she found Forcus and Eithni waiting for her by the hearth. Grief swelled in Tea's breast when her gaze met Forcus's. She clenched her jaw and forced back burning tears.

"Is it true?" she whispered. "Is Loc dead?"

Forcus stared back at her before nodding. His handsome face was set into austere lines this morning. Tall and intimidating, with wavy brown hair that fell over one of his pale blue eyes, Forcus was bare-chested, although he wore a heavy fur mantle over his shoulders to ward off the chill.

The sight of Eithni next to him shocked Tea. Her sister had lost a lot of weight since she had last seen her. She looked fragile; her heart-shaped face was drawn, her skin pale, and her hazel-green eyes hollowed. She stared at Tea with a look akin to horror.

Tea's belly twisted, and her gaze flicked from her sister back to Forcus.

Eventually, he spoke. "Loc fell during a boar hunt, just before Mid-Winter Fire," he began gently. "One of the beasts gored him in the belly."

Tea stared back, unable to take his words in. She could not imagine her brother, who had been a formidable warrior and skilled hunter, dying in such a fashion. She had always thought that Loc would meet the same end as his father, in battle—a warrior's end.

She glanced back at Eithni, seeking confirmation. However, Eithni had dropped her gaze to the floor. Tea saw that she was trembling.

"I don't understand," Tea managed finally. "Why did no one send word? I should have been here for his burial."

"There was no need," Forcus rumbled. "We did not want to disturb you in your *new life*."

The sarcastic inflection on these last two words brought Tea's head up sharply. The heat of shame filled her, making her forget her chilled limbs and the ice-grip of grief. "He was my brother," she said softly. "I had the right to know."

She looked back at Eithni, willing her to raise her head and meet her eye once more. She barely recognized this waif as her sister. Eithni had never possessed Tea's force of character, but she had never been like this—a pale shadow.

"Eithni." She took a step toward her. "What's wrong?"

Her sister did not reply, and she kept her head lowered as if she had not even heard Tea speak.

"Your sister has taken Loc's death hard," Forcus told her. "I have given her what comfort I can, but she finds it difficult to rally."

Tea fixed her stare upon him. His expression was shuttered, making it nearly impossible to gauge his feelings. Yet she saw the tension in his big frame. Despite the gentleness of his words, she sensed he was not pleased to see her.

"Where are Wid and the others?" she asked. She looked around the empty space, as if expecting to see her dark-haired cousin emerge from one of the alcoves, yet he did not.

"Away hunting," Forcus replied.

Tea's gaze narrowed. "The lads in the stables tell me that you are chieftain now." She stared him down. "Surely as kin, Wid should have taken Loc's place?"

Forcus raised a dark eyebrow. "Wid is a cousin to Loc through the male line, not the female. Since your family has no males on the female line, I have as much right to rule as chief as him."

Tea stared at Forcus, scowling. Sometimes she forgot that Forcus was a lot older than her. He was not that many winters younger than her parents. The age gap between them had not mattered when they were lovers—he had always seemed younger, immature compared to her father—yet now she saw him in a different light.

He did not look sorry that Loc was gone, despite that Tea had always thought them as close as brothers.

Not only that, but she wagered that he had taken his place as chieftain by force after her brother's death.

Loc is gone.

Grief slammed into Tea's belly like a battering ram, driving through the wall she had kept in place since entering the broch. She turned away from Forcus, tears burning down her cheeks, her shoulders shaking as she struggled to keep herself from crumbling. She stumbled back a few paces and collapsed upon a bench next to the wall, doubling over as sorrow hit her once more.

Her brave, good-hearted brother was gone. It seemed that wherever she went, grief followed her.

This was no homecoming.

Chapter Twenty-six

Lies

TEA WEPT FOR a while, bent double and oblivious to the rest of the world. She forgot that Eithni and Forcus were watching her, cared not that the servants who were now setting out wooden bowls on the tables for the noon meal also saw her grief. Hot tears poured down her face, and she covered her eyes with her hands, blocking everyone out.

After some time she became aware of her surroundings once more. She straightened up, wiping away the last of her tears, and glanced back at Forcus and Eithni.

Forcus had not moved. He stood there observing her from under hooded lids. She could see his derision for her woman's tears; in the past he had always admired her coldness, her hard approach. It possibly disappointed him to see that she was not made of stone after all.

Next to Forcus, Eithni had sat down upon a stool. Her pale, thin hands were clasped on her lap, and Tea saw that her sister's face was also wet with tears. It was the only sign that Tea's sorrow had touched her—or that she shared it.

Tea blinked, her eyes swollen and her face raw from the salt of her tears. Now that she had mastered herself, once the paroxysm of grief had passed, her befuddled mind started to clear. She remembered the reason that had brought her back to Dun Ardtreck, the reason that news of Loc's death had obliterated.

Wiping her eyes, Tea rose to her feet and faced Forcus once more. "Do you wonder why I'm here?" she asked him, her voice husky from crying.

He smiled. "I knew you would not suffer to remain at Dun Ringill long—the wife of that Eagle maggot. You are indeed your father's daughter."

He had meant the words as a compliment, but Tea found it difficult not to flinch.

"That's not why I left," she replied. "Raiders bearing the mark of The Wolf have been attacking and killing upon the Strathaird Peninsula—Galan's territory. I came to find out why Loc has broken the peace, but now I see he did not."

Forcus's smile widened into a grin. "I sent those warriors," he confirmed, his broad chest expanding with pride. "It is reckoning for your father, one he should have had moons ago."

Tea stiffened. "This was vengeance?"

"Aye, and it's only the beginning. I've got men out gathering more warriors as we speak—and my people here are eager to march to war. I will not stop until Dun Ringill falls—until Galan mac Muin crawls before me. Then I will sink my blade into his guts."

Tea's breathing hitched in her chest. His words hit her like a physical blow. Despite her anger toward Galan, she could not bear the thought of any harm coming to him. Forcus's threats made her feel ill. Bile crept up her throat. She swallowed, clenching her fists by her sides.

To think she had been like Forcus once, full of mindless hate. To think she had once thought about hurting Galan. Now she knew with absolute clarity that she would defend his life with her own.

He needs to know that Loc didn't betray him, she thought suddenly panicked.

She watched Forcus then, stunned by the viciousness that twisted his handsome face, turning him suddenly ugly. She understood her father's hatred for the People of The Eagle, and even her own, but she did not see why Forcus loathed them so. A chill passed through her as she observed him.

Now that he was chief of their tribe, everything Loc and Galan had worked for would be destroyed. Their people had only known but a few months of peace, and now war was about to tear them apart once more.

Faileas was breathing hard when Galan reined him in at the crest of the last hill before Dun Ardtreck. He had never travelled to the fort before, and he paused to see it now: an austere fortress shaped like a giant beehive, looming over the rocky slopes upon a craggy headland. It was a lonely, cold spot, and he wondered what it would have been like to grow up here.

"What now?" Cal pulled his pony up next to Galan, his gaze also riveted upon the towering bulk of the fort.

Galan did not reply immediately. Instead, he scanned the broch before searching the rocks and slopes below it, looking for signs of warriors guarding the fort. He could see the outlines of figures on the walls and spears bristling against the sky.

Somewhere inside that stone bulk was his wife. A woman who now likely hated him. He wanted to make peace with her first, yet the man who now ruled here saw him as the enemy.

Forcus mac Vist would not welcome him into his broch.

Turning his attention back to his warriors, Galan took in their faces. Ru, Namet, Lutrin, and Cal—all had proved their loyalty to him by riding here. Yet what he was about to ask would test that loyalty further.

Galan urged Faileas forward so that the twenty warriors riding behind could also see him. "I must go inside," he told them, his voice ringing out over the hillside. "I must find my wife and face Forcus mac Vist." He paused here, weighing his words before he spoke. "I don't ask the same of you. If any of you wish to remain behind, you may."

His warriors stared back at him. Ru was the first to respond, his bearded face fierce. "You are our chief, Galan. We would follow you to the bottom of the sea, if you asked it."

The others in the band silently nodded their agreement with Ru, fire in their eyes.

Galan stared back at them, humbled by their courage. "It won't be easy," he pointed out. "An ambush or a trap might await us."

"Then it's one you shouldn't go into without us," Cal replied. "Enough said. We will not let you ride into Dun Ardtreck alone."

"Leave us." Forcus's voice lashed across the feasting hall, causing the two servant girls laying the table to cringe. They stared at their chief, their faces paling.

"But ... the stew," one of them began hesitantly. "It's ready."

"Get out now," Forcus growled, "and tell the others not to come in until I call for them."

The girls nodded and fled from the hall, leaving Forcus alone with Eithni and Tea.

Forcus turned to Eithni, addressing her for the first time since Tea had entered the broch. "Eithni—fetch us some ale."

Tea stiffened at the commanding edge to his tone, his barely concealed distaste. Since when had Forcus taken such a vehement dislike to Eithni? Tea remembered him being respectful toward her in the past.

Eithni nodded and, eyes still downcast, made her way over to the scrubbed oaken table behind them, where a ewer of ale and a row of cups sat. Tea noted that her sister walked with an odd shuffle this morning, almost as if she was in pain. Tea's gaze narrowed. "Eithni, are you hurt?"

Her sister's shoulders stiffened, but she did not reply.

"She's fine," Forcus spoke on Eithni's behalf. "I told you, the girl took Loc's death badly. She's not as tough as you. She refuses to eat."

Tea saw now that Eithni's slender shoulders were shaking, as if she was trying to keep her emotions back. Her hands trembled as she picked up the ewer and began to pour the ales. She was shaking so badly that she spilled ale onto the table.

Unable to watch her sister's suffering any longer, Tea rushed across the floor. Reaching Eithni's side, she put an arm around her, drawing her close.

"I'm so sorry, love," she murmured into her sister's hair. "I'm so sorry I wasn't here to comfort you." She squeezed Eithni's body close, tensing at her fragility. Her sister had never been so thin.

Eithni gasped and sank against Tea, her head bowing close to her sister's.

"Run," she whispered hoarsely. "Get out now."

"Eithni!" Forcus's voice boomed across the space. "Just pour the ale and hold your tongue, girl."

Tea released her sister and turned to Forcus, viewing him through a narrowed gaze. "What gives you the right to speak to Eithni so? She's the daughter and sister of chieftains. She has a revered place at Dun Ardtreck, and yet you address her like a slave.”

Forcus sneered. “I’m chief,” he said simply. “Eithni seems to resent that fact—but you would both do well to remember who commands here.”

Tea stiffened and drew herself up to her full height. Eithni had stopped trying to pour the ale; instead, she stood cringing against Tea, her body quivering like a drawn bow-string. Her obvious distress made a wave of protectiveness surge through Tea. She did not know what Forcus had done to her sister, but she knew that something terrible must have happened for Eithni to act this way.

Tea would not let him speak to either of them this way. Now that the shock of Loc’s death had sunk in, a cold rage had replaced it. “The women of this family have as much right to command as the men,” she reminded him. “I only suffered Loc’s sending me away because he was my blood kin. You are nothing to us ... you have no right to terrify my sister.”

Forcus stared at her, his eyes glittering. “You always were a mouthy wench,” he said, slowly advancing. “I once used to put that mouth of yours to better use— maybe I will do so again.”

His coarseness made Tea clench her jaw, yet she gave no other reaction.

He advanced on her, stalking her like the wolf he was. She watched as his fists clenched at his sides.

“I liked your fire once, but I tire of it now,” he growled. “Neither of you compare to your mother. I plowed you both, hoping to find Fina—yet you are both but pale shadows in her memory.”

Tea recoiled at his words.

Plowed you both.

Suddenly she knew why Eithni trembled and cringed in her arms.

"You stinking turd," she hissed, pushing Eithni behind her and facing Forcus, balling her own fists at her side. "How dare you lay a finger on my sister."

He continued to advance on her. He was a big, intimidating man, easily as strong as Galan. However, she stared him down, refusing to cower before him.

Forcus stopped a few feet away, his gaze trapping hers. Behind Tea, she heard Eithni's whimper of fear. "Please Tea … just run."

"I'm not running," Tea shot back, anger surging through her. "This is our home. I'll not let him touch you again."

"He lies," her sister gasped, her voice stronger now, almost as if Tea's body providing a barrier between them gave her strength. "He lies about everything."

"Silence, bitch!" Forcus's voice slashed toward them. "Swallow that forked-tongue!"

Tea's belly clenched. She did not look Eithni's way, instead keeping her gaze riveted upon Forcus, watching him. "Go on, Eithni," she commanded. "Tell me of these lies."

"Loc," Eithni choked their brother's name out. "He did not die on a hunt. He and Forcus argued about keeping the peace. And then Forcus drew his blade and sliced Loc open here, in his own hall, and let him bleed to death in front of the hearth."

Bile rose in Tea's throat. She swallowed with difficulty, fighting the urge to be sick. Her mind spun, but she kept her gaze upon Forcus and saw an ugly change creep over his face.

Until now he had been playing a role, keeping up a pretense, but suddenly the mask fell away. Now that Eithni had spoken, Tea watched him transform. Slowly smiling, he relaxed his clenched fists by his sides.

"So now you know." He paused here, his expression turning feral. "And since you know that much, you and Eithni should learn the rest."

Galan knew they would only have one chance to get inside the broch. The men on the walls would spot his band as they galloped up the incline toward the entrance to the fort; however, The Wolf tribe would need time to rally themselves.

Speed was essential if he was ever going to get through the gates.

Faileas thundered up the incline, sending villagers, fowl, and dogs scattering. Galan had already realized that Dun Ardtreck was harder to attack than Dun Ringill. Perched high on a cliff-face with only one entrance in a cleft between two boulders, it was a bottle-neck. Once they closed the gates, he and his men would be locked out.

Shouts echoed down from the walls above—they had been spotted.

Even so, the two warriors guarding the gate were still scrambling to close the gates when Galan reached them.

Roaring the battle cry of the Eagle and flanked by Cal and Lutrin, he rode Faileas against the heavy oaken gates. Their heavy-set ponies drove through the gates like a battering ram, trampling men underfoot.

Inside, warriors rushed at them from all angles, howling with rage as they scrambled for their weapons.

Sword drawn, Galan leaped down from his stallion and met them head on. Behind him, the rest of his band poured in through the breach. He heard their shouts and tasted their bloodlust. The madness of battle took fire in his veins. Galan roared his people's battle cry once more, and slashing his blade before him, he began cutting his way through the throng.

The Reaper had come to Dun Ardtreck, and he would leave none untouched.

Chapter Twenty-seven

The Secret

SILENCE SETTLED INSIDE the broch—a hollow, breathless silence that told Tea she should run.

She did not.

Instead, she continued to watch Forcus. Apart from a slender knife at her waist, which she used for preparing vegetables or gutting animals, she had no weapon. Her breathing stilled as she calculated if she could reach for an axe hanging on the wall behind her in time, should he leap for her.

The rest.

What she had learned so far was bad enough—she needed to hear no more.

"Your mother was nearly a decade older than me, but I wanted her," Forcus began, his voice roughening. "Even after she wed Domech, I still wanted her."

Tea wished for Forcus to stop talking, but now that he had begun his tale, the words poured out in an unstoppable tide. Years of pent-up frustration and rage were finally set free.

"She knew how I felt, but she kept me at arm's length," Forcus continued. "For years I watched her, longed for her. Then, one summer she visited an ailing aunt at Dun Skudiburgh. For once Domech and her brats did not accompany her, and I finally had my chance. I would convince her she had chosen the wrong man."

Forcus started to pace then, circling the women as memories of the past consumed him. Tea and Eithni stood, frozen in place while he began to speak once more.

"I was gentle with Fina on the way there, for I didn't want to frighten her. I wanted her to come to me willingly—some part of me still believed she had never really wanted Domech, that it was me she'd yearned for all those years. But on the way home, I finally couldn't stand it any longer. I'd spent too long watching her, aching for her. One night I went to Fina in her tent and tried to kiss her. She struck me across the face, furious— and at that moment I realized that I'd been living in a dream of my own making. She'd never wanted me. Overcome by fury, I took her by force."

Forcus stopped for a moment, breathing hard as if even the memory of it excited him. He turned to the two women he circled, his gaze hungry.

"It was the most beautiful experience of my life. I put my hand over Fina's mouth, so she would make no sound, ripped off her clothes, and had my fill of her. However, when I was done, she no longer breathed. Too late, I realized that, in my maddened lust, I'd smothered her."

Forcus's words fell like hammer blows. Tea reached behind her, fumbling for Eithni's hand. Her sister's fingers, ice-cold, laced through hers and squeezed.

"Once I realized she was dead, I had to act quickly," Forcus continued, oblivious to Tea and Eithni's horror. "I couldn't let anyone know what I'd done. I waited till the deepest night, and then I crept out and killed the man who had taken the watch. When I was sure I wouldn't be seen, I carried Fina out into the moor and carved the mark of The Eagle into her flesh, making it look as if she had been raped and savaged by the enemy."

Forcus looked up, his gaze pinning Tea to the spot. "I knew Muin mac Uerd wanted her. Years earlier, barely out of boyhood, I attended the gathering of the tribes—I'd seen the way he looked at her. The next morning, I feigned shock with the rest of them when we discovered the man taking the last watch dead, and The Wolf chief's wife's mutilated body." Forcus's mouth twisted. "The rest you know."

An icy silence settled, as if the interior of the broch had turned into a great stone cairn burying the three of them alive.

Tea could hear nothing but the thundering of her own heart. Her mind scampered, struggling to take his words in.

It was Eithni who spoke first. "Beast," she rasped. "May The Reaper torment you for what you have done."

Forcus snorted, his gaze narrowing with derision. "What a disappointment you've been, Eithni. You look so much like your mother, but you're a sniveling shadow compared to her." He shifted his attention back to Tea. "You on the other hand look too much like your father for my taste. However, I like a woman with fire, and I would have saved you from that marriage if you'd let me."

Tea's belly twisted at his words. She spat on the ground between them in answer, so filled with rage that she could not even speak.

Forcus laughed. "What? Not regretting the handfasting so much now? I see that Galan mac Muin has succeeded in changing you." His eyes widened as realization dawned. Forcus's laughter boomed through the empty space, echoing high in the rafters. "You didn't come here to escape him, did you? You came to confront your brother about the attacks."

"I certainly hope that's why she's here."

Galan's voice, low and hard, cut through the laughter.

The mirth died on Forcus's lips, and he swiveled to see a tall, leather-clad figure stride into the broch. Galan's drawn sword-blade dripped with blood, and his face was hawkish. Behind him Tea spied Lutrin and Cal enter the broch, weapons drawn. For the first time, the sounds of fighting outside—the clang of iron and shouts—intruded.

Tea's heart stilled a moment at the sight of Galan, her breath catching in a mixture of relief and fear that he had followed her.

Forcus drew his own sword, iron scraping against leather. "Come to die upon my blade, Eagle?" he enquired, taking a step toward Galan.

Tea did not know who would have won that fight—having trained with both men she knew them to be of equal ability. However, Forcus was rested, while Galan had ridden a day to reach them and had been forced to fight his way into the broch. Even so, Galan looked formidable, his face all sharp angles, his eyes gleaming.

But Forcus was deranged and deluded—and that made him dangerous.

Tea could not let him kill Galan, could not let him take someone else from her. Even if her next act cost Tea her own life, she had to do it.

She whipped her boning knife from its sheath and lunged.

Forcus was distracted, his attention fixed upon The Eagle chieftain who strode across the rush-strewn floor to face him. He caught movement to his left at the last moment and swiveled to defend himself from Tea.

Too late.

Her knife slammed up under his ribcage, sending him reeling backward. Tea's left fist struck out and slammed into Forcus's jaw, the force of her rage behind it. Forcus took another step back, tripped over a stool and sprawled.

Roaring, he let go of his sword and fell on his back. His fingers fastened around the bone handle of the boning knife embedded in his torso, and he yanked it free. With frightening speed, he twisted, rolling to his feet.

Tea had moved faster. She dove for the sword, her fingers clasping firmly around its worn leather hilt. With a shout of fury that deafened all that heard it, she lunged at Forcus and thrust the blade into the base of his neck.

The warrior gave a choking, gurgling noise and fell to his knees. He stared at her, his pale blue eyes widening in shock. Tea stepped closer still and drove the blade deeper, watching as the life faded from those cruel eyes.

"For my mother," she whispered hoarsely.

Galan stood a few feet away, staring at the woman who stood over the slumped figure of Forcus mac Vist. He barely recognized Tea's face, the fury that contorted her proud features. Her eyes glittered as she stared unseeing down at the man she had just killed. Tears ran down her face, and her body started to quiver.

Even so, she held the hilt of Forcus's blade tight, keeping his body upright long after the life had drained from him.

For my mother.

Galan had heard Tea's last words but did not understand them. His gaze flicked to where Eithni, ashen-faced and hollow-eyed, approached her sister and wrapped her arms about her.

Something had happened in here prior to his arrival—he could see that. He had sensed it the moment he had stepped through the door. Tea and her sister had been standing by one of the long tables, their bodies rigid, their faces like stone. Forcus had reminded him of a circling predator, the low rumble of his voice the only sound in the empty space.

Galan slowly approached the women. Tea was weeping openly now, as was Eithni. They clung to each other as if they were cast adrift on a wild sea. Tea still grasped the hilt of the sword, her knuckles white from the force of her grip.

Galan stopped next to her and bent down, gently placing his hand over hers.

"It's over now, Tea," he said gently. "He's dead—you can let go."

His heart twisted when she nodded, her head bowed with the force of her grief. He felt the hand under his relax its grip on the hilt, and he relieved her of the weapon.

Deftly, Galan withdrew the blade from Forcus's neck, and the warrior's body slumped over onto its side. Dark blood pooled out under him, soaking into the rushes.

Galan turned his attention back to his wife. It had been such a relief to see her, unhurt and well, but that relief had lasted only a moment. He hated to see her so distressed. Tea was strong; even when she had been upset after Luana's death, he had not seen her lose control.

Yet now he did.

He hunkered down next to the sisters, aware that Cal and Lutrin had followed him inside. They stood a few feet away, their faces tense and worried.

"What happened here?" Cal finally asked, casting a glance back over his shoulder toward the door. Outside, the rest of Galan's men were dealing with the warriors guarding the broch. It had been a brief but bloody battle—bodies of Wolf warriors now littered the fort.

"I don't know." Galan's gaze shifted back to Tea. Her dark hair had come undone from its long braid down her back and had fallen across her face like a raven's wing, obscuring her grief from view. Whatever had occurred within these walls, it appeared to have broken his wife.

Chapter Twenty-eight

Upon the Wall

NIGHT FELL OVER the Minginish Peninsula of The Winged Isle. Mist had rolled in just before dusk, settling softly over the craggy cliffs around Dun Ardtreck. The broch perched, cold and silent, over the empty fort and the clusters of round houses and huts that carpeted the slopes below.

Indoors, the mood was no less somber.

Galan and his warriors sat at the chieftain's table with Tea and Eithni, listening in silence as Tea recounted what had happened here. Ashen-faced servants moved around them, bringing ewers of wine and bowls of turnip and barley pottage to the table.

Galan listened intently, the pottage he had just eaten churning in his belly as Tea spoke of Forcus's treachery. He had not realized that Tea and Forcus had once been lovers. If Tea had told him earlier, he might have felt a stab of jealousy. But there was no time for that now; Tea's tale made everything else fade into the background—and when she finished an uncomfortable hush settled.

Next to Galan, Ru shifted on the bench, casting his chief a pained look. None of them knew what to say. Sometimes, the best answer was merely silence.

Galan looked down at his barely touched cup of ale, considering everything that Tea had told him. Forcus had deserved a worse end than the one he had received, for all he had done. He had raped and murdered Tea's mother, raped her sister, and slain her brother. Galan now understood the rage he had seen on her face as she killed the warrior, and the grief that had consumed her afterward.

Mingled with shock, however, he felt a strange sense of relief.

His father was innocent.

Self-reproach swiftly followed on the heels of his relief when he realized that Tea's discovery was far worse for her than the belief that Muin mac Uerd had murdered Fina. It had been easier to believe The Eagle chieftain, an enemy of their tribe, had done it. Knowing that one of their own, a man whom her father and brother had trusted implicitly—and her former lover— had turned on them was much harder to accept.

Galan glanced up, his gaze resting on Tea's face. She did not look at him—in fact, she had barely met his eye since his arrival here. He knew she was avoiding him deliberately and that they would need to speak in private soon. Still, he had been waiting till he knew what had happened here, so that he could start to make sense of the events of the past few days.

"I'm sorry, Tea," he said finally, his gaze flicking between her and Eithni. "For you both."

Tea's sister sat hunched under a thick fur mantle, her small, thin body trembling. Galan clenched his jaw at the sight of her shock and distress; he could see that Forcus had damaged her. He remembered seeing Tea's sister at the handfasting, but he did not recall her being so timid.

Ever since his arrival, Eithni had cringed away from him and his warriors. He had seen the fear in her eyes.

Tea nodded, still not meeting his eye. The bowl of turnip pottage before her had started to grow cold. "So now you know," she said, her voice toneless, her eyes empty. "Your father was not to blame after all."

Galan deliberately held his tongue here. It would not be wise to answer her. Despite her pale, shocked appearance, rage still pulsed within Tea. She was looking for an excuse to explode, to lash out, and he did not blame her. Tea's anger would need to be released, just not here in front of her sister and his men.

Tea wrapped a fur cloak around her shoulders, drawing the heavy warmth close, and left the broch. Behind her a carpet of figures lay sleeping on furs around the fire pit, yet she could not sleep.

Leaving the broch, she crossed the yard. Galan's warriors had lit two peat braziers, illuminating the misty darkness. The outlines of Eagle men and women keeping watch moved in the shadows, but Tea ignored them.

Instead, she climbed the stairs to the stacked-stone outer wall of the fort. The air smelt of brine and was heavy with moisture. Around her the thick mist pressed in, tendrils drifting like smoke across the slick stone.

Tea barely noticed any of it; her thoughts had turned inward. She stared out into the night and tried to control the seething rage and grief that still cramped her belly. Weeping had brought little relief—her tears had burned away now leaving an aching hollow in the center of her chest.

Forcus had destroyed her family.

She wished she could have killed him ten times over for his crime, yet that would not be enough. Vengeance would not give her Loc or her mother back—or have mended her father's broken heart.

Tea inhaled deeply and turned her face to the sky. A light misty rain had started to fall. It settled on her skin in a cool balm. Somewhere beyond that porridge-like fog there would be a full moon tonight.

"The Mother give me strength," she murmured. Tea's life had never been an easy one, but she had never been tested as much as now.

The scrape of a footstep on stone alerted her that she was no longer alone.

Tea's eyes snapped open, and she turned to see a man's shadowy outline mount the steps behind her. Galan approached.

Drawing her mantle tighter around her, she waited for him. The faint glow of the braziers was behind him, casting his face into darkness, but she sensed his purpose. She had known he would seek her out so that they could speak alone.

"Couldn't sleep either?" he greeted her quietly, his voice a low rumble. The sound of it caressed Tea, causing the tension in her shoulders to ease slightly. Her reaction to him made anger stir in her already knotted belly. She cursed her body's response to this man; he had always been able to work magic upon her.

"No," she replied before turning her attention back to the darkness beyond. The mist was so thick she could not even see the fires of the settlement below. The crash and hiss of waves on the rocks beneath the fort reached her, a sound she would forever associate with this place. The sound of her childhood. "Is the fort secure?" she asked finally.

"Aye. Those we didn't kill threw down their arms when they saw the fight was lost. I've left some men in the village as well, so we'll have a bit of warning if more of Forcus's warriors return."

They lapsed into silence then and stood for a while upon the wall, listening to the night. Eventually, the silence stretched out so long that Tea inclined her head toward him. Was he ever going to speak?

"I wronged you, Tea," he said finally, "and I'm sorry for it."

Here it was—the barrier that now lay between them like a great mountain.

"It took so little for you to turn against me," Tea replied, glad that the darkness hid both of their faces. She did not want to see the contrition on his face, or for him to see the pain on hers. She inhaled deeply, forcing down her fury. She would not lose control, even though she felt like raging at him. "When you heard about the raiders, you were only too ready to think the worst of me, and of Loc."

"You're right to be angry," he replied, speaking slowly as he considered his answer. "There is no excuse I can make." He paused here, and although they stood at least three feet apart, Tea sensed his tension, the intensity of the emotions he held in check.

She watched him in the darkness and saw him reach up and drag a hand through his unbound hair. It was a gesture she had come to know well, one he only made when upset.

"I used to look down on my father for his blind pursuit of vengeance," he admitted finally. "I saw his behavior as weak, narrow-sighted. When he died and I took his place I told myself I would be different—fair-minded and wise—that I would not make his mistakes. I would rule with my head, not my gut." He broke off here, the intensity of his gaze pinning Tea to the spot, even in the darkness. "That was my arrogance, my mistake. When it comes down to it, we're all animals … we all act on instinct when threatened. For all my high words and lofty ideals, the moment I felt my people were threatened, I let instinct take over."

Tea listened quietly. She knew how proud Galan was—to admit his failings to her was hard for him, but it did not change what had been done.

"I understand that," she replied, "but the fact remains that you turned on me. How do I know you won't do so again?"

Her words sounded flat and harsh in the damp, dark stillness. Galan stepped closer to her. "I won't."

She shook her head, her throat closing as her anger bubbled up. "You think you can bend me to your will." She ground the words out between clenched teeth. "But your words come too late."

He reached out, his hand clamping down over her arm, his grip firm and strong. "You're my wife, Tea. I'd drown the world in blood and then set it alight to make you happy. Don't you understand?"

She stared up at him, her pulse thundering in her ears. "I'm no longer yours, Galan. Go back to Dun Ringill with your warriors—I'm staying here. My people need me now, more than ever."

His grip on her arm tightened. She could feel the panic in him, the turmoil churning just beyond that cool, contained shield he wore. She was close to breaking it down.

"When I return home, I'm taking you with me," he growled. "I didn't come here to face your brother's killer—I came here for you."

She tore her arm from his grip, hurting herself in the process. She did not care; the pain only galvanized her. "It was a wasted trip."

Tea brushed past him and ran down the steps into the yard below. Her heart was pounding now, for she expected him to follow her, to catch her so he could plead, cajole, and argue with her.

But he did not.

Tea ran to the stables, past the line of ponies that dozed in the stalls. She recognized Faileas and the other ponies of Dun Ringill but kept going until she reached the stall at the far end where her bad-tempered dun mare stood. The pony snorted as Tea entered the stall, but for once did not flatten her ears back or try to bite her.

Tea would not have cared if the pony had. Gasping for breath, for it now felt as if the night was closing in on her, she sank against the mare's fury neck, burying her face in its mane. She had thought she had exhausted the well of tears inside her, but it appeared she had not.

Not caring who heard her, Tea wept.

Chapter Twenty-nine

Farewell to Loc

THE INHABITANTS OF the broch broke their fast together the following morning, with fresh griddle bread and fowl broth. It was a tense meal, for Tea and Eithni said little, and the servants whispered to each other. When Galan's men spoke between themselves, they too used hushed voices, almost as if they did not want to break the silence that had settled over the table.

Toward the end of the meal, Galan shattered the quiet. "My warriors and I cannot remain here long," he said, his gaze meeting Tea's across the table. It was the first time they had looked at each other since their conversation on the wall the night before. Tea noted the lines of tension etched either side of his mouth—lines that had not been there a few days before. "Dun Ringill has few warriors left to defend it—but Dun Ardtreck has even fewer. We should search for Wid and those men loyal to him and Loc."

Tea nodded. "Thank you." She shifted her attention to Eithni, who sat beside her. "Do you know where Wid has gone?"

Eithni shook her head. "After Forcus slew Loc, he gave Wid a choice. Fight him, join him, or leave. Wid left with a group of warriors and families loyal to him, and they rode east. That's all I know."

Tea's throat constricted at this news. She knew why Wid had chosen to leave; however, Forcus would have seen his decision as weak. A true Wolf would have stayed and fought. Still, her cousin was the rightful chieftain of her people, and she wanted to see him back here.

Galan turned to the tall, sinewy warrior seated opposite him. "Lutrin—take Cal and ride east this morning. When you find Wid, tell what has happened here and bring him home."

Tea met Galan's eye across the table. "You should not leave Dun Ringill undefended," she said firmly. "As soon as Wid returns, you must leave."

Galan held her gaze, his mouth thinning. "Aye, I'll depart soon enough." His gaze narrowed then. "But I won't be going home alone—you're coming with me."

Tea put down the cup of broth she had been holding with a hard thump upon the oaken table, causing Eithni to start. "No, I won't."

"You're my wife, Tea—we were handfasted."

"Handfastings can be broken," she shot back. "I release you from your obligations."

He leaned over the table, his grey eyes darkening to slate. "Obligations ... is that how you see things?"

She lifted her chin, her heart fluttering at the power of his gaze that stripped her bare and called her a liar. "That's all it was," she replied coldly. "A pact between two tribes—one that is now broken."

Two women, one tall with dark hair pulled back into a severe braid, the other small with unbound hair the color of walnut, made their way down the hillside beneath Dun Ardtreck. Both women wore heavy fur cloaks, their breath steaming in clouds before them in the chill air. They strode purposefully, making their way toward the row of stone cairns to the south-east of the fort.

The fog seemed to have thickened with the dawn, lowering so that it blotted out the top of the broch from view. Tea coughed as the damp, gelid air burned her lungs; it was so raw out here this morning that her nose felt numb. She glanced at Eithni, who huddled inside her cloak. Her face was pale and pinched, although her hazel-green eyes were brighter than the day before.

Unspeaking, they made their way to the bottom of the hill before climbing a rocky incline to the row of cairns of their forefathers. The mound nearest the fort was the freshest, the ground around it still muddy from its construction—it was also the most hastily-built. Unlike their father's cairn next to it, which was a perfectly rounded sphere of stone, this one had been stacked in careless haste. One side of it was already starting to crumble.

Tea's gaze narrowed. "Was this the best they could manage?"

Eithni sighed. "Forcus's men made a hurried job."

"When Wid returns, I'll ensure this is built properly," Tea replied. "Our brother deserves better."

The two of them stood in front of the cairn, just before its entrance—a deep cleft that cut into the center of the tomb. Farther in there was a stone slab, preventing animals or grave robbers from entering. Within, lay her brother's body.

Tea clasped her hands before her. "Did anyone sing a lament for him?"

Eithni shook her head. "No one attended his burial—Forcus wouldn't let me, and Wid had already been driven out. There was no one here to see him safely into the afterlife."

Tea's eyes prickled with tears at this news, and she felt another surge of hatred toward Forcus. Loc had never done him any harm; instead, he had always seen the warrior much like an elder brother. He had trusted and respected Forcus, but his killer had not even granted him a proper burial. Tea balled her hands into fists and breathed deeply until the crimson tide of fury passed.

"Then I shall sing one for him," she said finally.

Inhaling deeply, dredging down into the depths of her soul, Tea began to sing. Lingering, quavering, long notes filled with sadness and regret lifted high into the fog, drifting across the still, mist-shrouded landscape.

> *Brave Loc mac Domech*
> *Believer in peace*
> *Go to your long sleep.*
> *Brave Loc mac Domech*
> *Warrior, brother and chief*
> *Slain.*
> *Betrayed.*

Tears streamed down Tea's face as she poured out all the love she felt for her brother, and her regret at how they had parted. He had tricked her, but she forgave him for it. Loc had believed in peace when all others opposed it. Her lament was her way of reaching out to his spirit, of letting him know that she was sorry, and that she loved him more than words could ever express.

On and on she sang, until her throat was hoarse. When she finished, she felt wrung out, exhausted. This was the third lament she had sung in a year, and she would end up a husk if she had to sing any more.

Straightening up and wiping the tears from her face, Tea turned her attention to Eithni, who stood quietly beside her. Her sister's eyes were dry, although they glittered with deep emotion as she stared at her brother's tomb. A nerve flickered in her smooth cheek. Tea worried about Eithni. During their walk here, she had noticed that her sister's gait was uneven, and she limped slightly.

"Eithni," she began gently, "what did he do to you?"

Her sister looked up, her face hardening. "I can't speak of it, Tea," she replied, her voice shaking slightly. "Even to you ... I can only say that he was a beast, and that he used me in ways that will scar me forever, inside and out."

"But, the way you walk ... did he—"

"I can't!" Eithni choked out the words, backing away from her sister. "I'll heal in time, but you mustn't rush me. Maybe one day I'll be able to tell you what he did, but now I'm not strong enough. Please don't ask me again."

Tea nodded, her heart hammering at the thought that Forcus had damaged her sister. It made her feel ill.

She realized what a lucky escape she'd had during their time together. Forcus had never been a good lover—she had realized that fully after laying with Galan. Unlike her husband, Forcus had been rushed and rough in his treatment of her. She had been a maid the first time they had lain together, and he had hurt her. Things had gotten easier after that, but she had never really enjoyed their coupling. It had been one of the reasons she had ended things between them. However, she now realized things could have been far worse for her.

Tea stepped forward and drew her sister into a hug. "I'm so sorry, Eithni. I didn't mean to upset you. I was only worried."

Eithni wrapped her arms around Tea's waist and squeezed in a wordless answer, her slender body relaxing against hers. When the two sisters drew apart, the panic had faded from Eithni's eyes.

"Just promise me that if you need a healer, you'll tell me," Tea said firmly. "You can be so stubborn."

"I *am* a healer," Eithni replied with a shake of her head. "And if I'm stubborn you are doubly so."

Tea snorted, linking her arm through Eithni's, before they turned and picked their way down the rocky incline. "I wasn't talking about me."

"No, but I see your pig-headed ways have not mended. What has your husband done for you to treat him so viciously?"

Tea stiffened. Of course, Eithni was talking of the conversation she had overhead that morning. She did not know of what had passed between Galan and Tea the night before.

Tea sighed. She did not want to go into this, but nor did she wish to rebuff her sister, not when Eithni was currently so fragile. "When I first went to Dun Ringill, things were difficult between us," she said finally, "but after a while we grew close." Tea paused here, her jaw clenching. "Yet when word of raiders bearing the mark of The Wolf reached him, he turned on me."

Silence stretched between them for a few moments. They had reached the flatter ground and started along a narrow path that wound through the village back toward the gates of Dun Ardtreck.

"And is he sorry for it now?" Eithni asked eventually, once she had considered Tea's words.

"Aye—he says so, but I don't see him the same way. It's for the best, Eithni. My place is here—Wid is young and untested, he will need someone to help him rule Dun Ardtreck."

Tea realized that Eithni was watching her closely now, her gaze narrowed.

"What is it?" Tea demanded, uncomfortable under such intense scrutiny.

"You gave your heart to him, didn't you?"

Tea made a dismissive, scoffing noise. "You've seen how handsome he is. Galan is an easy man to like, but that doesn't mean I'm smitten."

“I think you are.”

Tea frowned. “Well, I’m not—I just want him to go.”

“He seems like a good man.”

Tea’s chest squeezed painfully at her sister’s words. If only things were as easy as her sister saw them.

“He is,” Tea eventually replied, her voice barely above a whisper, “but that changes nothing.”

Chapter Thirty

Final Words

WID RETURNED TWO days later, bringing with him a host of warriors, as well as the families who had fled Dun Ardtreck with him. Tea's cousin had not been idle in his time away. He had been gathering men from the east—warriors from the People of The Stag—who agreed to help him reclaim Dun Ardtreck. He had been planning an attack on the fort in a few days' time, when Lutrin and Cal found him.

Greeting him before the gates of the fort, Tea clasped Wid in a hug. He was a hulking young man who at seventeen winters was already an impressive size. A mane of jet curls tumbled over his shoulders, and he smelled of leather and ponies. When he pulled back, Wid's face was wet with tears.

"I failed you," he said, his voice rough with emotion.

"Your decision to go saved the lives of many," Tea replied firmly. She did not admit to him that she had initially been angry at him for refusing to fight Forcus, instead leaving the broch. However, in the days since she had realized the wisdom of his act. "Never regret it."

"But I should have guessed Forcus's ruse." His young face twisted with grief. "I should have prevented Loc's death."

Tea reached up, her hand cupping his whiskery face. "You couldn't have known—none of us suspected him."

Behind Wid a crowd of weary travelers trudged up the hill—men, women, and children who had fled Dun Ardtreck days earlier now returned home. It gladdened Tea's heart to see them. Now the tense melancholy that had lingered here for days would lift.

A few feet behind Tea and Wid stood Galan. He waited silently, his warriors gathered behind him, allowing Tea and her cousin to be reunited before the young man turned his attention to him.

Tea watched Wid leave her side and stride up to Galan, stopping before him. The two men's gazes met and held for a few moments, before Wid stepped close and hugged Galan. His eyes shone when he stepped back.

"I thank you."

Tea watched a smile curve her husband's mouth. "What for?"

"Things would have gone ill for Tea and Eithni if you had not followed your wife here."

Galan's smile turned wry. "Tea didn't need my help—she slew Forcus herself."

"Yes, but you and your men liberated the fort."

Galan inclined his head, finally accepting the younger man's thanks. "So the peace between our tribes still stands?"

Wid's face turned serious. "You realize that Loc and I had nothing to do with those raids?"

"Aye," Galan replied, his gaze flicking to Tea. Their gazes met for a moment, before he fixed his attention on Wid once more. "I know that now—one of the raiders we captured alive told us that Forcus was responsible. I don't blame you."

Wid held his gaze. "I am of the same mind as Loc was—I want peace between The Wolf and The Eagle."

Galan smiled, and this time warmth reached his eyes. The two men reached out and clasped arms. "As do I."

The fog remained in a dense shroud over The Winged Isle for two further days after Wid's return—two difficult days in which Tea avoided Galan as much as she was able.

Fortunately, there was plenty of work to keep her occupied. Wid initially seemed a bit lost, so she took control of the fort. She welcomed back some of Loc's warriors who had returned from a deer hunt to find Loc dead and Forcus's men guarding the fort. Loc's men had been denied entry unless they swore loyalty to Forcus, and when the warriors refused, they had been driven off.

Tea set men to work sharpening blades and mending the shields and weaponry damaged in the attack. Meanwhile Galan and his warriors repaired the oaken gates they had broken down during the attack.

Eithni oversaw the cleaning of the fort. Forcus and his men had left it a mess, and it took a full day to clean out the broch, replacing the soiled rushes with clean ones and scrubbing all the wooden surfaces with hot water and lye. Eithni also organized a great feast to celebrate Wid's return, and the accompanying ceremony that would make him the new Wolf chieftain.

They held the chief-making ceremony at noon the second day following Wid's homecoming. Tea stood upon a raised stone dais at the far end of the broch, watching as her cousin's men pushed their way through the crowd, bearing a great oaken shield. They brought it before Wid, who seated himself on it.

With a great cheer, the warriors lifted Wid high into the air—a gesture that showed their new chieftain to the gods. Clinging on to the edge of the shield, Wid laughed, and for the first time in many days, Tea found a smile curving her own mouth.

However, the joy she felt at seeing Wid made chief was tinged with sadness. Just months ago she had witnessed Loc go through the same rite—yet his time ruling the tribe had been so tragically brief. He had never had the chance to take a wife or father children—and he would have made a good husband and father.

The gathered crowd inside the broch roared their approval, the noise shaking the great stone tower to its foundations. Tea's eyes misted with tears, but she blinked them away. She would not let her grief tarnish this occasion. Like her people, she had to look forward and make a fresh start.

A great feast followed the ceremony. The long tables arranged in a square around the great central hearth groaned under the weight of the dishes: roast boar stuffed with walnuts and apples, braised onions and carrots, many types of breads, huge wheels of goat's and ewe's cheese, roast fowl, and turnips mashed with butter.

Tea sat down next to Eithni. Her sister had finally regained some color to her face, although she still walked awkwardly and sometimes winced when she rose to her feet after sitting a while. Tea worried for Eithni at times, but she was relieved to see her sister smile at the sight of the feast set before them.

Glancing away from her sister, Tea felt Galan's gaze upon her, boring into her from across the room. She did her best to avoid eye contact. Determined that she would not ignore him completely, as she had done since Wid's return, Galan had sat down directly opposite, ensuring that every time Tea raised her gaze she would see him.

He was watching her now, his eyes smoke-grey in the flickering light from the cressets that lined the broch's walls. Outside, it was day, but the fortress had few windows, meaning that it was dark indoors even on the sunniest of days.

Tea helped herself to some roast fowl, meeting Galan's eye briefly as she did so. She saw that his expression was troubled. She knew her avoidance of him would hurt Galan, but she was not ignoring him in order to cause him pain. Indeed, it was painful to look upon him, to look into his eyes.

Every look brought back memories.

That period after Mid-Winter Fire had been the happiest in her life. Like a flower opening after a long and bitter winter, she had given herself to him and let warmth touch her heart. She knew he was sorry, but his regret had come too late—she had already walled up her heart again.

Her true purpose was not to be a wife, but a warrior. She would not wed again—instead, she would co-rule with Wid. She would make the People of The Wolf strong. Loc could rest easy now; the peace would last whether or not Tea and Galan remained handfasted. There was no need for her to return to Dun Ringill.

A roar went up at the far end of the table, drawing Tea's thoughts from Galan. Wid's men had filled a huge drinking horn with mead and passed it to him. They cheered raucously, a few of them already well into their cups, as the new chief brought it to his lips and tipped back his head, drinking until the horn was drained. Face flushed, Wid handed the horn back to one of his men to be refilled.

Tea turned her attention back to her end of the table, to find Galan still watching her. Bristling, she resolutely kept her gaze fastened upon the wooden platter in front of her.

Let him stare all he wanted—it would do no good.

The feasting and drinking went on throughout the afternoon and into the evening. A harpist set herself up on the dais above the revelers and began to play, a scop at her side. The scop was a young man who had come from a neighboring village for the chief-making. Small and frail, with a shock of jet hair, the lad had a hauntingly beautiful voice as he sang of the gods, of great chieftains and their wives, of battles, loss, and reckoning.

After the scop had sung for a while, a flutist playing a bone whistle climbed up onto the dais and, together with the harpist, they played songs for dancing. The rich food and surfeit of ale and sloe wine made Tea feel drowsy. The noise of the reveling and the smoke from the burning peat had given her a thick head, and she longed for some peace and fresh air.

She stood on the edge of the dancers, watching as Wid staggered around, passed from maid to maid, each of them eager to dance with the young, handsome chief. After a while Galan approached her.

Tea was aware of his presence by her side before she even glanced in his direction. From the first time she had seen him, she had noticed Galan's charisma; how he filled every space he walked into. Her skin prickled with awareness as he stepped close to her.

"Tea," his voice was low, barely audible above the clapping, cheering and drunken laughter that echoed through the broch. "I would speak with you."

She inclined her head to him. "What … now?"

He nodded.

She stiffened. "Can you not do so here?"

He frowned. "I can barely hear my own thoughts above the din—come upstairs with me a moment."

Tea watched Galan leave her side and stride around the edge of the circular space, before he climbed the stone steps leading up to the top level. Her belly clenched. She did not want to follow him, yet she found her feet doing just that. She made her way around the perimeter of the dancing and hesitantly climbed the steps.

The top level of the broch was a sacred place: the private quarters of the chieftain. Her mother and father had once dwelled up here, and then Loc. Now this space was Wid's. Thick furs covered the wooden floor, and wall hangings, richly decorated with gold, obscured the damp stone walls. A pile of furs dominated one corner of the space—a disturbing reminder of the alcove Tea had shared with Galan in Dun Ringill—and three cressets filled with burning oil cast a gilded light over the room.

Galan was waiting for her in the center of the space.

The sight of him caused the pit of Tea's belly to tighten in instinctive arousal. Damn him for being so attractive. Dressed in tight plaid leggings, his torso bare, his long straight hair flowing like oil over his bare shoulders, he watched her as if she were a deer and he was the hunter.

Tea stopped a few feet from him, clenching her hands by her sides to prevent herself from trembling. "What did you wish to say?" she asked.

Galan held her gaze, tension emanating from his strong body. "The mist is clearing," he said finally. "I will leave with the dawn tomorrow."

Tea stared back at him, her chest constricting at this news. This was what she wanted—why then did she feel so hollow inside?

He continued to watch her. "I want you to come back to Dun Ringill with me, Tea." He stepped closer to her. "Let us start again."

Tea raised her chin and clenched her jaw. Their gazes fused, and her insides twisted. Galan's mouth thinned when she did not answer him.

"I won't ask again, Tea." He spoke her name like a caress, the gentleness of his tone made her suppress a shiver. "I won't beg or bully you to be with me—I ask you this final time to forgive me, to come home."

Tea inhaled deeply, her heart slamming against her ribs. "Why do you have to make this so hard," she gasped. "I've already given you my decision. Why won't you just accept it?"

Two strides brought Galan to Tea; he reached out and took hold of her upper arms, holding her fast. "I can't. Not without knowing that's really what you want." He pulled her against him, his mouth covering hers.

The kiss was brutal, wild—and for a few moments Tea succumbed to it. Desire crashed over her, sweeping her up in a great wave, and she drowned in the taste and feel of him. She knew then that she would never want another man as she did Galan.

But even her hunger for him was not enough to make her forget herself—or cast aside the decision she had made.

Tea tore herself free of Galan's embrace and staggered backward. "It *is* what I want," she panted. "Go from here, Galan—leave me be."

The pain in his eyes nearly made her relent. For a brief moment his shield slipped, and she saw his naked grief. He looked as if she had just driven a blade into his chest. Unable to bear the sight of his pain, for it mirrored her own, Tea whirled and dove for the stairs.

Galan did not go after her.

Chapter Thirty-one

Absence

"THEY HAVE GONE."

Eithni's words sounded bleak in the chill morning air. Tea, unable to bear the sight of Galan and his men leaving, had left the broch before dawn. She had climbed out to a spot on the cliffs behind the fort—a place where she and her siblings had played as children—where no one would bother her.

Of course, Eithni remembered the hiding place.

Tea sat perched on the rock, her knees pulled up under her chin, her fur mantle pulled tight about her. Far below, the surf pounded the rocks, throwing up spray that settled over her in a fine mist. It had been a mistake to hide here, for this place reminded Tea of the spot where she and Galan had made love, during one of their afternoon excursions from Dun Ringill. She had been so happy that day, barely able to believe how kindly the gods had treated her.

Grief constricted her throat. How quickly things changed.

She had not slept the night before. The rest of the broch had slumbered while she stared with burning eyes up at the smoke-blackened rafters. Grief and anger warred for the long night, but this morning she felt nothing—a chill numbness had seeped through her.

Eithni sat down next to her on the rock ledge. She did not try to disturb her. Instead, the sisters sat in silence, listening to the rumble and crash of the waves below. The sky above was lightening. After days of fog, it felt as if the world had suddenly expanded.

Eventually, when the first rays of sun bathed them, Tea felt Eithni's gaze settle upon her. "Come, Tea. You'll be frozen through—let's go back, and I'll get you some hot broth."

Tea nodded, grateful that Eithni did not try and speak to her of Galan. The last thing she needed right now was her sister singing The Eagle chieftain's praises. Wid too clearly worshipped him and was completely mystified as to Galan and Tea's estrangement. She did not look forward to her cousin's looks of reproach this morning. He had believed she would relent in the end.

I'm stubborn—like my father, she thought as she stiffly rose to her feet and followed Eithni off the ledge. In the past, such a comparison would have filled her with pride. This morning the thought depressed her, for Domech mac Bred's last years had been unhappy ones. *And I'll end up alone and bitter like him too.*

Smoke was rising from the broch's roof as the two women made their way back inside the fort. Somewhere inside the walls a rooster crowed, the mournful cry carrying over the cliffs.

Tea felt Galan's absence the moment she stepped back inside the broch. Despite that she had barely spoken to him during his time here, she had been aware of his presence at all times. Even when he had not been looking at her, or when he had been speaking to one of his warriors, she had sensed his nearness.

A chill went through Tea at the realization that she would miss him.

She followed Eithni to the chieftain's table, where Wid was breaking his fast with a barley and oat pottage, enriched with fresh cream and honey. He watched Tea, his brow furrowed, as she took her place at the table.

"Are you well, cousin?"

Tea nodded, avoiding his gaze, and reached for the cup of goat's milk one of the women handed her.

"Galan asked after you," Wid continued. The sound of her husband's name nearly made Tea wince, although she managed to suppress the urge.

"I thought it best if I stayed away," she murmured. She raised the cup to her lips and took a sip.

"He did not leave us with a smile on his face," her cousin continued. "Like me, he does not understand your behavior."

Tea glanced up, meeting Wid's gaze. He was only three years younger than her, the same age as Eithni, but she suddenly felt decades older. "I can't pick up where we left off—he needs to accept that," she replied. "Dun Ardtreck is my rightful place. I should never have left it."

Wid stared back at her, the look on his face telling her he was still unconvinced. However, perhaps seeing that his cousin was on a knife-edge this morning, he held back further comment.

Tea was grateful for that.

Galan led the way south. He pushed Faileas hard, urging the stallion into a fast canter across the desolate moors. He had lingered at Dun Ardtreck far longer than he should have—he needed to return home and secure his borders.

The austere landscape suited his mood. He felt as if all color had leached from the world, all joy. Until last night he had hoped that Tea would change her mind, yet he had not bargained upon her obstinacy.

Anger—at Tea, at himself, at life—churned through Galan. The tempo of Faileas's pounding hooves thrummed through his body, giving him focus for the moment. He wanted the distraction. The last thing he needed was to be alone with his thoughts.

Leaving this morning had been harder than he had anticipated. The desire to go looking for her, to tie her up and throw her across the back of his pony, had swept over him as he saddled his stallion. He had not expected her to see him off, but her absence had still hurt.

Enough.

He needed to focus on leading his people. His tribe had to come first. Wid had promised that the peace would endure, and now that Tea co-ruled with her cousin, Galan felt sure that the People of The Wolf would not break their word.

The knowledge should have brought him solace, yet it did not.

For the first time he envied his brothers and their campaign against the Caesars to the south. He wished that he was with them, rushing at that great wall, roaring the battle cry of The Eagle.

Now that he had lost Tea, he wished only for oblivion.

"Fernilea and Carbost both need fortifying," Wid announced, setting down his cup of ale with a thud.

Across the table one of his warriors, Beli, frowned. "Is that really necessary?"

"Aye—The Stag have given us little trouble of late, but their numbers grow in the north. If they send out raiding parties across the water and attack from Loch Harport, those villages have little defense."

Beli's frown deepened. "I thought you found The Stags friendly when you asked them for help?"

"I did, but that was only because we were uniting against a common enemy. Forcus was a danger to us all."

"So you think we should be wary of them?"

Wid shrugged. "I think it pays not to be complacent. Just because we've made peace with The Eagle, does not mean we should not mind our borders." Wid then turned his attention to the tall, statuesque woman with long dark hair who sat next to him at the chieftain's table. "What do you think, Tea?"

All eyes at the table fastened upon Wid's cousin. The noon meal had just finished and the warriors had been deep in discussion. However, the distant look on Tea's face told Wid that her thoughts were elsewhere.

Irritated that she appeared to be ignoring him, Wid frowned. "Tea?"

Blinking, Tea came out of her reverie. "Sorry, Wid. What?"

"Did you hear what we were discussing?"

Her features tensed. "No, can you repeat the question?"

Wid gave a huff of impatience. "I asked you if you believe we should keep an eye on the People of The Stag. Their numbers grow along our northern borders."

Wid watched his cousin struggle to focus on the topic at hand. She had become distant of late, often disappearing into her own world when she thought no one was watching. It was unlike Tea to do so at a conference with the other warriors. Dun Ardtreck's safety was important to her—she was usually the first to bring up discussions about its defense.

"I agree," she replied softly. "My parents' union forged peace between the tribes for a while, but ever since my mother's death contact has diminished. Some of the villages have stopped trading with us."

"Then we should see to it that Fernilea and Carbost have stone outer defenses built," Wid replied. "Just in case an attack ever comes from the water."

Tea nodded her approval, before her gaze settled upon Beli. "Take a group of ten strong men and start work on Fernilea tomorrow," she ordered. "The sooner those villages are defended the better."

"Aye, Tea." Beli dipped his head in respect, before rising to his feet. "I will see it done."

Now that the discussion had ended, the other warriors rose from the table and made their way back outdoors. Wid and Tea remained seated at the head of the chieftain's table and watched them go. Presently, Eithni joined her sister and cousin. She had brought a basket of dried herbs, powders, and clay bottles with her, which she began to sort out upon the table.

The three of them sat in companionable silence. A girl refilled their cups with watered-down ale before returning to help the other servants chop onions and turnips for that evening's supper. The rise and fall of conversation in the feasting hall moved around them. A few yards away, a dog yelped as one of the cooks accidently stood on its foot.

Tea looked down at her cup of ale, her thoughts turning inward once more now that the conference had ended. She felt drained today and wished she could just crawl into her alcove and sleep the afternoon away.

Feeling her cousin's gaze boring into her, she glanced up. Wid was surveying Tea over the rim of his cup. "What ails you, cousin?"

Tea stiffened. "Nothing—I'm perfectly well."

"You're not yourself ... all of us can see that."

Tea gritted her teeth, forcing down irritation. This was not the first time Wid had brought this subject up in the month since Galan's departure. She grew tired of having to defend herself.

"I'm just weary," she murmured. "Once the spring arrives, I will feel better."

Wid's gaze narrowed. "That's your flimsiest excuse yet."

"It's not an excuse."

Wid gave her a hard look. "You pine for Galan mac Muin," he said eventually. "He was a fine match for you—a great warrior and leader. You'll find no better man upon the isle."

A few feet away Eithni went still. Her eyes widened, flicking from her cousin to her sister.

Tea drew herself up, glaring at Wid. "I don't wish to find a better man—or any man," she informed him coldly. "The match was my brother's idea, not mine. Besides, you need me here."

Wid shook his head. "You have been a great help to me, Tea—and for that I will always be grateful—but we both know I can rule Dun Ardtreck without you."

Tea went rigid. "You don't want me here?"

Wid's swarthy complexion darkened. "No, I don't *need* you here."

Eithni shifted uncomfortably on the bench. "Of course we want you here," she murmured, casting her cousin a look of censure. "We're all worried about you, that's all. You've been so pale and drawn since Galan left."

"There's no need," Tea snapped, setting her cup of ale down with a thump. "I wish you'd stop fussing like a couple of crones."

"Tea." Wid snapped, the last of his patience dissolving. "Neither of us are fools. I see your red-rimmed eyes every morning. You haunt this broch like a shade. What has happened to you?"

Tea stared at her cousin, shocked by the bluntness of his words. Did she really cut such a pathetic figure?

The days since Galan's departure had been the bleakest of her life. Yet she had thought no one had noticed her melancholy.

“I just need time,” she choked out the words and rose to her feet. “Can’t you give me that?”

Chapter Thirty-two

You Must Go to Him

TEA FLED FROM the broch, hurrying down the steep steps to the yard below.

Fowl scattered before her as she strode out of the fort, through the cleft in the rock face. The village was deserted, as most folk were indoors resting after their main meal of the day. Relieved that she was alone, Tea took the winding path along the cliff face to the west.

A chill wind blew in from the north-west, stippling the dark waters of Loch Bracadale. Tea barely felt the cold, such was her desire to be away from her sister's pity and Wid's concern.

Out of breath, she reached the edge of the rocky cliff-face and turned her face up to the buffeting wind. Tears streamed down her face, and her shoulders shook with the force of the emotion she kept in check.

Curse you Galan—why can't I forget you?

Then she saw a slight figure, swathed in a thick fur cloak, hurrying up the path behind her. Eithni's unbound hair twisted and billowed around her pale, heart-shaped face. Her eyes had deepened from their usual hazel to a blazing green, as she reached her.

Tea's first reaction was anger. She scrubbed at her tears and turned on her sister. "Can't you give me a moment alone?" she snarled.

Eithni put her hands on her hips, her gaze narrowing. "Not when you're making the biggest mistake of your life. If you love Galan, then you must go to him."

"You don't understand," Tea shot back. "It's not as easy as you think."

"Yes it is—you're the only one making it complicated."

Tea stared at her a moment, before folding her arms across her chest. "You don't know what you're talking about."

Eithni drew herself up, her eyes glittering with fury. "I'm no goose, Tea—but I'm beginning to think you are. Do you know that when we went to the Lochans of the Fair Folk, and I saw the man you were to marry, I was jealous? I couldn't believe how lucky you were—to marry such a fine warrior, a man who wanted peace not bloodshed for his people. I hoped I'd one day be as fortunate as you, but Forcus tore that hope from me—he destroyed any dreams I'd once had."

Tea held her sister's gaze, her body going cold at these words. She did not want Eithni to continue, but now that her sister had begun to speak, the words rushed out in an unstoppable tide.

"The gods have always been kind to you, Tea, yet you throw their benevolence back in their faces. If you keep taking it for granted they will stop giving. Our parents and Loc are gone—we won't see them again until we pass into the realm beyond—but Galan is still alive. You still have a chance at happiness ... don't throw it away."

Tea stared at her, shocked by the bluntness of Eithni's words. Had she really been as blind as her sister accused her of being?

Was she really that ungrateful?

Galan had just returned from a scouting expedition with his warriors, when the bandruí approached him.

Their party had found nothing suspicious, no sign of any further raids, yet Galan was in a dark mood this afternoon. He had barely spoken to his men during the day, preferring to keep his own counsel. Sensing their chief's ill-humor, his warriors had wisely given him space. Galan did not share in their conversation as they unsaddled and rubbed down their ponies.

After seeing to his stallion, Galan strode across the yard toward the fort. He felt in need of a strong cup of mead and time alone in his alcove. Initially, when he had first returned to Dun Ringill from Dun Ardtreck, he had been unable to sleep there—for memories of Tea were too raw, too fresh. However, a month on, he now spent time there once more. The space gave him the solitude he craved.

Noting Galan's unwelcoming expression, Ruith's gait slowed as she drew close to him. Despite her advancing years, the seer still moved with the grace of a much younger woman. Barefoot, her lithe frame shrouded in a heavy woolen cape, she strode across the frozen earth without seeming to notice its chill. There had been a hard frost that morning and the ground had just started to thaw.

The bandruí reached Galan and fell in step next to him. "Good afternoon."

Galan grunted and lengthened his stride. He did not wish for company right now, could this woman not see that?

"Galan, I must speak with you."

He cast her a dark look. "Speak then."

"Please stop a moment. I require your full attention."

Irritation surged, but Galan did as bid. He stopped and turned to her. Ruith was much shorter than he was, and so she had to crane her neck up to meet his gaze. In her eyes he saw consternation. The seer was not a soft, gentle woman—she was known to speak plainly and to be fierce when riled. The empathy he saw now in her gaze was new.

"You are so changed, Galan," she observed.

Galan shrugged, his irritation mounting further. "Is that what you have to say to me?"

Ruith shook her head, her features tightening. "I cast the bones this morning. It is a good time to seek answers from the gods. The sun grows warmer and the days begin to lengthen—soon the first signs of spring will be here."

Galan folded his arms across his broad chest and regarded her under hooded lids. "And what did the bones tell you?"

He knew his tone was bordering on disrespect. Had he spoken to the bandruí in such a manner as a lad, his father would have knocked him to the ground. Muin had always revered the seer, and Ruith's mother too, who had lived among them as bandruí before her.

However, if he had given offence, Ruith did not show it. She was tough—life had weathered but not broken her—so his words appeared not to touch her.

"That there has been great upheaval to the south," she told him, her face solemn. "For good or bad I do not know."

Galan's chest constricted at this. He thought of Tarl and Donnel and wondered if his brothers still lived. They had always been so close that he almost believed he would have known if either of them had fallen: that he would feel the connection, the thread that bound them, snap.

"They must have attacked the wall," he mused.

Ruith nodded. "That is not all. The marks of the Crossed Arrow and the Rising Sun fell together when I cast the bones. Change is coming—newcomers to the isle."

Galan tensed at this news. "Invaders?"

The bandruí shook her head. "I know not—yet perhaps it is wise to shore up your defenses."

Galan gave a curt nod. "I will see to it."

He went to move on, but the seer reached out and grabbed his arm, forestalling him. "Wait. There is something else."

He turned and looked back down at her face. Ruith's expression had softened, and a smile curved her lips.

"The mark of The Eagle and The Wolf fell side by side," she said gently, although her grip was like iron upon his arm. "And the Cauldron fell beneath them."

Galan stiffened. He knew what she was insinuating. The Cauldron was a positive mark for their people, one associated with healing and rebirth—with miracles.

He stared at the bandruí, holding her gaze for a few moments longer. "She's not coming back, Ruith," he said finally. "Tea made her feelings clear. She'll remain at Dun Ardtreck with her people. I'll not see her again."

"But the bones—"

"The bones have been wrong before," he snarled, tearing free of her hold. "I will not cling to hope when there is none."

With that, he pivoted on his heel and strode away, leaving the bandruí staring after him.

Night settled over Dun Ardtreck. The sky was clear and once the last vestiges of the day had faded, the glittering stars came out to play one by one.

Tea sat alone in her alcove and packed the few essential items she would carry with her to Dun Ringill.

You must go to him.

Her argument with Eithni had drained her, but in the end her sister had succeeded in convincing her to leave Dun Ardtreck, to return to Galan. Initially, the decision had caused relief to wash over her, followed by a fluttering of excitement in the pit of her belly that she would see Galan again. Now that the rest of the day had passed, she was beginning to doubt her decision.

What if Galan hates me now?

She would not blame him if he did.

What if I go to him and he turns me away, humiliates me?

Tea shook her head, to clear the litany of self-sabotage that marched through her. She had to stop doing this to herself, or she would turn herself mad. The decision had been made, and now she had to find the courage to face her husband once more. If, in the interim, he had cast her out of his heart, then she would have to face that fact.

Of course, Wid was delighted that she had decided to return to Galan.

She had initially been offended that he seemed so eager to be rid of her. Yet she knew Wid was of the same mind as Loc: that the union would serve to strengthen alliances between the two tribes. He had offered four of his warriors to escort her to Dun Ringill at first light. If they rode hard, they would reach Galan's fort by nightfall.

Tea rolled a woolen tunic up and placed it into the single leather pack she would bring south, before she reached for the new linen shift that Eithni had sewn for her. She doubted she would sleep tonight, for she already felt sick with nerves.

Movement behind her, made her turn. Eithni entered the alcove and let the hanging of sewn goat-skins fall closed after her.

One look at her sister's face, and Tea knew she had something to tell her.

"What's wrong?

Eithni smiled, although her features remained strained, her gaze intense. "When you go tomorrow, I want to come with you."

Tea stiffened, her gaze widening. "Why would you want that? Dun Ardtreck is your home."

Eithni shook her head. "Not after what Forcus did it isn't. Everywhere I turn there are memories. I can't look at the hearth in the hall without seeing Loc lying next to it, bleeding to death. I can't sleep in my alcove without remembering what Forcus did to me there. I need a fresh start—I want to come with you."

Tea studied her sister a moment. Truthfully, her sister's request pleased her. She had missed Eithni over the past few months and knew that her skills as a healer were needed at Dun Ringill.

"But surely Wid won't allow it—you're the healer here."

Eithni shook her head. "I asked him earlier, and he understands why I do not wish to stay. There is another young woman in the village whom I've been training in herb lore. She will make an able healer. There's no need for me to stay on that account."

A smile crept across Tea's face. "Then I would love to have you with me, Eithni." She climbed to her feet and hugged her sister. "You'd better go and pack."

Eithni pulled back from Tea, excitement tightening her delicate features. "No need to worry about that—I already have."

Chapter Thirty-three

The Return

TEA AND EITHNI set off with the dawn, accompanied by four of Wid's most trusted warriors—three men and a woman. It was a bright, cold morning, and a sparkling carpet of frost covered the bare hills around Dun Ardtreck. The ponies' breath steamed in the air, which felt raw to breathe. Both Tea and Eithni had dressed warmly for the day's journey. Tea rode the same dun mare she had brought from Dun Ringill, and Eithni sat astride a small, grey pony that her father had gifted her two summers earlier.

Tea and Eithni trotted side-by-side, with two of Wid's warriors before them and two riding close behind. All four were heavily armed, bearing ash spears, long fighting daggers, and heavy shields. After the events of late, Wid was taking no chances with his cousins' safety. Tea appreciated his concern, although she could not imagine they would encounter any problems on the journey south.

As they crested the last hill, before Dun Ardtreck would be lost from sight, Tea pulled up her mare, twisted

in the saddle, and looked north once more. The broch
perched high and proud upon a rocky crag, its conical
outline silhouetted against the lightening sky. Upon the
walls before it, she could make out a man's shape—Wid
had climbed up to see them off.

Lifting a hand in silent farewell, Tea felt a pang of
melancholy. She was not sad to leave Dun Ardtreck—her
return here had taught her that this fort was no longer
her home—but sad for all that had befallen her people of
late. It would still take a while for them to rally from
Loc's loss and for Wid to settle into his new role.

You might be back here sooner than you think, she
reminded herself as she reined her mare south. *If Galan
doesn't want you—you'll return to Dun Ardtreck.*

Pushing the thought from her mind, she urged her
mare into a canter. Next to her, eagerness flushed
Eithni's face. Unlike Tea, she had not looked behind her
for one last glimpse of Dun Ardtreck. Instead, she was
looking forward—south—to a new future.

They reached the Black Cuillins around noon and
stopped briefly next to a trickling brook. As she nibbled
at a piece of bread and cheese, Eithni's gaze slid over the
looming dark peaks. Without asking, Tea knew her sister
was thinking of the handfasting she had attended here
months earlier, and of all that had happened since.

Sensing Tea's gaze upon her, Eithni eventually tore
her attention away from the mountains and glanced over
at her sister.

"I wish I could go back in time," Eithni murmured. "I
would not have done as Loc asked."

Tea held her gaze. "I was furious with you both for a
long while afterward," she admitted, "but it matters not
now. It's in the past, and we should leave it there."

Eithni nodded, although her gaze was still troubled.
"I know—I just want you to know I'm sorry. Loc was as
well. He knew he had taken things too far."

Tea smiled, sadness tightening her throat. "I wish I could go back in time too," she whispered. "I would have hugged him goodbye."

The women rode fast, covering ground swiftly, and arrived at the shores of Loch Slapin late afternoon. Despite that the bitter months were still upon them, the days had started to lengthen slightly. The shadows had grown long, the shade of Dun Ringill's outer perimeter walls stretching across the grass to meet them. Yet the sun was still a hand-span above the western horizon.

The sight of the fort, after over a month away, caused Tea's pulse to quicken. The familiarity of its squat shape, outlined against the glittering waters of the loch behind it, made tears prick her eyes.

Without realizing it, Dun Ringill had become her home.

"It's a beautiful spot," Eithni observed as they rode through the gate into the village surrounding the fort. "Look—you can still see the Black Cuillins from here."

It was true—to the north the shadowy layers of the great mountains etched against the sky, whereas grassy hills spread out to the west and the dark lake lay to the south. Unlike Dun Ardtreck, which sat perched like a hawk's eyrie above the world, the fort of Dun Ringill appeared to be part of the surrounding landscape.

As she rode in, Tea's gaze went to Ruith's hovel, which sat a short distance from the gate. She had been hoping to catch a glimpse of the seer, for she had missed her, but there was no sign of Ruith this afternoon.

It did not take long for folk to notice the newcomers. Halting their chores, they stopped and stared at the two women flanked by armed warriors who trotted up the incline to the stone arch leading into the fort.

At first a few of the women thought the newcomers were their missing Eagle warriors—the ones who had ridden south in the fall—and they rushed forward to greet them. Moments later the women stopped in their tracks, disappointment spreading across their faces when they recognized their chief's estranged wife. Tea did not blame them for their cool welcome. She was beginning to worry that Galan's reception would be even colder.

Tea's heart was pounding by the time she led the way into the stable yard. The moment she had been both waiting for, and dreading all day, had arrived.

It was not Galan who emerged from the fort to greet her but Cal, one of his men. He was the warrior she had liked the most, the one wed to Deri.

This afternoon the warrior's craggy face was stern, and Tea feared the worst. She swung down from her pony and passed the reins to her sister. Then she went to Cal, who walked down the stone steps to meet her.

"Good afternoon, Cal," she greeted him breathlessly.

"Tea," Cal replied. Close-up, she saw his expression was stunned. "You have returned."

Tea smiled, in an attempt to mask her nervousness. "I have—where is Galan?"

"He's not here."

Disappointment flared, although Tea did her best to hide it. Trust her to have ridden all this way, only to discover Galan was away on a hunt, or scouting with a war party.

"When will he be back?"

"Not for a few days," Cal replied, his gaze searching her face as he spoke. "He's out repairing the villages that the raiders destroyed—we're building stone defenses around them to make them stronger should more attacks come in future."

Tea's chest constricted. She could not wait a few days. She needed to see Galan today—before her courage failed her.

"We are doing the same around Dun Ardtreck," she replied with a nervous smile. "Do you know which village he's working in at the moment?"

Cal raised a dark eyebrow, regarding her a moment before answering. "He and the others left for Kil two days ago. I imagine they're still there. It's a small hamlet in a vale north of here."

"Can I reach it by nightfall?"

Cal's gaze widened. "Aye—if you ride fast."

Tea nodded. "I can." She turned and strode back to her dun mare, before swinging up onto her back.

Tea turned to Eithni. "You and Wid's warriors stay here. Cal's wife, Deri, will make you welcome and prepare you supper."

Eithni stared at her. "You're going on your own?"

Tea nodded.

"Tea—wait." Cal stepped forward. "I can send warriors with you."

"No." Tea was already riding across the yard, back toward the archway. "This is something I must do on my own."

Galan heaved the stone high, placing it upon the wall, before wiping sweat off his brow with the back of his arm.

He was exhausted—he had been out here since dawn, with only a brief rest at noon. Unlike his men, who had paced themselves during the day, Galan had pushed himself to the point of collapse. His head throbbed, his limbs ached, and the muscles in his back and arms felt as if they were on fire. Yet he did not care—none of it touched the emptiness inside him. He enjoyed the physical exertion, even the pain, for it provided a welcome distraction.

He did not want to dwell on his thoughts.

The sky was darkening, the last of the daylight leaching from the western horizon. The pungent tang of peat smoke filled the chill air in the valley, accompanied by the aroma of spit-roasting mutton. The village women were preparing a hearty meal for the band of men that were rebuilding Kil.

Galan stepped back and regarded the wall. Around him his men—Ru, Namet, and Lutrin among them—were packing up for the day. The rumble of their voices rose and fell against the clang of iron pots and the wail of a babe in one of the hovels behind him.

They had accomplished much in the past two days, having rebuilt most of the round-houses and a few timber hovels where Galan and his warriors slept. The perimeter wall, made from stones the villagers brought from nearby mountain slopes, now reached chest height. A few more feet and it would be tall enough to provide protection from attacks. Although he had dismissed Ruith's prediction about his own future, Galan had paid attention to the bandruí's warning about newcomers.

He would not risk further harm to his people. He would build stone defenses for each of the outlying villages and leave a small garrison of his warriors at each one to defend it.

Leaving his men, who were making their way indoors to enjoy their supper, Galan walked out of the village and climbed the heather-strewn hillside to the north. There, he sat upon a flat rock and looked down upon the hamlet of Kil. The perimeter wall rose up in an oval around the village, although the patchwork of village plots and animal enclosures beyond would remain unprotected. Galan remained there a while, watching the village as the gloaming deepened.

The weight of responsibility felt heavy this eve; he now understood the burden his father had shouldered all those years. Being a chieftain was not easy—the lives of all these people were now his responsibility. It was not a charge he took lightly, and he still felt to blame for the damage that the raiders had done. His people looked to him to protect them, and he had failed them.

Galan was deep in thought, brooding upon the tasks that still lay ahead of him, when he caught sight of a pony and rider cresting the hill to the south. At this distance he could see little more than a silhouette against the indigo sky.

Senses alerted, he rose to his feet and strode down the hillside to intercept the newcomer. He stood before the opening to the wall—where a gate would be fastened once the fortification was complete—and watched the rider approach.

The stranger was a few yards away when they spotted him and drew their pony up short. Then the newcomer spoke. "Galan?"

Chapter Thirty-four

Courage

A LOW, HUSKY female voice reached him through the stillness of the gathering dusk. It was a voice he recognized instantly, one he had never thought to hear again.

Galan took a pitch torch from a bracket on the wall and, holding it aloft, approached. The flickering flames outlined a tall, proud figure, and a face he had dreamed of every night since leaving Dun Ardtreck.

"Tea," he murmured, shock almost rendering him speechless. "Is that really you?"

The flames danced along the angles of her face, tracing her high cheek bones, delicate nose, full-lips, and firm chin—although her eyes were cast in shadow.

"Aye," she said softly. Unmoving, he watched her swing down from the saddle and walk toward him. When they were around three feet apart, she stopped, her gaze meeting his.

Galan continued to stare at her. After the ordeal of the past weeks, he could not believe that his wife was actually standing before him—that she had come looking for him in Kil.

"What are you doing here?" he asked finally. "It's not safe riding out at dusk on your own."

She smiled before shaking her head. "I can defend myself—you know that."

Tea continued to hold his gaze, before her smile faded. Her eyes were dark in the torchlight, her face suddenly strained. "I'm here for you, Galan," she said softly. "I'm so sorry for the things I said ... for hurting you."

He took a step closer, his gaze narrowing. "You weren't sorry for it then," he said, trying to keep emotion from his voice. "Why now?"

She stepped closer too, so they stood barely a foot apart. He could smell the warm musk of her skin and the mixture of rosemary and lavender from the lotion she used on her hair. Hunger contracted his belly. This woman possessed him, body and soul, and she always would.

"Every day that passed after you left was worse than the last," she replied, her voice husky, her eyes gleaming with tears. "I thought I'd feel better, that your absence would bring me to my senses, but the opposite happened. All hope, all light, gradually faded." She broke off here, and Galan saw that her cheeks were wet with tears. "The world is a dark place without you in it, my love."

My love.

Galan could not breathe, could not move. Instead, he stared into her eyes and wished for those words to be true.

"Is that really how you feel?" he finally asked.

Tea nodded, her shoulders trembling slightly from the force of emotions she was keeping in check. She took a step back, breaking the spell she had cast over him. The chill night air rushed in between them, bringing Galan sharply back to his senses. His hand snapped out, catching her by the arm. He hauled her against him.

"Come here, woman," he growled and brought his mouth down hard over hers. There were not any words he could use to describe how he felt at that moment; none would make her understand how much he loved her. He would show her with his body instead.

She responded to his kiss with a wildness that made him forget everything else. He dropped the torch into the mud and scooped Tea into his arms. She coiled her arms around his neck, her mouth devouring his. He gave a low groan in answer, pivoted on his heel, and carried her into the village.

As chief, Galan did not have to share his sleeping space with the other warriors. The villagers had made him comfortable in a small hut with a sod roof—one of the few original dwellings that had not been destroyed in the raids. Inside the gate he met Namet, who had come looking for him.

"Tea's pony is outside," Galan told the warrior. "Can you see to it?"

Not bothering to wait for Namet's response, and ignoring the stares from his men and the villagers who were making their way toward the feasting hut, Galan carried Tea through the village to his dwelling.

He kicked open the wattle door and carried her across the threshold into the warm space beyond. A small brazier burned in one corner and goat skins covered the dirt floor. A pile of furs sat in the center of the space, next to a low table where the villagers had placed a cup, a jug of ale; and a platter of bread, cheese, and cured meat for their chieftain.

Galan ignored the food and ale—there was only one thing he was hungry for. There was only one thing that would fill the yawning emptiness inside him. He wanted to feast upon this woman, to show her how much he loved her, to brand himself upon her soul so that she never thought to leave him again.

He set Tea down, and they tore at each other's clothing. Garments of fur, leather, and wool thumped to the goat-skin rugs at their feet. Galan pulled Tea hard against him, feeling the smooth heat of her skin against his. He ran his hands down her back, exploring the firmness of her muscles, the softness of her curves. His shaft pulsed against her belly, and when he felt her fingers wrap around it, the last shreds of his self-restraint snapped.

Galan threw her down on the furs, lifted her long, shapely legs over his shoulders and entered her in one deep thrust.

Tea angled her hips off the furs to meet him, throwing her head back and crying his name as she did so.

Galan stared down at her, his gaze devouring her full, pink-tipped breasts, the dip of her waist, and the flare of her hips. His fingers stroked those breasts, feeling her nipples harden under his touch. She met his gaze, her eyes glittering with passion.

"I'm yours, Galan," she gasped. "Now and always."

"You are," he growled back, "and let me prove it to you."

Galan began to move inside her in hard, possessive strokes—each thrust claiming her as his.

The brazier died to embers, casting a dull red glow over the interior of the hut. Tea lay upon her belly, thoroughly sated, while Galan lay against her, one leg draped over her back, trapping her against the softness of the furs.

He lifted up her curtain of hair, which had come undone from its braids during their lovemaking, and nuzzled the nape of her neck. The feel of his lips on the sensitive skin there caused Tea to shiver with pleasure. She gave a soft moan and pressed herself back against him, her loins melting when she felt his manhood pressed hard against her.

She would never tire of this man, of the feel and taste of him. The sound of his voice—the low, powerful timbre of it—was like listening to music after their time apart.

"I love you, Galan," she murmured, barely able to concentrate as his hand slid up and stroked her breasts.

Galan rolled back, bringing her with him so that she could turn and face him. Tea looked up into his face—those strong features that could be hawkish when angry but at that moment were relaxed and handsome. His eyes were the color of wood-smoke as he watched her.

"It nearly killed me to leave you at Dun Ardtreck," he murmured. "I wanted to tell you I loved you, but I let the moment pass. I've regretted that ever since."

She reached up and stroked his cheek. Tea inhaled the scent of him. He smelled of fresh sweat, smoke, leather, and of virile male—a scent that made her pulse quicken, her stomach tighten with hunger.

"It would have made little difference," she admitted, self-recrimination biting her with every word. "I was too proud."

His mouth twisted. "My fierce warrior bride." He caught her hand and brought it up to his mouth, gently kissing the backs of her fingers. "What made you cast your pride aside?" His smile was so tender that it hurt her to breathe.

"You can only ignore your heart for so long," she admitted ruefully. "Not only that, but Eithni and Wid were never going to give me any peace. I had to leave to escape their nagging."

Galan laughed, and the sight of him smiling made Tea's chest constrict once more. The gods had shone upon her, and given her a man she not only loved but one whom she respected deeply.

Both Galan and Loc had shown her that battle courage was not the sign of strength she had always thought it to be. Galan was a warrior—he had been taught to fight and to kill—but he had risked the ire of his people and of hers to take another path. That was the mark of true bravery.

Epilogue

Honeyed Oat Cakes

THE CHIEFTAIN OF The Eagle and his wife rode back into Dun Ringill two days later. The defensive perimeter at Kil had been built, and Galan had sent his men on to the next village while he returned home with his wife. He would join his men again soon enough—but for now it was time for Galan and Tea to bring news of their reconciliation home.

A feathery mist crept in from Loch Slapin this morning, curling around the fort's stone bulk like smoke. The air was damp, reminding Tea that although spring was now not far away, winter still held The Winged Isle in its grip.

They rode in through the outer perimeter and up through the collection of roundhouses. Ruith was there, scattering grain for her fowl. Upon spotting Tea, a wide smile split the bandruí's face. She waved to them.

"Ruith will be insufferable over this, you know?" Galan told Tea as he waved back at the seer.

Tea looked away from Ruith and met his eye. "Why?"

Galan gave her a pained look. "Ruith cast the bones a few days ago and saw the marks of The Eagle and The Wolf side-by-side with the Cauldron beneath them. She tried to tell me all was not lost, but I wouldn't hear it."

"Your bandruí is a wise woman," Tea replied with a grin. "I'd advise you to listen to her in future."

Galan smiled back. "I intend to."

They rode up to the fort and dismounted in front of the entrance. Cal and Deri, who had been overseeing Dun Ringill in Galan's absence, came out to greet them, as did Eithni.

Tea hugged her sister tightly, noticing that she did not feel as fragile as before. She was still slender as a reed, but Tea no longer felt as if hugging her would snap her. Eithni's face was starting to fill out, and the color was returning to her cheeks.

Eithni's eyes glittered as she drew back from Tea. Her gaze flicked from her sister to Galan, and a smile of pure, unselfish joy spread across her face.

"I was beginning to worry," Eithni admitted, breathless from her run down the steps and across the yard to meet them. Shyly, she dropped her gaze before Galan, and Tea realized that this was one of the few times her sister had addressed him directly. "I'm so glad you have reconciled," she murmured. "Tea was miserable without you."

"That's enough," Tea cut in. The last thing she needed was Eithni to embarrass her. "Galan knows the story—there's no need to repeat it."

She glanced at Galan, to see he was smiling. "Tea tells me you had a part to play in her returning to Dun Ringill," he said. "I thank you for that."

Tea watched her sister blush. She did not blame her; Galan had that effect on women.

"Eithni wishes to stay here with us," Tea said, hooking her arm protectively through her sister's. "I'd like her to, as well."

"I won't be a burden," Eithni assured him, slightly nervous under the chieftain's penetrating gaze. "I'm a hard worker."

"She's a gifted healer," Tea added.

Galan's smile widened. "Even if she was not, she would still be welcome here, Tea. She's your kin." He turned his attention back to Eithni. "You may have one of the alcoves inside the fort—or I can have a dwelling built for you in the village if you prefer."

Tea watched a smile illuminate her sister's face. "I would love a home of my own."

Galan nodded. "Then you shall have one."

That evening Galan and Tea hosted a great feast. Barrels of ale, mead, and wine were opened, and the folk of Dun Ringill feasted on roast venison. Husband and wife sat together at the chieftain's table and dined off the same platter, feeding each other slivers of meat and morsels of bread. They drank sloe wine from the same cup.

It was a significant meal, a re-creation of their handfasting feast all those months ago. That occasion had been tense and marred by decades of feuding—while this one was joyous and marked the beginning of a new life for them both.

Tea ate slowly, savoring the flavor of the roast venison. She had not been able to eat venison or drink sloe wine since her handfasting without being reminded of that evening and the night that followed. For a long while she had wanted no memory of it, yet now things had changed.

When the oat-cakes, dripping in honey, were brought to the table, the feasters surrounding them cheered. One or two of the men hooted and called-out lewd comments.

"They've got good memories," Tea muttered, staring down at the cake on the platter before them. She had forgotten that a good many of the warriors here had been at their handfasting.

"Aye—and if you keep blushing they're not likely to let you forget it," Galan teased.

Tea glanced up to see him grinning at her, not remotely embarrassed by the cat-calling and hooting that echoed around the feasting hall. At the end of the chieftain's table, Eithni had gone pink in the face, while next to her Ruith wore a knowing smile.

Tea looked back at Galan and raised an eyebrow. "What do you suggest we do now?" she asked.

Her stomach fluttered at the smoldering look he gave her in answer. Galan then broke off a piece of seed cake and fed it to her.

Ignoring the cheering that now shook the rafters, Tea chewed slowly, before she smiled back at Galan. "Well then ... let's give the crowd what they want."

She reached out and caught his wrist, stopping his hand before he could lower it. Then she licked the honey from his fingers.

Initially, they had done this for show—to entertain the feasters—but as soon as Galan's smile faded, Tea knew they were no longer acting. They had gone full-circle; only, now things would be different.

This night would be a new start—a union untainted by blood feud.

Galan rose to his feet, bringing Tea with him. Then he scooped her into his arms. The revelers roared their approval, their cheers shaking the broch to its foundations. Ignoring them all, The Eagle chief turned his back on the feasting hall and carried his wife away to their alcove.

The End

Historical Note

As I mentioned in the Historical Background in the forward to this novel—the culture, language, and religion of the Picts is one largely shrouded in mystery. Unlike my novels set in 7th Century Anglo-Saxon England, which is a reasonably well-documented period, researching 4th Century Isle of Skye proved to be a challenge. Pictish culture is largely an enigma to us. However, they did leave behind a number of fascinating stone ruins, standing stones, and artifacts, as well as a detailed collection of symbolic art.

In addition to a host of online resources, I relied heavily on three books to ensure my depiction of the Picts, and the Isle of Skye, was as accurate as possible:

Picts, Gaels and Scots by Sally M. Foster (Batsford, 1996)
A Wee Guide to the Picts by Duncan Jones (Goblinshead, 2009)
Isle of Skye and Raasay by John Garvey (Matador, 2009)

I created the four tribes of The Winged Isle from Pictish animal symbols. This is not a far-fetched idea; many Iron and Bronze-age peoples identified themselves with animal symbols. The clans we identify with Scotland did not appear until a few centuries later.

A note about Luana's death. Although I call her death 'birthing sickness', we now know the condition as Eclampsia, a life-threatening complication of pregnancy. Eclampsia is a condition that causes a pregnant woman, today usually previously diagnosed with preeclampsia (high blood pressure and protein in the urine), to develop seizures or coma. Today this complication is preventable and treatable.

Galan mac Muin and his two brothers are, of course, completely fictional characters (although I'd like to believe they all lived, if only in my imagination!). The next novel in this series will focus on Tarl's story. This novel will hinge on a real historical event—the Barbarian Conspiracy—when the Picts, Scott,i and Atecotti banded together and attacked Hadrian's Wall.

See you back here for the next installment!

Acknowledgements

Although writing a novel appears like a solitary task, there are actually plenty of people involved in the process. Firstly, I'd like to thank my readers—without you I would never have started on this new series. You've let me know you enjoy my stories and given me the drive to keep writing!

I'd also like to thank Emma—the book you lent me on Pictish symbols (A Wee Guide to the Picts) was a goldmine!

My gratitude goes to the members of the Otago Chapter of RWNZ (Romance Writers of New Zealand) particularly Maria, Susie, Rachel, and Kura, who have all given me valuable advice, and to RWNZ as a whole. Last year's conference showed me that yes, I can make a living with my fiction!

Lastly, but most importantly, I'd like to thank my fiancé, Tim. He's crucial to all aspects of the novel production but especially the editing. I might not want to always hear what he has to say—especially when it involves extensive rewriting—but the novel is always a better one once he has worked his magic on it. Not only that, but his belief in me, and in what I'm capable of, makes me realize just how lucky I am.

About the Author

Award-winning author Jayne Castel writes epic Historical and Fantasy Romance. Her vibrant characters, richly researched historical settings and action-packed adventure romance transport readers to forgotten times and imaginary worlds.

Jayne is the author of the Amazon bestselling BRIDES OF SKYE series—a Medieval Scottish Romance trilogy about three strong-willed sisters and the men who love them. An exciting spin-off series set in the same story-world, THE SISTERS OF KILBRIDE, is now available as well. In love with all things Scottish, Jayne also writes romances set in Dark Ages Scotland ... sexy Pict warriors anyone?

When she's not writing, Jayne is reading (and re-reading) her favorite authors, cooking Italian feasts, and taking her dog, Juno, for walks. She lives in New Zealand's beautiful South Island.

Connect with Jayne online:
www.jaynecastel.com
Email: contact@jaynecastel.com